THE CONFERENCE OF THE BIRDS

THE CONFERENCE OF THE BIRDS

THE FIFTH NOVEL OF

MISS PEREGRINE'S

PECULIAR CHILDREN

BY RANSOM RIGGS

PENGUIN BOOKS

PENGUIN BOOKS

UK | USA | Canada | Ireland | Australia
India | New Zealand | South Africa

Penguin Books is part of the Penguin Random House group of companies
whose addresses can be found at global.penguinrandomhouse.com.

www.penguin.co.uk
www.puffin.co.uk
www.ladybird.co.uk

First published in the USA by Dutton Books
and in Great Britain by Penguin Books 2020

001

Edited by Julie Strauss-Gabel
Design by Anna Booth

Text set in Sabon LT Pro

Printed and bound in Italy

A CIP catalogue record for this book is available from the British Library

HARDBACK ISBN: 978–0–241–32058–7
INTERNATIONAL PAPERBACK ISBN: 978–0–241–32090–7

All correspondence to:
Penguin Books
Penguin Random House Children's
80 Strand, London WC2R 0RL

You who live your lives in cities or among peaceful ways

cannot always tell whether your friends are the kind who would

go through fire for you. But on the Plains one's friends

have an opportunity to prove their mettle.

—William F. "Buffalo Bill" Cody

THE CONFERENCE OF THE BIRDS

CHAPTER ONE

LIVE BORDERS

*D*eep in the green-glowing bowels of a Chinatown sea-food market, down a dead-end hallway lined with crab tanks, we crouched in a puddle of dark the light-eater had made, watched over by a thousand alien eyes. Leo's men were close, and they were angry. We heard shouts and crashes as they tore apart the market, looking for us. *"Please,"* I heard an old woman crying, *"I didn't see anybody . . ."*

We had realized too late that the hallway had no exit, and now we were trapped here, squatting by a drain in a narrow gap between stacks of doomed crustaceans, their tanks piled ten high in leaning towers that scraped the ceiling. Between the bangs and shouts, beneath our sharp, panicked breathing, was the unceasing rhythm of crab claws tapping glass, an orchestra of broken typewriters burrowing into my skull.

At least it would mask the sound of our breathing. Maybe that would be enough, if Noor's unnatural dark held and if the men whose heavy steps were growing louder didn't look too closely at the wriggling void with unsteady edges; an omission in the air, a wrongness unmissable if your eyes came to rest on it. Noor had shaped it by dragging her hand through the air around us, dark spreading in its wake as light collected on her fingertips like luminous cake frosting. She popped it into her mouth, and it glowed through her cheeks and her throat as she swallowed, and disappeared.

It was Noor they wanted, but they would've happily taken me, too, if only to shoot me. By now they had surely found H dead in his apartment, his eyes torn from their sockets by his own hollowgast. Earlier in the day, H and his hollow had broken Noor out of Leo's loop. They hurt some of Leo's guys. That, perhaps, would be forgivable. What was not: Leo Burnham, peculiar leader of the Five Boroughs clan, had been humiliated. A feral peculiar he laid claim to had been taken from him in his own house, the power center at the heart of a peculiar empire that spanned much of the eastern United States. If I were discovered helping Noor escape, that, more than anything, would write my death sentence.

Leo's men were getting closer, and their shouts were growing louder. Noor tended to her dark, straightening its edges between her finger and thumb when it began to spread out, filling the center when it thinned.

I wished I could see Noor's face. Read her expression. I wanted to know what she was thinking, how she was holding up. It was hard to imagine someone so new to this world enduring all this without cracking. In the past few days, she had been chased by normals with tranquilizer darts and helicopters, kidnapped by a peculiar hypnotist to be sold at auction, and broken free only to be captured by Leo Burnham's gang. She'd spent days in a cell in Leo's headquarters, then been sleep-dusted in the course of her great escape with H, only to awake in his apartment to find him dead on the floor—the gruesome shock of which had sent a warhead of concentrated light erupting from her like a fireball (one that nearly took off my head).

Once she recovered from that shock, I shared with her some of what H told me in his last breaths: that there was one last living hollow-slayer, a woman named V, and I was to deliver Noor to her for protection. The only clues to her whereabouts were a torn piece of map from H's wall safe and garbled instructions delivered by H's ghastly ex-hollowgast, Horatio.

But I hadn't yet told Noor *why* H fought so hard to help her, enlisted me and my friends to the cause, and ultimately died in order to free her from Leo. I hadn't told her about the prophecy. There had hardly been time—we'd been running for our lives ever since I heard Leo's guys in the hallway outside H's apartment. But more than that, I wondered whether, on top of everything else, it would be too much, too soon.

One of the seven whose coming was foretold . . . the emancipators of peculiardom . . . the dawning of a dangerous age . . . It would sound like the ravings of a lunatic cult member. After all the other demands the peculiar world had made on Noor's credulity—not to mention her sanity—I worried it would send her running for the hills. Any normal person would've run off long ago.

Of course, Noor Pradesh was anything but normal. She was peculiar. And more than that, she had some serious iron in her spine.

Just then she leaned her head toward mine and whispered, *"So, when we get out of here . . . what's the plan? Where do we go?"*

"Out of New York," I said.

A slight pause, then: *"How?"*

"I don't know. A train? A bus?" I hadn't thought that far ahead.

"Oh," she said with a hint of disappointment. *"You can't, like, magic us out of here somehow? With one of your time-portal things?"*

"They don't really work like that. Well, I guess some of them do"—I was thinking of connections to the Panloopticon—*"but we'd have to find one."*

"What about your friends? Don't you have . . . people?"

Her question made my heart sink. *"They don't even know I'm here."*

Then I thought, *And even if they did . . .*

I felt her shoulders sag.

"Don't worry," I said. *"I'll figure something out."*

Any other time, my plan would've been simple: Go find my friends. I wished desperately that I could. They would know what to do. They had been my rock ever since I entered this world, and without them I felt unmoored. But H had specifically warned me not to take Noor back to the ymbrynes, and anyway, I wasn't sure I *had* friends anymore—at least, not the way I had before. What H had done, and what I was doing right now, was probably destroying any chance of the ymbrynes making peace between the clans. And it had almost certainly done irreparable damage to my friends' trust in me.

So we were on our own. That made the plan simple, but dumb: Run very fast. Think very hard. Get very lucky.

And if we didn't run fast enough? Or get lucky enough? Then I might never get a chance to tell Noor about the prophecy—and she would go the rest of her life, however long or short that was, without knowing why she was being hunted.

I heard a resounding crash not far away, and then Leo's guys were shouting again. It wouldn't be long now before they reached us.

"There's something I need to tell you about," I whispered.

"Can it wait?"

It was the worst time. It was also maybe the only time.

"You need to know. In case we get separated, or . . . something else happens."

"Okay." She sighed. *"I'm listening."*

"This is probably going to sound ridiculous, so before I tell you, just know that I know that. Before he died, H told me about a prophecy."

Somewhere close by, a man was trading shouts with Leo's guys—he in Cantonese, they in English. We heard a loud slap, a cry, a muffled threat. Noor and I both stiffened.

"In the back!" Leo's man shouted.

"It has to do with you," I continued, my lips almost touching her ear.

Now she was trembling. The edges of the dark shivered around us, too.

"Tell me," she breathed.

Leo's men rounded the corner into the hallway. And we were out of time.

The men started along the hall toward us, dragging some poor market worker behind them. The beams of their flashlights played over the walls, refracting off the glass of the crab tanks. I dared not raise my head for fear it might leave the confines of Noor's dark. I tensed, mentally preparing for a very unbalanced fight.

Then, halfway down the hall, they stopped.

"Nothing in here but fish tanks," one of the men grunted.

"Who was with her?" said a second man.

"A boy, some boy, I don't know—"

There was another slap, and the man they were holding groaned in pain.

"Let him go, Bowers. He don't know nothing."

The market worker was pushed away roughly. He stumbled to the floor, then picked himself up and ran.

"We wasted too much time here," said the first man. "The girl's probably long gone by now. Along with the creeps who took her."

"Think they could have found the entrance to Fung Wah's loop?" asked a third.

"Could be," said the first man. "I'll take Melnitz and Jacobs to check it out. Bowers, do a full sweep here."

I counted their voices: Now there were four, maybe five of them. The one called Bowers walked right past us, his gun holster hanging at our eye level. I looked up without shifting my head. He was heavyset and wore a dark suit.

"Leo's gonna murder us if we don't find her," Bowers muttered.

"We're bringing back that dead wight," said the second man. "That ain't nothing."

I tensed in surprise, my ears pricking. *Dead wight?*

"He was dead when we found him," said Bowers.

"Leo don't gotta know that," the first man said, laughing.

"What I wouldn't give to have killed him myself," Bowers said.

He reached the dead end to our right and turned back in our direction again. His flashlight spilled over us, then shone into the tank beside my head.

"You can go kick his corpse if it'll make you feel better," the third man said.

"Nah. I wouldn't mind givin' that girl a kick, though," Bowers growled. "And more than that." He started back toward the others. "You see the way she was helping the wight?"

The first man said, "She's just a feral. She don't know any better yet."

"Just a feral—exactly!" said the second man. "I still don't understand why we're wasting so much time on her. Just to add one more peculiar to our clan?"

"Because Leo don't forgive and forget," said the first man.

I felt Noor squirm beside me, then take a deep, steadying breath.

"Get me in a room alone with her," growled Bowers. "I'll show you how special she is."

He came even with our hiding place, then turned a slow circle, shining his light across the walls and the floor. My eyes came to rest on his holster. His flashlight panned across the tank to our left, then came to rest directly on us. The beam stopped inches from our noses, unable to penetrate Noor's dark.

I held my breath, praying that all of us, even our hair, was hidden. Bowers's expression soured, as if he were trying to make sense of something.

"Bowers!" someone shouted from down the hall.

He turned but kept his flashlight trained on us.

"Meet us outside when you're done here. After Fung's we'll do a three-block perimeter."

"Pick out a couple fat crabs!" said the first man. "We'll bring back dinner. Maybe that'll put Leo in a better mood."

The flashlight beam swung back to the tank. "I don't see how people can eat these things," Bowers grumbled to himself. "Spiders of the sea."

The others left. We were alone with the flunky. He was five feet away, grimacing at the crab tank. He peeled off his jacket and started to roll up his shirtsleeves. All we had to do now was wait, and in a few minutes . . .

Noor's hand clenched my arm. She was trembling.

At first, I thought she was melting down from stress, but then she drew three tiny breaths in quick succession and I realized: She was trying not to sneeze.

Please, I mouthed silently, though I knew she couldn't see me. *Don't.*

The man reached gingerly into the tank closest to him. His meaty hand felt around for a crab while he made gentle gagging sounds.

Noor went rigid. I could hear her teeth grind as she tried to hold in the sneeze.

The man yelped, then yanked his hand out of the tank. He swore and waved his hand wildly in the air while a fat blue crab held fast to one finger.

And then Noor stood up.

"Hey," she said. "Asshole."

The man spun toward us. Before he could get a word out, Noor sneezed.

It was a percussive blast: All the light she'd swallowed flew out, splattering the opposite wall and the floor and the man's face in radiant green spray, enveloping him in a ball of glowing light. It wasn't bright enough to hurt him—and not nearly enough to burn—just enough to shock him into brief inaction as his mouth formed a perfect, egg-shaped O of astonishment.

The small, dark void that had enveloped us disappeared in an instant. The man shouted, and for a moment we were frozen, as if under a spell: me crouched on the floor; Noor standing beside me, her hand over her nose and mouth; the man with one hand held up, a wriggling crab still dangling from it. And then I scrambled to my feet, and the spell was broken. The man moved to block our way, and with his free hand he reached for his gun.

I tackled him before he could use it. He fell back and I toppled down on him. We grappled for the pistol. I caught an elbow in the forehead, and a sharp pain ricocheted through me. Noor came from behind and thwacked him on the arm with a metal pole she'd found. The man hardly flinched. He got both hands against my chest and shoved me aside.

I ran toward Noor to push her away from him. As I reached her, the man squeezed off two shots. The sound was incredible, less a bang than a sonic blast. The first shot I heard caromed off the wall. The second shattered the tank next to him. One moment it was whole and the next it was falling to pieces, crabs and water and broken glass spilling everywhere, and then the many tanks stacked atop it toppled sideways and forward across the hall. The topmost one exploded as it hit the column of tanks on the opposite wall; the others shattered on top of Bowers. They must've held a hundred gallons apiece and weighed a collective ton, because in the space of three seconds he was both crushed and half drowned. Meanwhile, a chain reaction of impacts sent nearly all the tanks in the hallway crashing to the floor in a tremendous explosion of noise and glass, freeing their crustacean prisoners in a tidal wave of fetid water that rushed along the hall and knocked us both off our feet.

We coughed and choked; the water was disgusting. I looked at Bowers and winced. His face was shredded to strips and glowing with green light. His body was alive with scuttling crabs, but he was very dead otherwise. I turned away quickly and picked through the wreckage toward Noor, who had gotten washed down the hall.

"Are you okay?" I asked, helping her up and checking her for cuts.

She looked herself over in the dim light. "My limbs are still attached. You?"

"Same," I said. "We'd better go. The other guys will be coming."

"Yeah, they probably heard that in New Jersey."

We linked arms to steady each other and moved as fast as we could toward the mouth of the hall, where a neon sign in the shape of a crab buzzed and flickered.

We'd hardly made it ten feet when we heard heavy footsteps pounding in our direction.

We froze where we stood. Two people, maybe more, were coming for us at a dead run. They had heard us, all right.

"Let's go!" Noor said, and started pulling me forward.

"No—" I stopped. Planted my feet. "They're too close." They'd be here any second, and the hallway ahead was too long and cluttered with broken tanks; we'd never make it in time. "We've got to hide again."

"We have to *fight*," she said, gathering what light there was into her hands, but there wasn't much left.

That had been my first instinct, too—but I knew it was wrong.

"If we fight, they start shooting, and I can't let you get shot. I'll give myself up and tell them you ran somewhere else—"

She was shaking her head vehemently. "No way in hell." Even in the dark I could see her eyes flashing. She let the tiny ball of light she'd raked up dissipate and retrieved two long shards of glass from the floor. "We fight together or not at all."

I let out a frustrated sigh. "Then we fight." We crouched down, shards of glass held out like knives. The footsteps were loud, and so close we could hear the approaching runners' heavy breaths.

And then they were here.

A figure appeared at the end of the hall, silhouetted against neon. Someone stocky, broad-shouldered . . . and familiar, though I couldn't immediately place them.

"Mr. Jacob?" a voice I recognized said. "Is that you?"

A shimmer of light fell across her face. Her strong, square jaw, her kind eyes. I thought, for a moment, that I must be dreaming.

"Bronwyn?" I said—almost shouted.

"It *is* you!" she cried, her face breaking into a wide grin. She ran toward me, bounding around drifts of broken glass, and I dropped the shard of glass just before Bronwyn wrapped me in a big, breath-stealing hug. "Is that Miss Noor?" she said over my shoulder.

"Hi," Noor said, sounding a bit stunned.

"Then you succeeded!" Bronwyn said. "I'm so happy!"

"What are you doing here?" I managed to squeak.

"We might ask the same of you!" said another familiar voice—and as Bronwyn let me go I saw Hugh coming toward us. "Blimey, what happened in here?"

First Bronwyn, now Hugh. My head was spinning.

Bronwyn set me down. "Never mind that. He's all right, Hugh! And here's Miss Noor."

"Hi," Noor said again. Then, quickly, "So there's, like, four guys with guns coming for us right now—"

"I coshed two on the head," said Bronwyn, holding up a pair of fingers.

"I chased off another with my bees," said Hugh.

"More will be coming," I said.

Bronwyn picked up a heavy-looking metal bar from the floor. "Then let's not dally, shall we?"

◆   ◆   ◆

The subterranean seafood market was a baffling maze, but we navigated its wriggling nooks and crannies as best we could, each twosome struggling to remember just how we'd gotten down here and which of the Chinese-language signs around us meant *exit*. The place was both cramped and sprawling, packed tight with crates and tables, divided by hanging tarps, nests of dangerous-looking electric wires and bare bulbs that swung overhead. It had been crowded a short time ago, but Leo's guys had pretty well cleared it out.

"Try and keep up!" Bronwyn called over her shoulder.

We slid after her under a table squirming with live octopi, then chased her down an aisle of fish laid out in boxes of steaming dry ice. Turning left at a junction with another aisle, we saw two of Leo's men—one was splayed on the ground, and the other was crouching next to him, attempting to revive him with little slaps on the face. Bronwyn didn't slow her pace at all, and the man looked up in surprise just as she delivered a running kick to his head and sent him sprawling onto the ground beside the other one.

"Very sorry!" she called behind her, and in reply there came a pair of shouts from far across the market—two more of Leo's guys had spotted us and were now charging in our direction. We took a sharp turn and ran up a narrow stairway, then slammed through a door and burst out into daylight, briefly blinded after having spent so long in the gloom. Suddenly, we were on a busy sidewalk at rush hour in the present day. Cars and pedestrians and street vendors were everywhere, zipping around us in a dizzying whirl.

There's an art to fleeing casually. It's not easy, running from something that might kill you while not attracting stares. Seeming to be engaged in something no more dramatic than an afternoon jog, especially when two of you are soaked head to toe, two of you are dressed in nineteenth-century clothes, and all of you keep shooting nervous glances down every alley and back over your shoulders. Apparently, we hadn't got the hang of it, because we were getting even more stares than two costumed and two wet teenagers should have warranted, especially in New York, where strange people populated most sidewalks.

We jaywalked, we ignored red lights and DON'T WALK signs, edging into the street until there was a stall in traffic, or sometimes just going for it in a mad dash and letting the cars honk and swerve, because getting run over was better than being dragged back to

Leo's loop. His goons had been on us like a bad cold, tailing us through the grit of Chinatown and up the streets of a touristy Italian neighborhood, then nearly catching up to us when we got stuck on the median strip of busy Houston Street. They were easy to spot in their old suits. Finally, just when I was beginning to wonder how much longer I could run, Noor poured on more speed to catch up with Bronwyn and pulled her around a corner. Hugh and I followed them, and a short time later Noor hauled Bronwyn to the side again, this time through a door into a seemingly random store. It was a cramped little bodega that sold beer and dry goods.

As the owner shouted something at us, we all saw two of Leo's guys dash past the front door without stopping. Then Noor pushed us down a narrow aisle, through a door into a stockroom, past a surprised employee on a smoke break, and out through a swinging metal door into an alley lined with dumpsters.

It seemed we had shaken them off—for a moment, anyway—and we allowed ourselves to stop for a minute and catch our breath. Bronwyn had hardly broken a sweat, but Noor, Hugh, and I were gasping.

"That was quick thinking," Bronwyn said, impressed.

"Yeah," Hugh said. "Nicely done."

"Thanks," said Noor. "Not my first rodeo."

"We should be safe here for a minute," Hugh said between breaths. "Let's give them some time to think we're long gone, then move."

"I should probably ask where you're taking us," I said.

"I'd certainly love to know," Noor said, one eyebrow rising.

"Back to the Acre," said Hugh. "Closest loop entrance ain't pleasant, but it ain't far . . ."

I couldn't stop looking at my friends. Part of me had worried I might never lay eyes on them again. Or that, if I did, they would act like strangers.

And then Hugh drew back his fist and punched me in the arm.

"Ow! What was that for?"

"Why didn't you *tell* us you were doing some daft rescue mission?"

Noor was gaping at us.

"I *tried*," I said.

"Not very hard, you didn't!" said Bronwyn.

"Well, I dropped some awfully big hints," I said defensively. "But it was pretty clear no one wanted to help me."

Hugh looked ready to punch me again. "Maybe not, but we *would* have!"

"We never would have let you do something like this alone," Bronwyn said, sounding angry at me for the first time. "We were worried sick when we found you gone!" She turned to Noor and shook her head. "He was in a sickbed just yesterday, mad boy. Thought somebody'd kidnapped him in the night!"

"To be honest, I wasn't really sure you'd care that I was gone," I said.

"Jacob!" Bronwyn's eyes went wide. "After all we've been through? That's just hurtful."

"Told you he was a Sensitive Sally." Hugh shook his head. "Give your old mates some credit, man. My God."

"Sorry," I said meekly.

"I mean, *really*."

Noor leaned toward me and whispered, *"No friends, huh?"*

"I don't know what to say." My heart was suddenly so full it seemed to crowd out the words from my brain. "I'm really glad to see you guys."

"And we you," said Bronwyn. She hugged me again, and this time Hugh did, too.

And then a gunshot rang out from one end of the alley and we all startled, then broke apart to see two men in suits booking it toward us.

So much for shaking them off.

"Follow me," Noor said. "We can lose them in the subway."

✦   ✦   ✦

I shot down the subway steps three at a time. Hugh slid on the metal banister. In the crowded vestibule we shoved through knots of rush-hour commuters. Noor shouted, "Like this!" behind her and then jumped a turnstile—we all followed suit.

We came to a train platform and ran along it. I looked back and saw Leo's guys, distant but still chasing us. Noor stopped, planted a hand on the floor, jumped down onto the subway tracks, and shouted for us to follow. She yelled something about a third rail, too, though her voice got lost in the noise of a sudden station announcement.

We had no choice but to go after her.

"You're gonna get yourselves killed!" somebody yelled at us, and I was inclined to agree—but right now this seemed preferable to the alternative.

We were dashing across four sets of tracks, stumbling over hidden pits and dark rails, when it occurred to me that Noor had obviously done this before, that she knew the city like the back of her hand, and that someone so hard to catch must have had lots of experience running away. And I wondered why and from what, and I very much hoped, as I noticed a train coming, that I'd get a chance to ask her.

The train was uncomfortably close as Hugh and I crossed the last track, the wind and noise it pushed strengthening by the second, and then Bronwyn and Noor hauled us up onto the opposite platform just before it thundered past, brakes squealing like some creature from hell.

Moments later the train disgorged its passengers, and suddenly there seemed to be a thousand people on the platform, but finally we were able to push our way on board. We crouched down on the floor so we couldn't be seen—the car was nearly empty—and then the doors slid shut.

"Gee," Bronwyn said, looking suddenly worried. "I hope this train's going in the right direction . . ."

Noor asked where we were supposed to be heading, and Bronwyn told her. Noor raised her eyebrows. "Weird luck," she said. "That's just a stop away."

It was amazing: Of the four of us, she knew by far the least about what was happening, but her certainty and calm had already become a guiding force.

An announcement blared and the train took off from the station.

"How did you find me?" I said to Bronwyn and Hugh.

"Emma realized what you were probably up to, after all your talk about *her*." Hugh nodded to Noor and said, "Nice to properly meet you, by the way, I'm Hugh . . ." He reached over and shook Noor's hand.

"It was a fairly simple matter to find you after that," Bronwyn said. "Oh, and we had some help from a dog. Remember Addison?"

I nodded.

"Sharon's Panloopticon toadies tracked you to New York, and Addison's nose was able to track you to that market," said Hugh. "But that's as far as he would go."

Bless that little dog, I thought. I was losing count of how many times he'd risked his life for us.

"You were easy to find from there," said Bronwyn. "We followed the shouting."

"Did Miss Peregrine send you?" I said.

"No," said Hugh. "She doesn't know about this."

"She probably does by now," said Bronwyn. "She's awfully good at knowing things."

"We thought more than two of us leaving might attract too much attention."

"We all drew straws," said Bronwyn. "Hugh and me won." She glanced at Hugh. "Think Miss P will be mad at us for coming?"

Hugh nodded vigorously. "Steaming. But proud, too. Assuming we can get him back home in one piece."

"Home?" Noor said. "Where's that?"

"A loop in late-1800s London called Devil's Acre," Hugh said. "Closest thing we got to a home, anyhow."

Noor's eyebrows furrowed. "Sounds . . . delightful."

"It's rough around the edges, but it has a certain charm. It's better than living out of a suitcase, at any rate."

Noor looked a bit doubtful. "And it's a place for people like you?"

"For people like *us*," I said.

She didn't react, or tried not to, but I saw a flicker of something behind her eyes. An idea, perhaps, that was starting to register. *Us.*

"You'll be safe there," said Bronwyn. "No men with guns chasing you . . . no helicopters . . ."

I was about to agree, but then I remembered H's warning about the ymbrynes, and the things Miss Peregrine had said to me in the last conversation we'd had, about certain sacrifices being necessary for the greater good. One of those sacrifices being Noor herself.

"What about all the things H told us we need to do?" Noor said to me.

She had lowered her voice a bit, unsure of whether Bronwyn and Hugh knew, or should know, about this.

"All *what* things?" Hugh asked.

I said, "Before he died, H gave me some information about Noor and the people who've been chasing her, and he said we needed to find a woman named V. That there were important things about this that only she knew."

"V? Isn't that the hollow-slayer your grandfather trained?" asked Bronwyn.

Bronwyn had been at the diviners' loop when V's name had first come up. Of course she remembered.

"The same," I said. "And H—well, his hollowgast—showed us a map and gave us some instructions on how to find her—"

"His *hollowgast*?" gasped Bronwyn.

I pulled the paper map fragment out of my pocket and showed them. "He wasn't a hollowgast anymore. He was turning into something else."

"You mean a wight?" said Hugh. "That's the only thing hollows *turn into*."

Noor gave me a confused look. "You said the wights are our enemies."

"They are," I said. "But H was *friends* with this particular hollow . . ."

"This is getting more and more surreal," Noor said.

"I know. And that's why I think we should go with them to Devil's Acre," I said. "We need help, and all the peculiars I know and trust are there."

Whether or not they would ever trust *me* again, or would be willing to help after what I'd put them through, was another matter. But I had to try. I needed my friends, H's warning be damned.

If Miss Peregrine was really capable of sending the girl we had just helped rescue back into the hands of her captors for some political reason—or *any* reason—then she wasn't the Miss Peregrine I thought I knew. And if I couldn't keep Noor from harm in a loop full of friends, how was I supposed to help her navigate the wilderness of peculiar America?

"Millard's a cartography expert," said Bronwyn.

"And Horace is a prophet," I added. "Part-time, at least."

"Yeah," Noor said, her eyes sliding to me. "You never finished telling me about that."

The prophecy. I wanted to tell her in private, not in front of other people. It seemed we were no longer in immediate danger.

"It can wait," I said.

Hugh and Bronwyn both gave me curious looks.

"If you say so," Noor said, but she was starting to sound impatient.

The train began to stop. We were at the next station.

◆　　◆　　◆

We ran up out of the subway and back onto daylit streets. Noor took a moment to help Bronwyn get oriented.

"It's not far now," Bronwyn promised, guiding us diagonally through four lanes of traffic as horns blared.

We cut through a basketball court with a game in progress, through a sad green space overwhelmed by a looming pair of old condo towers. With each block the neighborhood was getting worse, rusty and chewed-up, until finally we were in the shadow of a huge brick building covered in scaffolding and ringed by chain-link fences skinned with green tarps. Bronwyn stopped and pulled a tarp back, revealing a hole in the fence. Noor and I traded a quick, hesitant glance.

Bronwyn and Hugh waved at us to follow and then disappeared through the hole.

Hugh popped his head back out. "You two coming?"

Noor squeezed her eyes shut for a second—no doubt fighting some version of *What the hell am I doing?* in her head—then climbed through. Though she might not have believed me, I often fought that same battle. A voice inside me had been shouting *What the hell are you doing?* more or less daily since I'd gone to Wales on a hunch to chase down ghosts from old photos. I'd gotten better at tuning it out, and it had gotten a lot quieter. But it was still there.

On the other side of the fence was a different world—or a much sadder and grimmer one, at any rate. Stepping through was like peeling back a corpse's shroud. The building had been built and finished long ago, then left to ruin. I stood in the wild grass and allowed myself one long breath to take it in—ten stories tall and wide as a city block, leaded windows all broken, bricks scabbed and veined with dead vines. Grand steps led up to a doorway framed in fancy wrought-iron curlicues. Above it, carved into a heavy marble slab, were the words PSYCHIATRIC HOSPITAL.

"How fitting," Noor said under her breath. "I must be losing my mind."

"You're not." I'd been waiting for this: for everything to start sinking in. "I know it feels like you are, but you're not, I promise."

Bronwyn and Hugh were twenty feet ahead, waving with increasing urgency for us to follow.

Noor wasn't looking at me. "I was drugged. I ate bad mushrooms. I'm in a coma. This is all a dream." She rubbed her hands on her face. "Anything makes more sense than—"

I said, "I can't prove you're not dreaming. But I do know what you're going through."

Bronwyn was running back toward us now and mouthing, *Come on, come on, come on.*

The fence rattled behind us, and someone swore. Then another voice said, "I know there's a way through here somewhere," and someone else grunted in reply.

It was a couple of Leo's guys. They had tracked us all this way.

If Noor had been contemplating some other course of action, that rattling fence banished it from her mind.

We raced through the high grass with Bronwyn and Hugh, up the steps past signs that blurred in my vision but said things like CONDEMNED PROPERTY and NO TRESPASSING, to an entrance that had been boarded over and broken open again. The splintered wood and bent nails gnawed at us like teeth as we contorted ourselves into the breach, once more to be entombed in a place we might never leave.

◆　　◆　　◆

The building was so dark and packed with trash that we couldn't quite run, not without impaling ourselves on some sharp obstacle or tripping into a hole in the floor, so instead we scurried sideways like crabs, taking long, kicking steps and sweeping our arms in front of us, following Hugh and Bronwyn. They were familiar with this place. We could hear Leo's guys in the yard, coming through the fence, pounding up the steps. Bronwyn had blocked the hole through which we'd entered by shoving an old fridge in front of it—it seemed to have been left close by for just that purpose—but we knew that wouldn't slow Leo's guys for long.

We stumbled into a large room lit by filthy, half-boarded windows, where we could finally see. We dodged moldering wheelchairs and nightmarish hulks of rusting medical equipment, our feet splashing through a shallow sea of toxic-looking water that stretched from wall to wall.

Noor was humming quietly to herself. I glanced at her, and she stopped.

"Nervous habit," she said.

I hopscotched around a patch of caved-in floor, then held out my hand to help her across. "What's there to be nervous about?" I said, managing a mirthless grin.

She took my hand and leapt. She wasn't laughing. "Please tell me there's a back way out of here."

"Better than that," said Hugh over his shoulder. "It's a Panloopticon door."

Before Noor could reply, there came a sound so eerie and out of place it sent shivers through me: a sour, dissonant chord of unmusical music. Rounding a stack of sodden yellow mattresses, we saw where it had come from: a gutted piano. It was an upright model that had been knocked onto its back and lay blocking the room's only exit, to a hallway lined with doors. The piano's intestines had been ripped out and nailed to points all around the hallway entrance, the heavy strings rising like a forest of metal hair standing on end. To get out of this room we would have to climb over the piano and squeeze through the strings. Someone had done it already—that must have been the awful chord we'd heard—which meant that that someone had just left this room or was in it with us now.

And then, out from behind a tipped-over baby incubator not far away, a figure rose to standing.

"Ah. It's you."

His face was covered by a mat of hair so thick it could only be called fur, and he gave us a cockeyed grin.

It was Dogface.

"Back so soon?" he said to Bronwyn and Hugh.

"Yes, but we can't stay," said Bronwyn.

"We need to get out now," said Hugh.

Dogface leaned against the piano. "Exit fee is two hundred."

"You said the fee was round-trip!" Hugh said angrily.

"You must have misheard me. You did seem to be in an awful hurry when I was explaining our pricing . . ."

We heard a distant shout, then the scrape of metal against stone. They were starting to move the refrigerator.

Dogface tipped his head toward the sound. "What's that? You haven't gotten yourselves into trouble, have you?"

"Yeah," I said irritably, "there's someone chasing us."

"Oh no," he said, clicking his tongue at me. "That's going to cost you a bit extra. We'll have to deceive them, cover for you . . . and are those Leo Burnham's flunkies? They sound angry."

"Fine. Whatever it costs," said Bronwyn.

We were dying to just knock him out of the way, but we knew he could cause us endless trouble if he wanted to.

"Five hundred," said Dogface.

Another scraping sound, this one longer than the last. They were making progress.

"I only have four hundred," said Hugh, digging in his pocket.

"Too bad." Dogface turned to go.

"We'll pay you tomorrow!" said Bronwyn.

Dogface turned back. "Tomorrow it'll be seven hundred."

There was a loud, splintering crash. They'd broken through.

"Okay! Fine!" Hugh said, an agitated bee escaping his lips.

"And don't be late with it. I'd hate to have to show them your little secret door."

They paid him all they had. Dogface counted it with excruciating exactness, then stuffed the bills into his pocket. He climbed onto the piano, pulled a lever inside it, then slipped silently through the muted strings. We followed, and when we'd reached the other side, he pushed the lever back into place.

The piano, I realized, was an alarm.

Dogface showed us the way. We rushed after him down a long hall—now that he'd extorted us, he started picking up the pace—but the hallway seemed to stretch on forever.

Along the way, a clutch of peculiars filed out from one of the doorways and began to follow us. They were unusual-looking, even by peculiar standards, and when Noor saw them she drew a sharp breath. A woman who was either legless or whose legs were invisible wafted after us on a cushion of air, the bottom of her long coat fluttering in the vacancy. "Aw, sweetheart, we're not gonna hurt you," she said, her voice soft and melodious. "We'll be friends."

"Don't know about *friends*," snorted a girl who was at least half warthog, two tusks and a snout protruding from her face, "but if you pay good, we won't be enemies."

Then came another legless lady—this one apparently unable to float, because she moved by taking great leaps forward on her hands. Then, with the litheness of a cat she jumped into the burly warthog girl's waiting arms. I could see her properly there: She lacked not only legs, but hips, waist, and half a torso. Her body, and the black satin blouse she wore, were cropped in a neat line near her belly button.

"Hattie the Halfsie," she said, giving us a little salute. "Which one of you is the famous feral?"

"Don't call her that," snapped a teenage boy with a huge, pulsating boil on his neck. "It's derogatory."

"Fine, *uncontacted*."

"She's not that either, anymore," said Dogface. "She's had to learn fast."

The warthog girl let out a snorting laugh. "Not fast enough, from the looks of her!"

Noor's jaw was locked tight, as if through sheer force of will she was forcing herself forward.

"These curious souls are the Untouchables," Dogface said, turning to walk backward for a moment, like a tour guide. "The ones no other clan wanted."

"Too peculiar to ever pass as normal," said Hattie.

"The most appalling, most unspeakable, most disgusting peculiars anywhere!" the boy with the boil said proudly.

"*I* don't think you're disgusting," said Bronwyn.

"Take it back!" said warthog girl, scowling.

Dogface twirled like a dancer and slid through an open door. "And this is our sanctum sanctorum. Well, the front door, anyhow."

We followed him into the room, and then Noor and I stopped cold. In the middle of the floor was an operating table, and honeycombed into the back wall were a dozen small freezer doors. This room was not only a dead end, it was the hospital's morgue.

"It's okay," Bronwyn said to Noor, gentle but urgent. "It won't kill us."

"Oh, *hell* no," Noor said, backing away. "There's no *way* I'm hiding in one of those things."

"Not *hiding*," Hugh said. "Traveling."

"She don't like it," said the warthog girl. "She's scared!"

The Untouchables all tittered in the doorway behind us.

Noor was already out of the room, crossing to another open door across the hall, the last alternative before going back the way we'd come.

Bronwyn and Hugh started after her, but I blocked them. "Let me talk to her," I said.

Climbing into a morgue freezer would've been a hard sell for anyone, peculiar or otherwise, but especially for someone so new to this world. I didn't particularly relish the idea myself.

I ran across the hall to join Noor in the other room. There was a bare metal cot lit by a beam of sunlight from a barred window. The corners were stacked up with discarded personal items that had belonged, presumably, to people who'd lived and died in the institution. Suitcases. Shoes.

Noor was agitated, turning from side to side. "I could've sworn I saw a door here. When we were running by before . . ."

"There's no other way out," I said.

Then I saw it, and my stomach sank.

"You mean this?"

She turned to look, and when she registered what it was, I thought she might cry. It was part of a mural on the wall. A trompe l'oeil; a door made of paint.

And then we heard the piano clang—once, twice, three times. Leo's men had climbed through.

"We have a choice," I said. "We can either . . ."

She wasn't listening. She was focused on the barred window and the sun beaming through it.

I started again. "We can either stay here and wait for them to *definitely* find us . . ."

She swept the air with both hands but succeeded only in scraping finger-trails of darkness through it, which quickly filled in again with light. I'd seen this sort of thing before: Some peculiar abilities function like muscles, and they can be strained, exhausted. Others get shy when the pressure's on.

She turned to face me. "Or I can trust you."

"Yes," I said, willing her toward me with every fiber of myself. "Me and a bunch of weirdos."

Leo's men were thundering down the outer hallway, searching rooms, rattling locked doors.

"This is absurd." She shook her head, then met my eyes, and something in her steadied. "I shouldn't trust you. But I do."

She'd accepted so much absurdity already. What was a little more, in the balance, when it might save us?

Bronwyn and Hugh were waiting at the door, looking panicked. "Ready?" Hugh said.

"Better be," said Dogface, leaning in. "By the way, if we have to cosh one of 'em for you, that's a thousand."

"Or Miss Poubelle can memory-wipe 'em for two," said the boy with the pulsating boil.

The men spotted us darting across the hall. I didn't look back, but I could hear their shouts and footfalls. The Untouchables had disappeared—they clearly didn't want to tangle with Leo's men, or make enemies of them, if they didn't have to.

In the morgue, one of the lower body freezers was now unlatched and hanging open. Hugh was standing beside it—and when he saw us coming he called to us, waved us on, and dove in.

We ran to the open freezer and squinted into the blackness inside. It wasn't just a cabinet for a corpse: it was a narrow tunnel that seemed to go on forever. Hugh's voice echoed from somewhere deep within, receding quickly. *"Whoooaaaaa!"*

I waited for Noor to go first. "This is stupid I'm so stupid this is so so *stupid*," she was chanting, but then she took a deep breath, steeled herself, and climbed in headfirst. She slid in partway but then got a little stuck, so I grabbed her feet and pushed, and in a moment the little compartment in the morgue wall swallowed her up.

Bronwyn went next, at my insistence, and then it was my turn. It was harder to make myself climb in than it should've been, considering I was the one who had convinced Noor to do it. It was such an unnatural action, shoving oneself into a morgue tray, that it took a few seconds of special effort for my rational mind—which knew that horrible, dark tunnely places made excellent loop entrances—to overcome my natural instincts, which were saying *no, no, no, you'll be eaten by zombies, nooooo.* The sound of angry men bursting through the door behind me helped a great deal, though, and before they got to me I was in, wriggling deeper and deeper as fast as I could.

A hand grabbed my foot. I managed to kick it off. I heard a struggle behind me, and there was a dull *thud* and one of the men cried out. I glanced back to see one of Leo's guys falling to the floor, the warthog girl behind him with a hunk of wood held in her hand.

I could hear Noor ahead of me, somewhere, grunting as she army-crawled forward on her elbows, farther and farther into the black. I pushed forward, then began to slide without effort. The tunnel was greased with something, and it angled downward slightly; after a few feet, forward momentum began to take me. It felt something like being born, I imagined, only faster and much longer—then I heard Noor scream. I felt myself being actively pulled through by something—not a hand but a bodiless force that gripped every part of me—like gravity. I felt that quickening in my blood and that lurch in my stomach that I knew so well.

We were crossing over.

CHAPTER TWO

*W*e tumbled out of a small closet onto the long, red-carpeted hallway of Bentham's Panloopticon. Bronwyn was collecting herself when Noor and I arrived, and Hugh was already waiting, looking slightly impatient.

"I was beginning to wonder if you'd decided not to join us!" he said as Bronwyn pulled Noor and I up effortlessly.

"Do you think they'll come after us?" I said, glancing nervously at the door.

"No chance," Bronwyn said. "The Untouchables like to get paid."

I turned to Noor. "How are you?" I said, quiet and close.

"I'm fine," she said quickly, seeming embarrassed. "Really sorry about my little freak-out back there." She was talking to the three of us and looking around at the plush hallway. "This place is definitely better than the one we just left."

Hugh started to say we should be going, but Noor interrupted him. "One more thing I need to say before we go anywhere or meet anyone else." She looked at us. "Thank you all for helping me. I'm grateful."

"You're welcome," Hugh said, maybe a bit too breezily.

She frowned. "I'm serious."

"We are, too," said Bronwyn.

"You can thank us when we get back to the house," said Hugh. "Come on, or Sharon's toadies will notice us and start asking questions I imagine we'd rather not answer."

"Right enough," Bronwyn said.

We walked quickly down the hall in a tight cluster. This section of the Panloopticon was relatively deserted, but after rounding a few corners, it began to get crowded. Peculiars dressed in outfits spanning every era and style were coming and going from loop doors. A sand drift was collecting outside one door, and a howling wind was spitting rain from another, held open a crack by a brick stuck in the jamb. People were lined up against the walls to have their travel documents checked and stamped by bureaucrats at small standing desks, and the echo of voices and footsteps and papers being shuffled made the place sound like a train station at evening rush hour.

Noor's eyes were wide and roving, and I could hear Bronwyn, a hand on her back, attempting to explain our surroundings in a low voice.

"Every one of these doors leads to a different loop . . . It's called the Panloopticon and it was invented by Miss Peregrine's extremely brilliant brother Bentham . . . then taken over by her extremely evil other brother, and our worst enemy, Caul—"

"It's actually proved quite useful," Hugh cut in. "This loop we're in, Devil's Acre, used to be a prison for miscreant peculiars . . . then became a lawless place and our enemies, the wights, made their headquarters here—"

"Until Jacob helped us smash them and killed their leader," Bronwyn said proudly.

At the mention of Caul, goose bumps had spontaneously broken out on my arms. "He's not exactly *dead*," I interjected.

"Fine," said Hugh, "he's trapped in a collapsed loop he can never, ever get out of, which is basically the same thing."

"And now the wights are all dead or locked up in jail," said Bronwyn. "And because they destroyed or seriously damaged many of our loops, a lot of peculiars had nowhere else to go and were forced to move in here."

"Temporarily, we hope," Hugh said. "The ymbrynes are trying to rebuild the loops we lost now."

Noor was starting to look overwhelmed, so I said, "Maybe we should save the history lecture for later."

We were passing a long row of windows, and Noor stared out as we walked. It was Devil's Acre on a supersaturated-yellow afternoon, the kind only intense air pollution can create: the Acre's crumbling buildings; snaking, green-black Fever Ditch; Smoking Street's eternal haze; and beyond it, old London, a confusion of spires and gray buildings receding into a cauldron of Industrial Age soot.

"My God," Noor said, voice just above a whisper.

I was walking next to her.

"This is London. Late nineteenth century. And you're feeling that thing again, aren't you?"

"The can't-be-reals," she said, slowing long enough to reach through an open window and wipe one finger along the ledge. As we sped up to keep pace with the others, she held it up. Her finger had turned black with soot. "But it *is* real," she marveled.

"Yes, it is."

She angled herself toward me. "Do you ever get used to it?"

"A little more every day." I thought about it. Tried to remember how hard it had been, even recently, to accept this world as real. "I still have moments where I look around and my head swims. Like I'm in the grip of some . . ."

"Nightmare?"

"I was going to say dream."

She nodded, a small assent, and I felt a shared recognition flicker between us: of a darkness mutually understood, and of a thin, golden thread of wonder and hope that ran through the fabric of this new world. *There is more*, it said. *There is more to the universe than you ever imagined.*

Then, in the corner of my vision, another kind of darkness appeared—and I felt a chill come over my whole body.

"So, you're alive." A slithering whisper in my ear. "I must say, I'm pleased."

I turned to see a wall of black robes. It was Sharon, towering behind us. Noor pressed her back against the window, but her face betrayed no fear. Hugh and Bronwyn saw what was happening and slunk over to an informational stand about loop costuming, trying not to be noticed.

"Are you going to introduce me to the young lady?" Sharon said.

"Sharon, this is—"

"I'm Noor," said Noor, thrusting out her hand. "And you are?"

"Just a humble boatman. How very nice to meet you." A gleaming grin appeared within the black tunnel of his hood, and his long white fingers wrapped around Noor's soft brown ones. I saw her try to suppress a shudder. He retracted his hand and turned to me. "You missed our meeting. I was very disappointed."

"I got busy," I said. "Can we talk about this later?"

"Of *course*," he said with exaggerated subservience. "Please, don't let me keep you."

We slipped away from him. Bronwyn and Hugh were waiting by the stairwell. "What did *he* want?" asked Hugh.

"I have no idea," I lied. And we hurried down the stairs.

◆　　◆　　◆

The streets of Devil's Acre were packed with peculiars, and on that particular afternoon the strange and sometimes alarming contrasts that defined the place were on full display. We passed an ymbryne teaching a group of young peculiars how to repair a ruined building using their peculiar talents. There was a redheaded boy levitating a stack of lumber with his mind, and two girls were reducing a pile of jagged rubble to gravel, very slowly, by grinding down the boulders with their teeth. We passed Sharon's cousins, too—the singing, hammer-swinging gallows riggers were leading a chain gang of miserable wight prisoners in leg shackles, followed by an ymbryne and a contingent, ten strong, of peculiars assigned to guard duty.

Noor turned to watch as they passed, singing at full volume.

"The night before the thief was stretched,
    the hangman came around
I've come, he said, before you're dead,
    a warning to expound . . ."

"Are they . . . ?"

"They are," I answered.

"And *everyone* here is . . ."

I met her eyes. "Yep. Just like us."

She shook her head in awe, and then her eyes widened and her chin rose, and I turned to see an extraordinarily tall man wobbling down the cobblestones toward us. He was fifteen feet high at least, and the top hat he wore added another foot or two. I couldn't have reached even the pocket of his tent-sized floral trousers if I'd reached my arms up and jumped.

Hugh hailed him as he passed. "Hullo, Javier, how goes the production?"

The tall man stopped too quickly and had to pinwheel his arms and steady himself against the roof of a building to keep from toppling over. Then he bent to look at Hugh. "Sorry, didn't see you down there," he boomed. "The production's hit a snag, unfortunately. Some cast members have been called away on loop-rehabilitation assignments, so we're restaging *The Grass Menagerie*, instead. They're over in the Green rehearsing right now . . ."

He gestured with his comparatively normal-length arm to a pocket of muddy grass across the street (the closest thing the Acre had to a park), where a troupe of Miss Grackle's student actors were tottering around in grotesque animal costumes, practicing their lines.

Noor gaped at them as we walked on, engrossed in the strange sight until Hugh kicked the stones and muttered to himself, "Too bad! I was looking forward to coaching the actor who plays me."

Noor turned, a half smile forming on her lips. "They're doing a play about you?"

I felt the heat of embarrassment start creeping up my neck. "Uh, yeah, one of the ymbrynes has a theater troupe . . . it's no big deal . . ."

I waved my hand dismissively and peered ahead, hoping to find a quick way to distract her and change the subject.

"Oh, don't be modest," said Hugh. "It's a whole play about how Jacob helped save us from the wights and banish Caul to an interdimensional hell."

"It's a big honor!" said Bronwyn, grinning broadly. "Jacob's really famous around here—"

"Whoa, check that out!" I shouted, hoping Noor hadn't heard that last bit. I pivoted and pointed at a small crowd of people in nearby Pye Square, where it looked like two peculiars were competing at something.

"It's a doorlifter contest!" Bronwyn said, successfully distracted. "I've been meaning to enter, but I need to train a bit first—"

"Let's not dawdle," said Hugh, but Bronwyn slowed to stare as we passed by, as did the rest of us.

There were a dozen people standing on a door that was laid across a pair of sawhorses, and a strapping young guy was facing off against a distinctly un-muscular older lady with a face mean enough to freeze water.

"That's Sandina," Bronwyn said. "She's amazing."

The small crowd was chanting her name now—"*Sandina! Sandina!*" The lady knelt below the door, planted her broad shoulders against it, and then rose slowly to her feet, groaning, the dozen people atop her swaying and cheering.

Bronwyn was cheering, too, and even Noor let out a little whoop, her face all surprise and wonder.

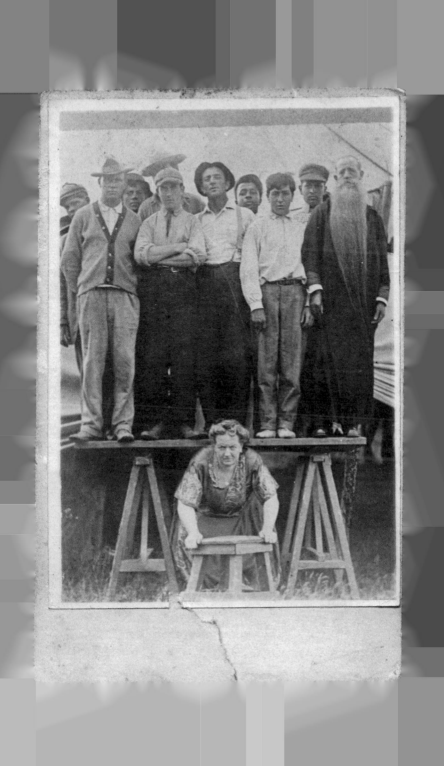

Wonder. Not horror. Not revulsion. And I started to think she might just fit in here.

I suddenly realized I didn't know where we were heading. Bronwyn and Hugh had said something about our "house," but last I'd checked, our friends were living in the rambling dormitories that occupied the ground level of the Panloopticon. When we started to cross a ramshackle footbridge over Fever Ditch, I finally asked where we were going.

"Miss P moved us out of Bentham's house while you were at the bone-mender's," Hugh explained, "away from nosy folk and their prying ears. Watch out for this board, it's loose!"

He hopped over a plank that fell away and splashed into the black water below. Noor stepped over it easily, but it took me a head-swimming moment to stretch out my leg and force myself over the gap.

We reached the other side, then walked parallel along the banks of the Ditch until we came to a rickety old house. Its design seemed to defy the laws of gravity and architecture: It was narrower by half at the bottom level than it was at the top, as if the house were standing on its head, and the second and third floors, which had expanded to reach out over empty space, were supported by a forest of spindly wooden stilts and crutches that stretched down to the ground. It was also humbler at the bottom, more or less a shack, while the second floor had big windows and carved columns and the third had a kind of half-built arched dome atop it—all of it hanging at unstraight angles and stained by time and neglect.

"It ain't the fanciest habitation," Bronwyn admitted, "but at least it's ours!"

And then I heard a high, familiar voice say my name, and I craned my neck to see Olive float out from behind a cupola on the roof. She was carrying a bucket and a rag and had a taut rope tied around her waist.

"Jacob!" she cried. "It's Jacob!"

She waved excitedly and I waved back, thrilled to see her and relieved for the kind greeting.

In her excitement Olive dropped the bucket she'd been holding, which landed on a part of the roof I couldn't see and elicited a shout of surprise from somebody else, though I couldn't tell who it was. Then the front door before us burst open so hard one of its hinges flew off with a *ping!*

Emma came racing out.

"Look who we found!" Bronwyn announced.

Emma stopped a few feet short of where I was standing and looked me up and down. She had on heavy black boots and rough blue work clothes. Her cheeks were apple red beneath a coating of grime, and she was puffing as if she'd just run down several flights of stairs. And she looked wild, her face a complicated blend of emotions: anger and joy and hurt and relief.

"I don't know whether to slap you or hug you!"

I broke into a grin. "Let's start with a hug?"

"You complete ass, you scared the life out of us!"

She ran forward and threw her arms around my neck.

"I did?" I said, playing innocent.

"One minute you're injured in bed and the next you're gone without a word to any of us? Of *course* you did!"

I sighed and told her I was sorry.

"Me too," she whispered, burying her forehead in my neck, then yanking it suddenly away again a moment later, as if she'd remembered she couldn't do that anymore.

Before I could ask what she was sorry *for*, I felt a jolt as another body collided with us. I looked down to see the arms of a purple-velvet smoking jacket wrapped around me.

"Wonderful, *wonderful* that you've returned to us alive and well," Millard was saying, "but may we have our reunion somewhere other than a public street?"

And he began shoving us toward the house. Tumbling through the tilting door, I glanced over my shoulder to find Noor, but saw only Bronwyn's and Hugh's beaming smiles. And then I was being led into a cozy, low-ceilinged living room-kitchen-stable (judging by the chickens clucking in one corner and the hay scattered around), and my friends were rushing into the room, one after another. Suddenly, I was being attacked by hugs and there was a loud, happy hubbub, everyone all talking at once.

"Jacob, Jacob, you're *back!*" cried Olive, stomping down a creaking staircase as fast as her lead shoes would allow.

"And you're *alive!*" shouted Horace, jumping and waving a tall silk hat.

"Of course I am!" I said. "It's not like I was going to get myself killed."

"You couldn't know that!" said Horace. "And neither could I, distressingly—I've had no dreams at all lately."

"America is a dreadful, dangerous place," said Millard, still glued to my side. "What were you thinking, going off like that without a word?"

"He didn't think we'd care!" said Bronwyn with incredulous flair.

Emma tossed her hands up. "Oh, for bird's *sake*, Jacob, do you even know us at all?"

"I'd already gotten you in so much trouble with the ymbrynes," I tried to explain, "and then there were all the things we said . . ."

"I honestly can't even remember."

Neither could I, come to think of it. Only how I'd felt afterward: hurt and angry that they had sided with Miss Peregrine over me.

"People say things when they're upset," Hugh snapped. "It doesn't mean they don't care if you live or die."

"We're family," Olive said, looking up at me sternly, hands on her hips. "Don't you know that?"

Something about her little face screwed up into a frown made my insides melt a little.

"Wah-wah-wahhh, my friends were mean to me!" whined Enoch, plodding down the stairs with a sloshing pail of water. "I'll play hero by myself and get into so much trouble I need rescuing! *That'll* show them!"

"Nice to see you, too."

"That goes for one of us. Thanks to you, we've been shoveling flaming manure and unclogging sewer drains for two days." He shouldered past me and flung the wet and chunky contents of the pail out into the street, then wiped his dirty brow with the back of his even dirtier hand. "They might be in a forgiving mood, but you owe me, Portman."

"Fair enough," I said.

He put out his hand. It dripped.

"Welcome back."

I pretended not to notice the filth and shook it. "Thanks."

"How'd the girl-saving go, anyhow? Complete failure, I assume, judging by the fact that she's nowhere to be seen—"

I turned around to look, alarmed. "Noor?"

"She was just here!" said Bronwyn.

I started to panic, then heard her voice—"Over here!"—and I turned to see Noor emerge from a patch of darkness that hadn't been there when we came in, a faint glow rolling slowly down her throat.

I let out the breath I hadn't realized I'd been holding.

"Impressive," said Millard.

"You don't have to hide," said Olive. "We don't bite."

"I wasn't," said Noor. "You guys seemed like you needed a moment to yourselves, that's all."

I went over to her, feeling guilty that I hadn't introduced her yet.

"Some of you have already met her, but for those who haven't—everybody, this is Noor Pradesh. Noor, this is everybody."

Noor gave a general wave to the room. "Hey, everybody."

As my friends gathered around to greet her, she seemed remarkably calm. A totally different person from the one who had nearly refused to go in the Untouchables' morgue drawer.

"Welcome to Devil's Acre," Horace said, offering a prim handshake. "Hopefully you don't find it *too* disgusting."

"It's pretty astounding, so far," said Noor.

"I hope you'll stay here with us," said Hugh. "After all you've been through, you deserve a rest."

"It's nice to finally meet you in person," said Olive. "The others have talked so much about you. Well, shouted about you, mostly . . ."

I patted Olive's shoulder and moved her along. "Okay, Olive, thank you."

Emma swooped in and gave Noor a hug, which looked a bit forced. "Don't take what we said before to mean we're not happy to have you. We are."

"Hear, hear!" said Millard.

Enoch wiped his hand on his trousers before extending it to Noor. "Pleasure to see you again. I'm glad Jacob didn't screw this up—worse than he did, anyway."

"He was great," Noor said. "He and the old man were . . ." She winced, remembering.

"What happened?" said Emma.

Noor looked quickly at me, then back at Emma. Her voice went gravelly as she said, "He died."

"H broke Noor out of Leo's loop," I said. "He was shot, but hung on until he got Noor back to his place. That's where I found them."

I felt callous saying it so quickly and matter-of-factly, but there it was.

"I'm very sorry to hear that," said Millard. "I never met him, but any compatriot of Abe's was doubtless a good man."

"My God," Emma said. "Poor H." She was the only other one of us who had met him, and the mournful look she gave me said *we'll talk later.*

"I owe him my freedom," Noor said quietly. And it seemed there was nothing more to say.

There was a brief, awkward moment of quiet, which Millard broke by saying to Noor, "In any case, I'm very glad you're not in the hands of that awful Leo Burnham anymore."

"Me too," said Noor. "That guy was . . ." She shook her head slowly, unable to find just the right words.

"They didn't hurt you, did they?" asked Bronwyn.

"No. They asked me lots of questions and told me I was going to be in their army and then put me in a locked room for two days, but they didn't hurt me."

"Thank God for that, at least," I said.

Then a small voice asked, "Was it worth it, Jacob? Risking so much for her?"

I turned to see Claire glaring at me from the doorway, her sour expression a sharp contrast to the yellow rubber boots and hat she wore.

"Claire, that's rude," said Olive.

"No, *Jacob* was rude when he disobeyed Miss Peregrine even though it might've meant a *war* breaking out that the ymbrynes have been trying *very* hard to prevent!"

"Well, did it?" I said.

"Did it what?"

"Start a war?"

Claire clenched her fists and made the angriest face she could. "That's not the *point*."

"Your and H's actions did not, as a matter of fact, spark a war." Miss Peregrine, striking in an angular black dress and upswept hair, had appeared on the landing of the stairs. "Not yet, at any rate—though you may have brought us to the brink of one."

The headmistress wafted down the steps and made a beeline for Noor. "So you're the famous Miss Pradesh," she said evenly. She dashed out her hand and shook Noor's once, quickly. "My name is Alma Peregrine, and I'm headmistress to these sometimes intractable children."

Noor gave a crooked half smile, as if she found Miss Peregrine vaguely amusing. "Nice to meet you," she said. "Jacob didn't mention anything about a war."

"No." Miss Peregrine turned to face me. "I don't imagine he did."

I felt my face go hot. "I know you must be angry, Miss P, but helping Noor was something I had to do."

I felt Noor's eyes on me, and everyone else's, but I didn't look away from the ymbryne. Miss Peregrine held my gaze a moment longer, then turned abruptly, walked to a door, and opened it to reveal a small sitting room.

"Mr. Portman, you and I have a few things to discuss. Miss Pradesh, you've had an exhausting few days. I'm sure you'd appreciate a chance to rest and freshen up. Bronwyn, Emma, please help our guest get settled."

Noor gave me a questioning look—a kind of *what the hell is going on?*—and I replied with a quick shake of my head that I hoped said *everything's fine*, and then Miss Peregrine shuttled me into the room and closed the door.

The room was lined with thick fur rugs, and the only furniture was a pile of pillows on the floor. Miss Peregrine walked to a cloudy window and looked out for what seemed like a long time.

"I should've known you'd do this," she began. "It's my fault, really, for leaving you alone and unguarded." She shook her head. "It's just what your grandfather would have done."

"I'm sorry for any trouble I caused," I said. "But I'm not sorry for—"

"Trouble can be handled," she interrupted. "But we could not handle losing you."

I'd been all ready to argue, to make an impassioned case for why I'd gone to help H rescue Noor from Leo Burnham, and she'd caught me off guard.

"Then you're not . . . angry?"

"Oh no. I am livid. But I learned long ago to control my emotions." She turned fully to face me, and I saw that her eyes were rimmed with tears. "It's good to have you back, Mr. Portman. Never do anything like that again."

I nodded, choking back tears of my own.

She cleared her throat, rolled her shoulders, and reset her expression. "Now, then. You are going to sit down and tell me everything. I believe you were saying something about how you *had* to do this."

There was a sharp knock at the door, and without waiting for an answer, it opened.

Noor came inside.

Miss Peregrine frowned. "I'm sorry, Miss Pradesh. We're having a private conversation. Jacob has something to tell me."

"There's something he and I need to talk about." She pinned me with her eyes. "This prophecy. You made it sound urgent."

"What prophecy?" Miss Peregrine said sharply.

"Apparently it's got something to do with me," Noor said. "So I'm sorry, but I can't let someone else hear about it before I do."

Miss Peregrine looked both surprised and impressed. "I completely understand. I suppose you'd better come in."

She gestured to a pillow on the floor.

◆　　◆　　◆

We settled among the pillows. Miss Peregrine looked regal even sitting on the floor, back straight and her hands lost in the black folds of her dress. I told her and Noor about the prophecy, or what I'd heard of it, anyway, and what had preceded its telling. I caught Miss Peregrine up on some details she didn't yet know, such as how I'd snuck out of the Panloopticon to find H in New York and what I'd found when I reached his apartment: Noor sleep-dusted on H's sofa; H mortally wounded on the floor.

Then I told them what he'd said to me just before he died.

I wished now that I had written down his exact words while they were still fresh in my mind; so much had happened since they were told to me that they were becoming a bit jumbled.

"H said there was a prophecy that foretold your birth," I said, looking at Noor. "You were 'one of the seven' who would be the 'emancipators of peculiardom.' "

She looked at me like I was speaking Greek. "What's *that* supposed to mean?"

"I don't know," I said, and looked hopefully to Miss Peregrine. Her expression was neutral. "Is there more?"

I nodded. "He said a 'new and dangerous age' was coming, which I guess is what the seven are supposed to 'emancipate' us from. And he said the prophecy was the reason those men were hunting Noor."

"You mean the weirdos who were stalking me at school," said Noor.

"Yeah. And who came after us at that building site in the helicopter. And shot Bronwyn with the sleep dart."

"Hmmm." Miss Peregrine seemed doubtful.

"Well?" I said to Noor. "What do you think?"

"That's it?" Noor's eyebrows rose. "That's the whole thing?"

"Highly unlikely," Miss Peregrine said. "It sounds like H was paraphrasing. Attempting to convey the basics to you before he bled to death."

"But what does any of that *mean*?" Noor said to Miss Peregrine. "Bronwyn said you're someone who knows things."

"I am, generally. But obscure prophecies are not my area of expertise."

They were, however, one of Horace's. And so, with Noor's permission, we called him into the room and told him about it.

He listened with intense fascination. "The seven emancipators of peculiardom," he said, rubbing a hand over his smooth chin. "It rings a bell, but I need more information. Did he say who the prophet was? Or where the prophecy came from?"

I struggled to remember. "He said something about an"—the exact word was escaping me now—"an . . . *Apocryphate*? Apocryton?"

"Interesting," Horace said, nodding. "Sounds like a text of some kind. Not one I've heard of, but it's something to go on."

"Is that all?" Miss Peregrine said. "H paraphrased a few lines of prophecy and then expired?"

I shook my head. "No. The last thing he said was that I should take Noor to find a woman named V."

"*What?*"

We turned to see Emma poking her head through the door. She put a hand over her mouth, embarrassed at her outburst, then decided to own it and just came in. "Sorry. But we've all been listening."

The door opened wider, and there were all my friends on the other side.

Miss Peregrine let out an irritated sigh. "Oh, come in, then," she said. "I'm sorry, Noor. There really are no secrets amongst us, and I have a feeling this may be a matter that will concern all of us."

Noor shrugged. "If anyone can tell me what the hell this all means, I'd write it on a billboard."

"An emancipator of peculiardom, huh?" said Enoch. "Sounds quite fancy."

I gave him an elbow in the ribs as he sat down next to me. "Don't start with her," I muttered.

"Wasn't my idea," Noor said to Enoch. "I think it sounds *nuts*."

"But H must've believed it," said Millard, his purple jacket pacing the floor, "or he wouldn't have risked his life to save Noor's. And he wouldn't have roped Jacob and the rest of us into helping find her."

"You were saying," Emma said to me. "About that . . . woman."

"V, yes," I said. "She's the last hollow-slayer left alive, H said. She was personally trained by my grandfather back in the sixties. There are references to her all through his mission logs."

"The diviners remembered meeting her more than once," said Bronwyn. "They seemed quite impressed with her."

Emma squirmed, unable to hide her unease.

Miss Peregrine drew a small pipe from her dress pocket and asked

Emma to light it for her, then took a deep draw and let out a puff of green smoke. "I find it very curious," she said to me, "that he advised you to seek the help of another hollow-hunter, rather than an ymbryne."

Rather than me.

"*Very* curious," Claire agreed.

"He seemed to think V was the only person who could help us," I said. "But he didn't say why."

Miss Peregrine nodded and blew out another green puff. "Abe Portman and I respected each other immensely, but there were a number of matters on which his organization and mine disagreed. It's possible he simply felt more comfortable sending you into the protection of one of his comrades, rather than me."

"Or he believed there were things you didn't know about the situation," said Millard.

"Or the prophecy," said Horace, and Miss Peregrine looked briefly annoyed at the reminder.

I knew, of course, that H did not fully trust the ymbrynes, but he had never explained why, and it wasn't something I was prepared to bring up in front of the others.

"He left us a map," said Noor. "To find V."

"A map?" said Millard, spinning to face her. "Do tell."

"Just before he died, H directed his hollowgast, Horatio, to give us a piece of a map from a wall safe," I said. "Then he let Horatio eat his eyes"—this prompted a disgusted groan from several of my friends—"which seemed to allow the hollow to consume his peculiar soul. A few minutes later, he started turning into, I don't know, a wight, I guess. Or the beginnings of one."

"And that's when I woke up," said Noor. "And Horatio told us something that sounded like a clue."

"Then he jumped out the window," I said.

"May I see that map?" said Miss Peregrine.

I handed it to her. Millard's jacket bent over Miss P's shoulder as she smoothed the fragment against her leg, and the room went quiet.

"This scrap isn't much to go on," Millard said after only a few seconds of study. "It's a tiny detail of a much larger document, which is mostly topographical."

"Horatio's clue sounded like map grid coordinates," I said.

"Those might help more if we had the whole map," said Millard. "Or if the map included place names. Towns and roads and lakes."

"Actually," said Miss Peregrine, bending closer while holding up a magnifying monocle to one eye, "they appear to have been erased."

"Curiouser and curiouser," said Millard. "You say the ex-hollow uttered something . . . what was it?"

"He told us we could find her in a loop," I said. "H called it 'the big wind,' and Horatio said it was 'in the heart of the storm.' "

"Does that mean anything to you?" Noor said to the room generally.

"Sounds like a looped hurricane, or a cyclone," said Hugh.

"Obviously," said Millard.

"What kind of mad ymbryne would loop such a terrible thing?" Olive said.

"One who really doesn't want visitors dropping in," said Emma, and Miss Peregrine nodded in agreement.

"Do you know of such a place?" Emma asked her.

Miss Peregrine frowned. "I don't, sorry to say. It's probably hidden somewhere in America. Again—not my area of expertise."

"It will be someone's," said Millard. "Don't despair, Miss Pradesh. We'll make sense of this yet. May I borrow this?" The map appeared to float as he held it up.

I looked at Noor and she nodded. "Okay," I said.

"If I can't crack it, I'll bet someone around here can."

"I hope so," said Noor. "When you go asking around, I'd like to come."

"Of course," said Millard, sounding pleased.

"And I can help you find out more about the prophecy," said Horace.

"You might speak to Miss Avocet," Miss Peregrine said. "I was her pupil once upon a time, and I remember she had a special interest in lunacy, divination, and automatic writing. Prophetic texts might fall under that aegis."

"Fantastic idea," said Horace, his eyes gleaming excitedly. He cocked his head at Miss Peregrine. "Though it would help if I could get off cleaning duty for a few days . . ."

"All right." The headmistress sighed. "In that case, you're excused from work, too, Millard."

"That hardly seems fair!" Claire whined.

"I'm sure *I* could be of help," Enoch said with a grin. "Perhaps we should interview the recently deceased H?"

I remembered the dead man packed in ice that Enoch had helped us question back on Cairnholm and shuddered. "No, thanks, Enoch," I said. "I would never do that to him."

He shrugged. "I'll think of something."

Everyone was chattering in low voices now, until Noor got to her feet and cleared her throat. "I just wanted to say thanks," she said. "I'm brand-new here, so I don't know if this sort of thing happens a lot or not . . . prophecies and kidnappings and mysterious maps . . ."

"Not *very* often," said Bronwyn. "We went almost sixty years without much happening at all."

"Then . . . thanks," she said, a bit awkward.

She was blushing as she sat down.

"Any friend of Jacob's is a friend of ours," said Hugh. "And this is how we treat friends."

There was a chorus of assent. And suddenly I felt very humbled, and very grateful, to have such friends as these.

CHAPTER THREE

*A*fter a while Miss Peregrine announced that it was dinnertime, and that we'd done a not-very-good job of hosting Noor thus far, and here was our chance to make up for it. We trooped through the house and up the rickety stairs to a dining room, where a long table made from rough planks was set with mismatched cups and plates and a set of windows that looked out onto the polluted river and the crumbling buildings on its opposite bank. In the amber glow of sunset it looked almost pretty.

Noor and I had, finally, a chance to wash up. In the next room there was a basin and a big pitcher of water beneath a cloudy mirror, and we were able to splash some water on our faces and clean ourselves up a bit.

But just a bit.

When we came back, Noor sat beside me, and Emma was lighting candles with her fingertip while Horace oversaw the distribution of food, ladled into bowls from a big black cauldron hanging in the hearth.

"I hope you like stew," he said, setting a steaming bowl before Noor. "The food's great in Devil's Acre, so long as you like stew for every meal."

"I'd eat anything right now," she said. "I'm starving."

"That's the spirit!"

We settled into easy conversation, and soon the room was filled with the hum of voices and the clatter of spoons. It was remarkably cozy, considering where we were. Making inhospitable places cozy was one of Miss Peregrine's many talents.

"What did you used to do in your normal life?" asked Olive through a full mouth.

"Go to school, mostly," Noor replied. "By the way, your use of the past tense there is interesting. . . ."

"Everything's going to change for you," Miss Peregrine said.

"It already has," Noor said. "My life is unrecognizable from what it was last week. Not that I'd really want to go back."

"That's precisely it," said Millard, jabbing a loaded fork in her direction. "It's very difficult to tolerate a normal life once you've lived a peculiar one for a while."

"Trust me, I've tried," I said.

Noor looked at me. "Do you ever miss your normal life?"

"Not even a little," I said. And I almost meant it.

"Do you have a mother and father who will miss you?" asked Olive. Olive was always asking about mothers and fathers. I think she missed hers more than anyone, though she had long since out-lived them.

"I've got foster parents," said Noor. "I never met my real ones. But I'm sure Fartface and Teena won't cry too much if I don't come back."

The word *fartface* prompted a few curious glances, but they must have assumed it was just a weird present-day people name, because no one said anything.

"How do you like being peculiar?" asked Bronwyn.

Noor had hardly been able to take a bite of food, but she didn't seem to mind. "It was scary before I knew what was happening to me, but I'm starting to adjust."

"Already?" said Hugh. "Back in the Untouchables' loop—"

"I have a thing about certain types of confined spaces," she said. "That, uh, door—" She shook her head ruefully. "Kind of threw me for a loop."

"Threw you for a loop!" Bronwyn shouted, laughing loudly and clapping her hands. "That's very good!"

Enoch groaned. "No loop puns, please, intentional or otherwise."

"Sorry," Noor mumbled, having used the interruption to finally get some food into her mouth. "Unintentional."

Horace stood up and announced that it was time for dessert, and he whisked off into the kitchen and brought out a big cake.

"Where did that come from?" Bronwyn cried. "You've been holding out on us!"

"I was saving it for something special," he said. "I think this more than qualifies."

He served Noor the first slice. Before she could take a bite, he asked her, "When did you realize you were different?"

"I've been different my whole life," Noor said with a subtle smile, "but I only realized I could do *this* a few months ago." She waved her hand over a candle, took its light between two fingers, and popped it into her mouth. Then she blew it out again like a long stream of glowing smoke, which slowly settled, like falling particles of dust, back atop the candle.

"How wonderful!" Olive cheered, as everyone oohed and clapped.

"Do you have normal friends?" asked Horace.

"One. Though I think I like her so much because she isn't very normal."

"How *is* Lilly?" Millard asked, a little sigh of longing escaping him.

"I haven't seen her since you did."

"Oh," he said, chastened. "Of course. I hope she's well."

Emma, who'd been uncharacteristically quiet, suddenly asked, "Do you have a boyfriend?"

"Emma!" said Millard. "Don't pry."

Emma went red and looked down at her cake.

"It's okay," said Noor, laughing. "No, I don't."

"Guys, I think we should give her a chance to take a few bites," I said, weirdly embarrassed by Emma's question.

Miss Peregrine, who had been quietly brooding for the past few minutes, dinged her glass and asked for everyone's attention. "I'm due back at the peace talks tomorrow," she said. "The ymbrynes are in the midst of very sensitive negotiations with the leaders of the three American clans"—she gravely directed this to Noor—"and the threat of war between them grows with each passing day. I'm sure H's brazen rescue and your disappearance have only made things more complicated."

"Oops," Noor said quietly.

"You're not to blame, of course. But there will be damage to contain and bruised egos to mollify. That is, if we can even get them back to the negotiating table."

"Everyone's calling the peace talks the *Conference of the Birds*," Bronwyn stage-whispered to Noor.

Noor gave her a blank look. "Yeah?"

Bronwyn raised her eyebrows. "Because the ymbrynes can turn into birds?"

"They can?" said Noor, looking at Miss Peregrine with surprise.

"I still don't understand what the big to-do is," said Enoch. "Would it really matter that much if the Americans waged war on one another? Why is that any concern of ours?"

Miss Peregrine stiffened, then laid down her spoon. "I hate to repeat myself, but as I've said, war is a—"

"Virus," said Hugh.

"It 'respects no borders,'" Emma said, as if repeating from a textbook.

Miss Peregrine rose heavily from her chair and went to the window. We could feel a lecture coming on.

"Of course, the Americans are not our priority," she said. "We ymbrynes care most about rebuilding our society—our loops, our way of life. But the chaos of a war would make that impossible. Because war *is* a virus. I can see you don't understand what that means. It's not your fault; none of you have ever witnessed a war between peculiar factions. But many ymbrynes have."

She turned and looked out across the Acre, the perpetual smoke that hung above it now stained an imperial violet.

"The oldest amongst us remember the disastrous Italian war of 1325. Two peculiar factions rose up against each other, and the battle raged not only across physical borders, but temporal ones. The peculiars fought in loops, and the fighting spilled—inevitably, fierce as it was—into the present. Scores of peculiars died, and *thousands* of normals. An entire city was burned to the ground! Razed flat!" She turned to face us and swept a flat hand through the air, as if to paint a picture of the destruction. "So many normals saw us fighting, there was no containing it. It sparked a pogrom against our kind, a bloody purge that killed many more of us, and drove peculiars out of Northern Italy for a century. It took an enormous effort to recover. We had to memory-wipe entire towns. Rebuild. We even enlisted peculiar scholars—Perplexus Anomalous was one!—to revise normal history books, so that the carnage would be remembered as something other than the War of the Freaks, which is what it was called for generations. Finally, Perplexus and his scholars were able to rewrite it as the War of the Oaken Bucket. To this day, normals believe thousands died battling over a wooden pail."

"Normals are so stupid," said Enoch.

"Not as stupid as they used to be," said Miss Peregrine. "That was seven hundred years ago. Today, if a peculiar war were to break out in earnest, it would be nearly impossible to cover up. It could spill into the present, where it would be filmed, disseminated worldwide, and we would be exposed, ruined, vilified. Imagine the terror of normals witnessing a battle between powerful peculiars. They would think the end-times were upon them."

"A new and dangerous age," Horace mused darkly.

"But don't the Americans know all this?" asked Emma. "Don't they understand what could happen?"

"They claim to," said Miss Peregrine. "And they swear up and down that they would adhere to the various conventions of war that dictate a peculiar battlefield must always be in the past, or in a loop. But wars are hard to control, and they don't seem as worried about the consequences as they should be."

"Like the Russians and Americans during the so-called Cold War," said Millard. "Blinded by mutual distrust. Desensitized to the dangers by constant exposure."

"*I promise our dinner conversations aren't always this depressing,*" Olive whispered across the table to Noor.

"What if that's the 'dangerous age' the prophecy mentions?" I said. "Could it be predicting a war between peculiars?"

"It's certainly possible," said Horace.

"Then maybe war is inevitable," said Hugh.

"No," Miss Peregrine said. "I refuse to accept that."

"Prophecies are not necessarily fate," Horace said. "Sometimes they're just warnings about events that could happen—or will *probably* happen—if you don't take action to change the course of things."

"Hopefully there's nothing to the prophecy *at all*," Olive said miserably. "The whole thing sounds scary."

"Yes, I'd rather not need emancipating, thank you very much," said Claire.

"I'd rather not have to *do* any emancipating," said Noor. "Though it says I'm one of seven, so I guess I don't have to do it by myself . . . but who are the other six?"

Horace spread his hands. "Another mystery. Pass the salt, please."

Olive's head fell into her hands. "Can we *please* talk about something nice for a while?"

Emma reached over to ruffle her hair. "Sorry, dear. One more thing is bugging me. This supposed secret society that's trying to get their hands on Noor. Who *are* they?"

"Wouldn't I love to know," Noor said.

"Doesn't the answer seem obvious?" said Millard.

I turned toward him, surprised. "No. Should it?"

He snapped his invisible fingers. "They're *wights*."

"But H told me specifically they were normals," I said.

"And Miss Annie from the diviners' loop said something about a secret society of American normals," Bronwyn added, "left over from the slave-trade days."

Sometimes I underestimated how closely Bronwyn paid attention to things.

"Yes, I was there," said Millard. "I don't doubt there was such a society in the past. But I seriously doubt any normals would have the wherewithal to pose such a danger to us now. We've been hidden in loops far too long."

"I very much agree," said Miss Peregrine.

"Last time we talked about it," I said, "you told me it sounded like the work of another clan. Not wights."

"Things have changed," she said. "There's been a dramatic uptick in wight activity lately. Just in the last few days, there have been multiple sightings."

"Attacks?" said Horace, his face paling.

"None yet, but reports of movement. All in America."

"But I thought only a small group of them managed to escape after the Library of Souls collapsed," Emma said.

Miss Peregrine was slowly circling the table, the shadows cast by a dozen candles flickering over her face. "That's true. But a small number of wights are capable of causing a great deal of trouble. And they may have had a few sleeper agents embedded in America, waiting to be called up. We don't know for certain."

"How many are we talking about?" asked Noor. "Between the

people at my school and the ones from the helicopter attack, there were a lot . . ."

"Maybe they weren't *all* wights," said Bronwyn. "They might have hired mercenary normals to help them. Or mind controlled them somehow."

"It would be just like wights to attempt such a brazen kidnapping," Millard said, "then make it seem as if someone else was responsible—normals or another American clan."

"They're masters of trickery and disguise, after all," said Miss Peregrine. "It was Percival Murnau himself who founded the Department of Obfuscation."

She said his name as if I should've heard of him. "Who's that?" I asked.

Miss Peregrine stopped beside my chair and looked down at me. "Murnau is—well, *was*—Caul's top lieutenant. He was the main architect of the raids that destroyed so many of our loops and killed so many of our people. We caught him the day the Library of Souls collapsed, luckily, and he's cooling his heels in our jail, awaiting trial."

"He's a nasty man," Bronwyn said, a tremor of revulsion in her voice. "One of my jobs is guarding his cell block. He'll eat anything that crawls into his cell—rats, bugs. Even the other wights don't go near him."

Horace dropped his fork. "Well, *my* appetite is killed."

"So, if it was these wights," said Noor, "then what do they want with me?"

"They must know about the prophecy, too," said Horace. "And believe it, or they wouldn't have gone to all the trouble of finding you."

"They found her months ago," Millard said. "They could've taken her anytime. They were *waiting*."

"For what?" I said.

"Obviously, for someone else to come after her," he replied.

"You think they were using me as bait?" Noor said, eyes widening a bit.

"Not *just* bait," said Millard. "They wanted you. But they wanted someone else, too, and were willing to be patient in order to get them."

"Who?" I said. "H?"

"Maybe. Or V."

"Or *you*, Mr. Portman," said the headmistress. She let that sink in as I swallowed the last of my cake. "I think you and Miss Pradesh need to be very careful. I think someone may be trying to get their hands on the both of you."

* * *

After dinner was over we all went upstairs to bed. The third floor was a warren of small rooms connected by zigzagging hallways that spread across the top level of the house, half reserved for the boys and the other half for the girls.

Noor was red-eyed with exhaustion, and I'm sure I looked just as tired. We hardly had the energy to keep ourselves upright.

"You'll bunk with Horace and me," said Hugh.

"And you can have my bed," Olive said to Noor.

"I could never. I'll sleep on the floor."

"It's no trouble," Olive said. "I usually sleep on the ceiling anyway."

"The facilities are quite basic, inasmuch as there are none," Hugh said. He pointed at a bucket at the end of the hallway. "That's the bathroom." He turned and pointed to another bucket at the other end. "And that's clean boiled water to drink. Don't get them confused."

The others left Noor and me alone just as Miss Peregrine appeared carrying a candlelit lantern. She had changed into a long-sleeved nightdress, and her hair was loose and trailed down the back of her neck. "I won't see you in the morning," she said regretfully. "But I'm only a Panloopticon door away. You can always send a messenger to the conference loop if you need to reach me."

"I wish you didn't have to go," I said. "We could use your help."

"If it were for anything less important, I would never go. But at the moment I have greater responsibilities. I'll be leaving before first light." She turned to Noor and smiled. "I'm so glad you've come, Miss Pradesh. I hope you feel welcome here. The circumstances of your arrival might not have been ideal, but I am no less glad at your presence."

"Thank you," Noor said. "I'm glad to be here."

Miss Peregrine leaned in and kissed Noor on both cheeks, something I'd only seen her do to other ymbrynes or honored guests. "Bird be with you," she said, and then she was gone down the hall.

"Tomorrow we'll dig into all this," I said. "If there's more to the prophecy, we'll find it. And Millard will help us decode that map." I held Noor's gaze for an extra beat. "This is very important to all of us."

Noor nodded. "Thank you." Let out an exhausted breath. I felt a pang of empathy for her and for how she must've been feeling.

"How are you?" I said. "Still feeling like you're losing your mind?"

"It's probably better that I haven't had much downtime to think about everything. For now, I'm just going with it. You know what my brain keeps defaulting to whenever I have a moment of quiet?"

"What?"

"That I have a calc test in two days, and I should be studying."

We both laughed.

"I think your GPA is going to take a little hit here. Sorry."

"It's okay. Everything's bizarre and confusing and so much of this is super scary and messed up . . . but despite everything's that obviously wrong right now, I actually feel *good*."

"You do?"

Her voice fell to a near whisper. "Like for the first time in a long time I'm not . . . alone."

Our eyes met. I reached out and took her hand.

"You're not alone," I said. "You've got people."

She smiled gratefully, then hugged me. I felt something small but powerful turn in my chest.

I bent my head, let my lips rest on top of her hair. Almost a kiss.

And then we said good night.

⁕   ⁕   ⁕

I had the old dream again. The same one I'd had so many times after my grandfather was killed. It's the night he died, and I'm running through the spiky woods behind his house screaming his name. Like always, I find him too late. He's lying on the ground bleeding, a hole in his chest. One of his eyes torn out. I go to him. He tries to speak to me. Usually in these dreams he does, and he says all the things he said that night: *Find the bird. In the loop.* But this time he's only muttering in Polish, and I can't understand.

Then I hear another branch snap and I look up from where I'm kneeling and there's the monster, covered in Abe's blood, horrible thick tongues waving in the air.

He's got Horatio's face. And he says, in a guttural hollowgast snarl I can plainly understand:

He is coming.

⁕   ⁕   ⁕

I jolted awake to the sound of an explosion.

Bolting upright in bed, I saw that Hugh and Horace were already up, crowding each other to get a look out the window.

"What's going on?" I shouted, stumbling out of my sheets.

"Something bad," Hugh said.

I joined them at the window. It was first light. Sirens were howling in the distance, and panicked shouts echoed from across the Acre. People in other buildings were throwing open their windows and looking out to see what was going on.

Bronwyn burst into the room, her hair mussed from sleep. "What's happened?" she said. "Where's Miss P?"

Emma shoved past her. "Everyone into the common room!" she shouted. "Head count, now!"

A minute later we were all together, all present and accounted for but Miss Peregrine, who had left for the conference before dawn. Something had happened elsewhere in the Acre—an attack, an explosion, *something*—but we weren't sure what.

Through the window we could hear someone authoritative-sounding going down the street and shouting, "Stay indoors! Do not come out until so instructed!"

"What about Miss P?" Olive said. "What if something's happened to her?"

"I can find out," said Millard. "I'm invisible."

"I can be, too," said Noor, and she raked the light from the air before her and stepped into it. "Let me help."

"I appreciate the offer, but I work better alone."

"It's not worth the risk," Emma said. "Miss P can take care of herself."

"So can I," Millard replied. "Whatever's happening, you can bet no one's going to tell us the whole truth about it. If you want to know anything worth knowing around here, you've got to find out for yourself."

He shrugged off his sleeping robe and it fell to the floor in a pile. Emma tried to make a grab for him.

"Millard, come back here!"

But he had already slipped away.

We paced around the common room, chattering nervously

while we waited. Noor was humming to herself, arms folded tight. Olive attached a rope around her waist and floated as high as she could out of a third-floor window, hoping to get a better view of anything that might be happening.

"I see smoke rising from Smoking Street," she said, when we reeled her back in a few minutes later.

"Smoking Street smokes," Enoch said. "That's why it's called Smoking Street."

"All right, I saw an *unusual* amount of smoke rising from Smoking Street," she clarified, slipping her feet back into her leaden boots. "Dark, black smoke."

"That's where the remnants of the wights' compound is," Bronwyn said anxiously. "And the prison where we've been keeping the ones we caught."

Noor huddled close to me. "This is bad, huh?"

"Seems like it," I said.

"Figures. Right when I show up, everything goes wrong." She pursed her lips and her eyes cut away to the window. "Sometimes I wonder if I'm just bad luck."

I was starting to tell her that was ridiculous when Millard came back, his bare feet slapping up the stairs and into the room at a run.

We all crowded around him.

"What's the news?" Emma said, but Millard had to catch his breath before he could get a word out, and I think he lay down on the floor.

Finally he managed to say, between gulps of air, "It's . . . the wights."

"Oh no," I heard Bronwyn say under her breath, as if this one bit of information had just confirmed her worst fears.

"What about them?" Enoch said, sounding uncharacteristically scared.

"They . . . broke out . . . of jail . . . and escaped."

"*All* of them?" I said.

"Four." Millard sat up and wiped his brow with the closest thing at hand, which happened to be an errant sock.

Horace brought him a cup of water and he gulped it down, then told the story in feverish bursts. They killed the peculiar who'd been guarding them—"Thank the birds you weren't on duty," he said to Bronwyn. Then they made a hole in the wall of their jail big enough to crawl through without attracting attention, snuck over to the Panloopticon, and escaped.

The explosion we'd heard was a bomb they'd set off in the Panloopticon hallway.

"What about Miss Peregrine?" I asked.

"She traveled back to the conference via the Panloopticon shortly before this all happened," Millard said. "One of Sharon's Panloopticon minions confirmed it for me."

"Thank goodness," said Olive.

"Someone had better go fetch her," Emma said. "She needs to know about this."

"That could be a problem," said Millard.

"Why's that?"

"Because the wights took the hollowgast who was powering the Panloopticon with them. And now the entire apparatus is shut down."

The air seemed to go out of the room. Everyone was stunned.

"What?" I said. *"How?"*

"Well, the wights and the hollows are natural allies—"

"No, I mean how did they use the Panloopticon to escape if they stole the hollow powering it?"

"There must have been a few minutes' reserve power remaining in the lines. Just enough for them to make an escape."

I felt my stomach drop.

"What does any of that mean?" Noor said.

"It means that wherever they went, we can't follow them," said Emma, shaking her head.

"It means," Millard said, "we're stuck here for a while."

"And Miss Peregrine is stuck at the conference," Claire said miserably, "along with several of the other ymbrynes."

Just then, there was a loud rapping on the window—which was strange, since we were on the third floor of the house.

Emma rushed over and slid the window open. I heard her say, "Yes?" and a moment later she turned back with an odd expression and said, "Jacob, it's for you."

I went over to see a dour young man standing on the second-floor roof. "Jacob Portman?" he said.

"Who are you?"

"Ulysses Critchley," he said. "I work for Miss Blackbird at the Ministry of Temporal Affairs. She wants to see you. Instantly."

"What's this about?" I said.

Ulysses gestured vaguely at the smoke rising from the other side of the Acre, now easily visible. "The fracas."

Then he turned, walked calmly off the edge of the roof, and fell out of view at about half-normal speed.

"You'd better go," Emma said insistently. "But I'm coming with you."

"Me too," said Enoch and Millard at the same time. Then Millard said to Bronwyn: "If you wouldn't mind carrying me? I'm a bit shagged out."

She insisted he put on a shirt and trousers before she scooped him up.

Then I remembered Noor and the prophecy and everything we were supposed to do today, and I turned to her. "I'm so sorry," I said. "Today was supposed to be all about—"

She cut me off with a wave. "It's okay. This is clearly something serious. But by the way, I'm coming, too."

I smiled. "If you insist." Then turned and shouted out the window to Ulysses: "We'll take the stairs!"

The others wished us luck, and we went out.

CHAPTER FOUR

*U*lysses Critchley had a gravity-defying peculiarity not un-like Olive's, though his unnatural buoyancy wasn't so extreme that he seemed in danger of floating uncontrol-lably into the sky. He resembled a sped-up version of an astronaut walking on the moon, each little leap he took matching three or four of our steps.

We followed him across the Acre. Clusters of worried pecu-liars congregated here and there in the streets, glancing darkly at the smoke rising in the sky. I kept hearing the word *wight* murmured. Even if they all didn't know exactly what had happened yet, they knew it was something bad. Our defenses had been breached. Our enemies were not as vanquished as we had hoped.

As we crossed Smoking Street, we saw Rafael the bone-mender and an assistant walking alongside two men carrying a stretcher, grim expressions all. We stopped at a respectful distance and waited for them to pass.

"*I wonder who it was,*" Enoch whispered. "*Hopefully no one good.*"

"I heard some of the other guards talking," Millard said qui-etly. "I think it was Melina Manon, the telekinetic."

"Ah, too bad," Enoch said. "She was a bit mad, but I rather liked her."

"Have some respect!" Emma hissed.

"She's a hero," Bronwyn said, and I saw her wiping away tears.

A jet of smoke vented up from a crack in the street, the sad parade disappeared from view, and we continued on. I didn't know where Ulysses was leading us until I saw Bentham's house.

We were going, of course, to the Panloopticon.

Some of the upper-floor windows had been blown out. A small crowd had gathered around outside a perimeter of caution tape. It seemed the building had been evacuated. Farish Obwelo the journalist was there, interviewing people while scribbling furiously in a notepad.

Ulysses paused at the entrance, looked up the side of the building as if he'd rather just pull himself up, then glanced back at us and sighed. "Come on, you groundbounds," he said, and led us inside.

We headed for the stairs. Before we could reach them, I saw Sharon coming toward us, his long arms extended. "Young Portman and friends!" he boomed. "Not a moment too soon."

Sharon's giant form was blocking the stairs.

"I'm taking them to Miss Blackbird," said Ulysses, annoyed.

"She can wait," Sharon said, and with a dismissive sweep of his hand, he pushed the boy aside and took us down a connecting hallway.

"Look here," Millard said, "Jacob has important business with Miss—"

"Our business is the same!" Sharon said so loudly Millard stopped talking.

We descended into the basement as Ulysses followed, scowling, then passed through rooms crowded with machines that had been rumbling and filling the air with noise the last time I'd seen them, but were now silent.

Then we were hurried through a room I'd never been in before, crammed with what looked like telegraph and radio equipment. Several people were sitting together wearing headphones and looks of deep concentration, and in the corner was a knock-kneed man who wore a tuxedo wrapped in radio wires, with antennae poking up from the top of his hat. A loud warbling whine was emitting from an electronic box hung from his neck. (Or was that sound coming from the man himself?)

"Monitoring secret channels for wight communications," Sharon said to me.

Ulysses cleared his throat nervously. "It's nothing of the kind!" he said. "Ignore all this, you've seen nothing!"

He rushed us out of the room, muttering to himself.

Finally, we came to the heart of Bentham's machine, a room dominated by gears and valves and intestinal-looking tubes that crawled over the walls and ceiling to converge on the roof of a box in the corner. It was about the size and shape of a telephone booth, but it was windowless, forbidding, and cast from iron.

"I wanted you to see firsthand what was done," Sharon said, gesturing to the box. It was, of course, the battery chamber. The huge lock that had secured its door lay smashed on the floor.

Sharon opened the door. The inside was empty. The leather straps were stretched out and worn ragged from the hollow's long struggle against them, and the chamber's interior walls were stained and splattered black with a residue only I could see: the hollow's tears.

"Your little friend is gone," Sharon said.

"He wasn't my *friend*," I said, surprised at the sudden wave of guilt I was feeling. Hollowgast were monsters, but they could feel pain and fear, and I remembered vividly the howls it made after it was strapped in and the chamber door closed.

"Regardless," Sharon said, "he is gone, and we have no more. Travel is impossible; operations here have ground to a halt."

"And? What do you want me to do about it?"

"I don't suppose," said a high voice from behind us, "you could get us another one?"

We turned to see a dour woman hunched in the doorway dressed all in black. She had a strange growth between her eyes.

"Miss Blackbird," Ulysses said, and bowed smartly.

I couldn't quite believe my ears. "You want me to . . . get *another* one?"

She forced her dour expression into a smile. "If it isn't too much trouble?"

"I'm sorry," I said, struggling for words. "I don't know where I'd find one . . ."

"Oh." Her smile collapsed. "Too bad."

Emma stepped in front of me. "Miss Blackbird, with all due respect, Jacob nearly lost his life getting the one you had. It isn't fair to ask him—"

She waved her hand. "No, no. You're absolutely right. It isn't fair. Now"—she pinned Emma with a sharp look—"who precisely are you?"

Emma straightened. "Emma Bloom."

She nodded quickly. "Of course, yes. Alma Peregrine's brood." Her eyes traveled quickly over my friends. "I've heard you're feisty. And you must be *la Lumiere*," she said, turning to Noor, then blinking as if she couldn't properly see her.

"Eyes bothering you, miss?" asked Ulysses.

"Yes, I'm afraid so. They're next to useless some days. But I can still depend on Number Three . . . Wake up, lazybones!" She tapped the growth on her forehead, and it split open to reveal a large, red-rimmed eyeball.

"What's *that*?" Bronwyn said, then looked mortified at her own rudeness.

"My third eye, and lucky for me he's still sharp as a tack." Her two milky eyes were staring straight at Noor, but the big one in the center of her head was looking at me. "Anyhow, not to worry about the hollowgast," she said. "They're a pain to deal with, and the cleanup is frightful. We do have a backup in the works; we suspected the hollowgast battery wouldn't last forever, so we've spent these past few months developing an alternative."

All three of her eyes now gazed expectantly at Sharon.

"May be a little while before we can bring it into operation, madam," Sharon said. "It isn't quite ready yet."

"A few days at most," Miss Blackbird said, her voice and smile cracking with stress. "Come, Portman, there's something else I want to discuss with you." She looked at my friends. *"Alone."*

◆　　◆　　◆

As we climbed the stairs to the Panloopticon's first floor, Miss Blackbird talked at me fast and close in a Scottish lilt that was sometimes hard to decipher. She briefed me on what had happened, most of which I'd already heard from Millard, while keeping one clawlike hand on my arm always, like she was afraid I might run away if she let go.

When we reached the second landing, the bitter stink of burned carpet hit my nose. Halfway down the hall I could see where the bomb had gone off—the walls and floor were blackened and a half dozen loop doors had been splintered and blown off their hinges. Another ymbryne was conferring with a girl in a black suit and matching apron—Ulysses's same outfit, a uniform for Temporal Affairs people—and various adults were buzzing around the still-smoking blast zone, collecting bits of debris in bags and taking measurements. It was, after all, a crime scene.

"I didn't really expect you to go off and capture us another hollowgast, Portman, that was just a bit of fun. Eh?" She smiled apologetically, as if imploring me not to share her bizarre request with Miss Peregrine.

"Sure," I said, and smiled back. *I won't tell.*

"One moment," she said, and she went to speak with the other ymbryne—a tall black lady in a wide-collared blazer and knit tie—and I pretended not to notice them glancing at me while they talked. Instead I turned to study the loop door next to me, which was hanging crooked in its frame. Its brass nameplate was scratched but still readable: YASUR VOLCANO, ISLAND OF TANNA, NEW HEBRIDES, JANUARY 1799.

Curious, I nudged the door with my foot. It swung open to reveal the usual bedroom common to most Panloopticon gateways—three walls, a floor, a ceiling—but the missing fourth wall did not, as promised by the plaque, lead to a vista of some tropical island volcano. It was simply blank.

"Sorry to keep you waiting." Miss Blackbird returned with the other ymbryne in tow. "This is Miss Babax, my co-chair of Temporal Affairs."

Miss Babax's face widened into an ethereal smile and she extended her hand to shake mine. "Such a pleasure to meet you, Jacob," she said in a smooth English accent. "We sent for you this morning because you might be our best hope."

Her gaze was intense and unwavering. I felt a tightness grow in my chest, the same one I got anytime people expected big things from me.

"We don't know what these wights aim to do," said Miss Blackbird. "But we need to recapture them before they hurt anyone else." Her third eye blinked rapidly.

"We've already lost one peculiar child," Miss Babax said. "It ends there."

"I'm with you," I said. "How can I help?"

"We know they have a hollowgast with them," Miss Blackbird said. "That makes 'em more dangerous. But it also . . ."

Her head tilted and she raised her thick eyebrows.

"Makes them trackable," I said. "By me."

She smiled. "Precisely."

"Your talents could prove invaluable here," said Miss Babax.

"I'm happy to help any way I can."

"Don't say yes just like that," Miss Babax said sharply, holding up a finger. "I want you to know what you're getting into." Miss Blackbird frowned; Miss Babax went on. "These aren't just any wights—they were the worst we had. Dangerous, devious, and depraved. Have you heard of Percival Murnau?"

"Caul's lieutenant?" I said.

"That's right," said Miss Babax. "He and his three butchers. They alone are responsible for at least half the destruction and mayhem the wights have visited upon us in recent years."

"If we were to read a list of their crimes, it would make your hair curl," said Miss Blackbird.

"I'm sure they're awful," I said, "but I've faced worse."

That tightness in my chest began to dissipate. Sometimes I forgot myself, and what I had already done and accomplished.

"Caul himself," Miss Blackbird said with a touch of awe, "and a whole army of his wights." She winked at me. "Which is the only reason I asked about you-know-what."

"But then Mr. Portman had an army of hollowgast under his command to fight them with," said Miss Babax. "Hollows are suddenly a rather endangered species."

"I think I can handle it," I said. "I know the hollow they took pretty well, too, which could help."

Miss Babax nodded seriously. "That is just what I was hoping you'd say."

"As soon as we get this damned Panloopticon contraption operational again," said Miss Blackbird. "Expect a call to action."

✦   ✦   ✦

Miss Blackbird showed me out, her hand gripping my arm again—a gesture that now struck me as more for her comfort than mine. I had become a lifeline of hope, and she was reassuring herself of my realness.

I'd left my friends down in the Pantloopticon's guts, and I wondered where they were. I asked Miss Blackbird, and she waved vaguely at the end of the entrance hall she was hurrying me down, and its big door, flanked by two burly guards.

"*Elders help me,*" she muttered. "*They're all here.*"

Outside the building, the crowd had grown huge. Peculiars from around the Acre had converged on the Panloopticon, looking for answers. The moment Miss Blackbird and I came out the front door, they began shouting.

In the very front of the scrum were Farish Obwelo and another reporter. The big eye in the middle of Farish's forehead stared fiercely at the one in the center of Miss Blackbird's, and the other reporter was sketching a picture of Miss Blackbird and me so quickly that his hand was just a blur.

"Madam, can you tell us how exactly the wights managed to escape?" Farish shouted.

"We're still conducting our investigation," Miss Blackbird said.

The other reporter bounced forward. "Is the prison you built secure? Could it happen again?"

"Very secure, and we're doubling our guards and reinforcing the battlements around it as we speak. Be assured, the rest of the wights aren't going anywhere!"

"Do you think they had help?" said Farish.

"*Help?*" She gave him a withering glare.

He tried another: "What's Jacob Portman got to do with all this?"

I felt my face go hot.

"No comment!" Miss Blackbird shouted.

"Do you think you've allowed yourselves to be too distracted by the situation in America to properly manage things here?"

Miss Blackbird's mouth dropped open, so shocked was she by the audacity of the question.

Sharon loomed behind us—I could feel his coldness at my back—and then he thundered in his overwhelming basso voice, "QUIET!"

The crowd noise faded to a murmur.

"The ymbrynes will address the crisis very soon! You'll be given all the facts! But right now we must CLEAR THIS AREA!"

The power of his voice alone might've been enough to achieve it, but the appearance of his gallows-rigging cousins from around the side of the building sealed the deal, and the crowd began to disperse.

"Keep away from those vultures," Miss Blackbird said, and she gave my arm a sympathetic squeeze before disappearing back inside the building.

I saw Noor waving to me from the thinning crowd—she was riding on Bronwyn's shoulders. I pushed toward them, and found Emma and Enoch, too, and Horace, who had apparently ventured across the Acre on his own to join us.

"So? What did old bonnie Blackbird want?" Enoch asked.

"The nerve of her, asking you to fetch another hollowgast," Emma fumed, "as if you were just some expendable errand boy!"

I saw Farish eyeing me with interest. "Jacob! A few questions!"

"Let's talk somewhere else," I muttered to my friends, steering them away. The last thing I needed was to end up in the *Muckraker*.

"You never mentioned you were famous," Noor said, eyeing me playfully.

"Local celebrity," Emma said proudly.

"Flavor of the week," Enoch grumbled.

Bronwyn smirked. "That's what you said *last* week."

We walked down Oozing Street, past the slaughterhouse turned B and B and a pub called the Shrunken Head, and when it seemed like we'd put enough distance between us and prying ears, I told them what the ymbrynes had asked of me.

"Are you going to do it?" asked Horace.

"Of course," I said. "If the wights are up to something, we need to find out what it is."

"Knowing them, they've been up to whatever it is for quite a while," said Emma. "Now they're just putting the wheels in motion."

"They wanted to break out of jail, just like all prisoners do," Enoch said. "That doesn't mean they have some evil agenda."

"The wights always have an evil agenda," Millard said.

He had disrobed at some point, and I'd almost forgotten he was there.

Enoch dismissed Millard with an *ehh*, then looked at Noor, and said, "What about her?"

"What do you mean?" I said.

Noor shot him a look. "Yeah, what do you mean?"

"I thought you were helping her, Portman."

"I am," I said.

"How are you going to do that while you're chasing after escaped wights?"

"I'll do both—"

"I can handle myself," Noor cut in. "I'll be fine."

"Oh yeah?" said Enoch. "What would you do if a grimbear attacked you?"

"A what?"

He winked at me. "Exactly."

Noor's expression turned to stone.

"A grimbear would never attack a peculiar child like *us*," said Bronwyn. "They only go after—"

"Thank you, Bronwyn, we know," I said. "And shut up, Enoch."

Enoch had embarrassed her, and I worried I'd only made it worse.

"So, do you think the wights might actually have had inside help?" said Millard, oblivious as usual to the emotional dynamics of the conversation.

"They must have," said Bronwyn. "That prison is solid as a mountain—I should know, I helped build it with my own hands. The only way they could've made that hole in the wall and gotten their hands on an explosive is if someone in Devil's Acre helped them. But who?"

"Are you kidding?" said Emma. "The list of suspicious characters around here is longer than my arm. Could have been ex–Ditch pirates, mercenaries, ambrosia addicts . . ."

"I thought most of them got run out of town," Enoch said.

"*Most* of them," Emma replied. "I think some of them are covering up their past and are just pretending to be on the ymbrynes' side."

"Some peculiars aren't even pretending anymore," said Millard. "Look at this."

He had stopped in front of a cart selling newspapers. Most were from the present, brought in weekly from outside the loop to keep us (sort of) up-to-date on the goings-on of the larger world, but there were a couple of peculiar newspapers, too. One was the *Muckraker*, and its headline read:

YMBRYNES BUNGLE LOOP SECURITY; WIGHTS ESCAPE

I snatched a copy from the rack. "How did they already print this?" I marveled. "It just happened!"

"Special edition," said the boy behind the cart.

"An old acquaintance of mine works for the *Muckraker*," Horace said mysteriously. "Once in a while he gets advance word of things."

I kept reading. A smaller opinion article below the fold was titled: ARE YMBRYNES TOO FOCUSED ON AMERICA'S PROBLEMS TO SOLVE OURS?

I was too angry to read it.

"Look at this," said Emma, drawing my attention to a billboard wall where the escaped wights' mugshots had just been posted. WANTED FOR MURDER was emblazoned across the top, and a long list of their crimes and aliases trailed below.

"Don't *they* look a rough crowd," said Horace. "Wouldn't want to meet them in a dark alley at night."

"They don't scare me," said Enoch. "These two are mild as milk. Like bank tellers."

I saw the wights he was talking about. One had thin round glasses and a long nose; the other looked downright professorial. The other two looked like brawlers, especially the one on top, who

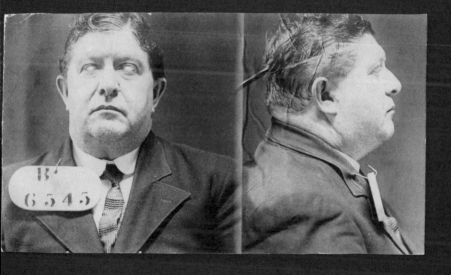

< RANSOM RIGGS >

had a thick nose, wiry hair, and was the only one with pupils—fake though they were. They were aimed upward and to the left, which gave the man an unsettling air of total ease, as if he were daydreaming about his next vacation. Or how he was going to strangle the photographer in the night.

The name printed below his mugshot: P. MURNAU.

◆   ◆   ◆

There was an announcement made over a loudspeaker that things were to go on as usual, and all peculiars would be expected to report to their jobs or classes.

Of course, we would be doing no such thing. We had much bigger fish to fry.

"I think we can see Miss Avocet today," Horace said to Noor. "But I'll need to make an appointment. She's awfully busy. I *might* be able to get us in this afternoon, if I beg."

"Please do beg, Horace," said Bronwyn.

"And if that doesn't work, threaten," said Millard. "If the rest of you could lend your hands and your eyes to me, it would help a great deal. I've got a few hundred loop maps to comb through in the peculiar archives, and at this stage it's all hands on deck."

"Of course," Emma said.

"I'm all yours," said Bronwyn. "I'll go fetch Olive and Claire, too. I'm sure they'll want to help."

"We're in, obviously," I said, trading a nod with Noor.

Emma narrowed her eyes at me. She nearly wagged a finger when she said, "Unless, of course, the ymbrynes need you. Right, Jacob?"

"Right," I said, trying to keep my voice mild. Emma had been acting weird ever since Noor arrived, but I decided to let it go.

Luckily, Noor didn't seem to notice. Either that, or she didn't much care. She turned toward Millard's half-clothed ghost and said, "Do you have any specific ideas? Or are we just searching blindly?"

"Not exactly blind," Millard replied. "I snuck out late last night and had a midnight chat with a friend. You remember Perplexus Anomalous?"

"You bothered him at midnight?" Enoch snorted.

"People as old as Perplexus hardly sleep," said Millard. "And ever since we saved him from aging forward, he's been very friendly toward me." Millard sounded proud of himself, and I could see why: He was making friends with one of his heroes. "Anyhow, I told him about our puzzle and the map fragment and the ex-hollowgast's mumbled clues, and Perplexus pointed out that if V's loop is in America—and it seems quite likely that it is—and if it is beset with large windstorms—as the phrases 'in the big wind, in the heart of the storm' would seem to imply—then it would make the most sense to search the midwestern United States. There's a rather wide stripe down the center of the country that's known colloquially as 'Tornado Alley.'"

"Of course," Noor said, nodding. "Nebraska, Oklahoma, Kansas . . . the *Wizard of Oz* states."

"What about you?" Bronwyn said, tossing Enoch a look.

He frowned. "I'd been imagining what a morning of relaxation and leisure might look like, if I'm being honest. Though I suppose that ship has sailed."

"How would you relax around here, anyway?" I said.

"Oh, the Acre has its pleasures. I could always view a hanging . . . or have a mud bath in Fever Ditch . . ." He gestured to the muddy stream beside us.

And on that depressing note, our group started to disperse.

"Hey, Enoch was joking, right?" Noor whispered to me.

"I think so?"

And then something wet hit me in the back with a *splat.*

"There he is!" someone shouted as I spun around, and a gob of mud struck me square in the chest. "Go back to where you came from, phony!"

It was Itch, the half-fish half-man, who held a nasty grudge against me. He was standing waist-deep in the creek, lobbing gobs of muck in my direction.

"Stop that!" Bronwyn shouted. She looked around for something to toss back at him, but she wasn't fast enough. A lady Ditch dweller chose that moment to rise from the mire and throw her own clump of mud in our direction.

"Loop freedom for all!" the woman shouted.

This one hit both me and Noor, who was standing too close to me.

My friends were all yelling at them, and Emma sparked a ball of fire in her hand and was waving it at them menacingly, but there wasn't much we could do other than scurry out of throwing range—which we did. I was dripping with the stuff. Noor less so, but she'd gotten hit, too.

"What the hell is their problem?" Noor said, scraping mud from her shirt.

"They're just angry and bitter that none of us have to worry about aging forward anymore," Bronwyn said.

"You two had better wash that stuff off, and good," said Enoch, wrinkling his nose. "It's toxic."

"I could definitely use a shower," I said, looking down at myself.

"You quite seriously need one, I'm afraid," said Millard. "This section of Fever Ditch is infested with flesh-eating microbes."

"Flesh-eating *what*?" I said, horrified.

"Don't worry, they're slow," Enoch said. "It would take them probably a full week to eat you whole."

"Okay, yeah, a shower would be good," Noor said, looking a bit freaked out.

I caught Bronwyn inching away from us.

"You need hot running water and soap," said Enoch. "But the only place you'll find that is . . ."

Emma and Enoch looked at each other.

"There is *one* possibility," Emma said, worrying her bottom lip, "though it's slightly complex and just a little bit risky."

"We don't exactly have a choice, do we?" I said, glancing apologetically at Noor. "I'm pretty sure we're going to need all of our skin, whatever we do."

Enoch shrugged.

Noor looked miserable.

And Emma was backing away from us as she shouted directions to a safe house just outside the Devil's Acre loop, in present-day London. It had modern bathrooms, hot water, the works.

"We'll be at the Mapping Department in the ministries building," Millard said. "Meet us there when you're clean. Just make sure you get every bit of that stuff off you."

"Yeah," said Enoch. "Because I, for one, enjoy having skin."

◆　　◆　　◆

Noor and I went down to the boat dock at Fever Ditch, trying not to think too much about the microscopic bugs slowly devouring our skin, and in exchange for a silver coin that Horace had given me, a grizzled old boatman piloted us down the slow black river in a glorified canoe. Rather than talk in front of a stranger we were mostly silent, and Noor spent much of the trip holding her nose and gazing up at the crumbling tenements we passed, where washerwomen hung laundry from the windows and raggedy kids shouted down the alleys.

"They're normal," I said. "Part of the loop."

Noor seemed fascinated. "You mean they do the same thing every day?"

"Every second of every day," the boatman rasped. "I been here seventy-two years and I know it all."

He jerked the tiller and the boat turned sharply left. A moment later, a boy running across an overhead footbridge tripped and fell into the water a few feet to our right, just where we would have been.

"Now he'll call that other mucksnipe a pigeon-livered ratbag," the boatman muttered.

The boy surfaced. "You pigeon-livered ratbag!" he shouted at someone up on the footbridge.

Noor shook her head. "That's *wild* . . ."

As we approached the long, dark tunnel that marked the loop exit, Noor started humming. The melody was sweet and simple, like a nursery rhyme, and I could see her shoulders relax as she hummed it.

I meant to ask her about it, but then the dark enveloped us.

We were gripped by the sudden rush of a loop changeover, and after a few seconds we emerged into a much-changed London, this one comprised of glass-walled buildings and clean streets.

The boatman dropped us at the bank without a word, happy to be rid of us.

We followed Emma's directions. We made a few turns, crossed a wide shopping street crowded with businesses and buses, made another turn down a residential block, and soon we were there: a simple two-story house on a street of nearly identical houses, all connected. I'd been keeping a keen feel out for hollows, because you never knew, but I'd felt no twinges out of the ordinary.

We rang the bell. A man I didn't know answered. He wore a black suit and apron just like Ulysses's—another Temporal Affairs minion. He looked us over for a moment, asked our names, then let us inside.

Miraculously, there were two bathrooms.

Nothing in my life had ever felt so good. I stood under the hot spray while the mud and grit and flesh-eating microbes ran off me and spiraled down the drain, I hoped, then I scrubbed my skin until it hurt. I dried myself with a heavy white towel, found a new razor and an unopened stick of deodorant in the vanity—and my heart sank a little as I realized we had only our dirty, Ditch-stained clothes to change back into.

Just then came a knock at the door, and the man who had let

us in told me there was a wardrobe of clothes in the next room, and I could choose anything I liked.

I wrapped a towel around my waist and went out to explore my options. I found a hunter-green button-up shirt that fit well, a pair of dark pants, and some brown lace-up ankle boots—an outfit I hoped would blend into various time periods.

I went out into the living room. Noor hadn't emerged yet, so I stood at the window and watched the street for a minute—the mailman pushing his cart from house to house, an old man walking a dog—and I marveled at how such a profoundly mundane world could exist right next door to ours.

"Hey," I heard Noor say, and then I casually turned and saw her walk into the room, and for a moment I couldn't believe it was the same person I'd arrived with. She'd put on a simple white henley shirt and blue jeans, and her hair was brushed and shining, and she was *beautiful*. We'd been mired in filth and running for our lives for so much of the time we'd been together, I had almost forgotten just how beautiful she was. This took me so by surprise, I realized, that I didn't have time to hide my reaction, and now—oh God—I was staring at her.

I cleared my throat. "You, uh . . . you look really nice," I said.

She laughed, and I think she was blushing. "You do, too."

There was a moment of silence which probably lasted only two or three seconds but felt infinite, and then she said, "Well, uh, we should probably be getting back, huh?"

A sudden clanging filled the house. The minion from Temporal Affairs dashed into the room.

"What is that?" I said.

"The doorbell," he replied.

Someone was ringing it like the end of the world was upon us.

The minion ran downstairs to answer it, and a short time later, after a thunderous noise of feet pounding up the stairs, Hugh and Emma appeared, out of breath.

"You need to come back," Emma said.

"We tried to call but the line was engaged," said Hugh.

"What's going on?" I said, trading a worried look with Noor. "Did you find V's loop?"

Noor looked hopeful, but Emma was shaking her head. "Not yet," she said. "It's Horace. He's with Miss Avocet right now. When he told her what he was after, she met with him right away. And they're waiting for us."

"Apparently they found something," Hugh said. "Something big. But they wouldn't say what."

We were all tripping over one another to reach the stairs.

◆　　◆　　◆

Emma and Hugh had a boat waiting for us at the dock, and this one had a motor on it. Emma barked at the boatman to drive like his life depended on it, and a minute later we were flying through the loop entrance so fast my head was spinning. We left a wide brown wake behind us in Fever Ditch, and had to hang on to the sides of the boat to keep from falling out, and when we finally docked in the center of town, I'd never been so happy to touch dry land.

Miss Avocet's office was inside the peculiar ministries building, formerly St. Barnabus' Asylum for Lunatics, Mountebanks, and the Criminally Mischievous. We rushed through its busy lobby with its registration windows and glum-faced bureaucrats, then up a few flights of stairs to a hallway.

Someone came rushing out of a door and ran straight into me, and papers went everywhere.

"No, no, drat! I had these all in order!" he said, and he'd already dropped to his knees to gather them up when I saw who it was.

"Horace!" Noor said. "It's us!"

He looked up sharply, his eyes a bit wild. He had papers poking out from under his arms and up in the brim of his hat like feathers, and between that and his overly formal tuxedo, he looked like a bewildered peacock.

"Oh!" he said. "Good! There's so much to tell. Where to start—"

We knelt and helped him gather up the papers.

"So that text H spoke about," he said, speaking fast. "Miss Avocet knew it. It's called the *Apocryphon*—and, as it turns out, it's a real book." He stuffed a few papers into a leather folder, which was already overflowing, then stuffed a few more into his vest. "It's extremely obscure, even in the already-obscure canon of peculiar prophecy. But when I asked Miss Avocet about it, she nearly fell out of her chair. She canceled all her meetings for the rest of the day and convened her best ymbrynes-in-training to work on this. She said she hadn't heard anyone mention the Prophecy of the Seven, or the *Apocryphon*, in many years—and she'd been dreading the day she would."

With all the papers gathered, he stood up and gestured to the door across the hall, which was twice as large as all the doors near it and labeled with a sign that read E. AVOCET, BY APPT ONLY.

I went to open the door, but it swung inward with a loud creak before I could reach the handle. It was dark and cavernous inside, and it took my eyes a moment to adjust to the gloom. The back wall was all windows, but they were completely covered over with newspapers so that they filtered only a slight orange glow. The office was lit instead by candles and candelabras—a hundred or more, dancing and twinkling everywhere—and in their dim pools of light I could see nothing but books and girls. Books in spiraling towers, books in laddered shelves to the ceiling, books in piles that tilted at impossible angles but somehow stayed aloft. For every pile there was a studious young woman in a long dress—twelve in all—poring over pages, writing in notebooks, necks bent at painful angles. These were students of Miss Avocet's ymbryne academy, from which Miss Peregrine herself had graduated a very long time ago. They were so absorbed in their work, they didn't even glance up at us as we passed.

We snaked around the piles until we reached an old, familiar face: Miss Avocet, seated at a desk that was drowning in papers.

"Ah, you're finally here," she said. "Come in, young ones. Fanny, make room!"

What I'd taken for a rug let out a rumbling growl, and a big brown grimbear lumbered up from the floor and slouched off into the corner.

"Don't be frightened, dear heart," Miss Avocet said to Noor. "He's tame as an emu-raffe, but he acts like he owns the place."

"I'm fine, thanks," Noor said, though the shock hadn't quite disappeared from her face.

Miss Avocet squinted. "I hope you don't mind the light. Whale oil smokes too much and gas lamps bother my eyes." Then she invited us to sit on the long velvet couch facing her desk. She pushed a pair of tiny wire spectacles up her nose and leaned forward on her elbows. The welcoming smile she'd greeted us with vanished, and her eyes gleamed with purpose despite their rheumy cataracts.

"I won't waste time, as I've got little to waste," she said, her voice shaking slightly. "The *Apocryphon*, as you might have surmised by its name, is regarded a bit dubiously by scholars of peculiar prophecy—when it is regarded at all. It is little-known. Not even a proper book: It was never written, merely written *down*. Its full title is *The Apocryphon of Robert LeBourge, Revelator of Avignon*, but I've heard it shortened to *The Apocryphon of Bob the Revelator*."

"What's a revelator?" Noor asked.

"It's a fancy word for prophet," said Horace.

"LeBourge was anything but fancy," said Miss Avocet. "Old Bob was an uneducated farmhand who spoke mainly in babbling incoherencies, and most who knew him thought he was possessed, an idiot, or some combination of the two. But sometimes this man who could hardly speak would tremble as if electrified and hold forth

in fully formed quatrains of sonorous, seemingly extemporaneous rhyming verse. That was amazing enough, but when people noticed that his verses sounded like predictions—and some of those predictions came to pass—he became famous, and people began writing down the things he said."

"They must have thought he was some kind of angel," said Noor.

"Devil, more like," said Miss Avocet. "He was plunged into boiling oil for the crime of divination, but suffered nothing from it. Another time he was hanged but only pretended to be dead, then escaped from the embalmer's room. He was peculiar, of course, and one of the more fascinating figures from our history." She turned her head slightly and said to the room, "Someone could write an excellent term paper on him, if one were so inclined!" Then she returned her eyes to us. "The *Apocryphon of Bob* is a collection of his pronouncements, recorded by whomever happened to be present at the time."

"What about the Prophecy of the Seven?" I asked.

"The Prophecy of the Seven appears only in a few translations of the text. It seems that speakers of a number of different languages were present at its utterance, and each recorded their own account in their own tongue. There is some disagreement amongst them, and the most widely known version of it is at best an educated guess at what Bob actually said—a necessarily compromised melding of them all, translated into English. Fortunately, my star pupil speaks many of those languages, and has been hard at work untangling the web."

An elegant young woman stepped forward, hands clasped around a notebook. She had winglike hair, dark skin, and eyes that radiated intelligence.

"This is Francesca," said Miss Avocet, "and if she passes my examinations at the end of this term, which I expect she will, she'll become Miss Bittern, our newest ymbryne." Miss Avocet was beaming with pride. Francesca smiled gently.

"Take it away, lass."

Francesca opened a notebook. "The Prophecy of the Seven was written some four hundred years ago," she began, "but it begins with several references to our own time period. Listen . . .

And now a word, in uncouth rhyme
Of what shall be in future time.
When folk shall fly as birds do now
And give away the horse and plow,
And round the world their thoughts will fly
Quick as the twinkling of an eye.
When creatures made of shadow creep
To stalk our children in their sleep
And ymbrynes cease their flocks to tend . . ."

She stopped and looked at us over her glasses. "You get the idea." She flipped ahead a few pages. "After some more of this, it says . . .

When the prisons are blown to dust
And chaos reigns
And the betrayers summon their king
The old ones from their sleep are torn
An age of strife will soon be born."

A chill traveled through the room, and for a moment even the candles seemed to shiver. Francesca looked up from her notes.

"And then it goes on to describe a war.

Every land on earth will sink
And reek and wallow in stench and stink
Of rotted trunks of beast and man
And vegetation crisped on land."

"Thank you, Francesca," Miss Avocet said, "I think we get the picture." She turned to face my friends and me. "As you can see, old Bob had a flair for drama."

"Does that mean the ymbrynes will fail?" Emma asked. "The peace won't hold?"

The big room went suddenly silent as all the ymbrynes-in-training stopped turning pages and looked up from their books.

"Absolutely not," Miss Avocet said acidly. "Here, let me see that." Francesca turned over the book, and Miss Avocet flipped through the pages, flustered. "This bit of translation is rather vague . . . It doesn't necessarily describe a war between peculiar clans, for instance. You have to let me check your work, Frannie."

"Of course, ma'am." Francesca nodded humbly. "Perhaps I made a mistake in the transliterations between Latin, Hungarian, and Old Peculiar—"

"Yes, that must've been it."

"I have faith in the ymbrynes," Francesca felt compelled to say.

Miss Avocet patted her hand. "I know you do, dear."

"But it means *something* terrible will happen," said Hugh. "With lots of dying."

"What about the seven?" Noor said.

I nodded. "Yeah, aren't they supposed to stop this from happening? 'Emancipate peculiardom'?"

"But 'emancipate' implies something terrible *does* happen," said Emma. "And the seven help *later*."

"That bit's near the end," said Miss Avocet. "Oh, *you* read it, your eyes are still young." She handed the book back to Francesca.

"*Emancipate* is another of those fuzzy words," said Francesca, "though it's clear that the seven are crucially important. The only line that all the translations agree on is this: 'To end the strife of war, seven may seal the door.' "

"The door to what?" Noor said.

Francesca wrinkled her nose. "Don't know."

"I don't mean to make this about me," Noor said. "But does it mention . . . *me*?"

"Yes. Near the end," said Miss Avocet, and she turned a strange, warm smile at Noor, as if she'd been looking forward to this. "It foretells the births of the seven. Well, it *begins* to, but the text we have does not appear to be complete."

"Then how do you know I'm one of them?" said Noor. "Did Bob include my Social Security number, or—"

"It's incomplete but for one entry," Francesca said. "It says that one of them shall be 'a babe who suckles the light.'"

I felt a tingle go down my spine.

Noor looked skeptical. "A babe?" she said. "Like . . . a baby?"

Now Emma was frowning, too. "Babies don't have peculiar abilities."

Miss Avocet nodded lightly. "As an almost iron-clad rule, they do not. It is exceedingly, exceedingly rare. But it can happen."

"I only started being able to do this a few months ago," Noor said, clawing a bit of light from the air. "So this can't mean me."

"Ah." Miss Avocet nodded heavily. "Now I must tell you a story. And I think you should sit down while I tell it," she said to Noor.

"I *am* sitting."

Miss Avocet pushed up her glasses and squinted at her. "Good." She tented her fingers beneath her chin, took a brief, dramatic pause, and then began. "Fifteen years ago, a baby was delivered to us. An infant who was clawing out the light from its nursery—and swallowing it."

Noor stared at Miss Avocet, completely still.

"I think that baby was you." Miss Avocet leaned forward. "Tell me, dear, do you happen to have a little moon-shaped birthmark behind your right ear?"

Noor took a beat and a long breath and then reached up her hand to brush aside the hair that was covering her ear. There behind it was just the birthmark Miss Avocet had described.

Noor's hand began to tremble, and she let her hair fall back into place.

I felt my chest tighten.

"It was me," Noor said quietly, her eyebrows knitted together.

"Yes. It's you." Miss Avocet smiled. "I was wondering when I might see you again."

"Oh my," Horace whispered, his hands clutched to his chest.

But Noor was shaking her head. "Who brought me here? Where were my parents?"

"An ymbryne from Bombay brought you to us. She said you weren't safe there. That your parents had been killed, and you were being hunted."

"By who?"

"Hollowgast, my dear. A particularly vicious strain of them that we had not seen here—until a few months after your arrival, that is. After several attacks, a decision was made that the safest course for everyone, including yourself, would be to send you on to America—in the hope that crossing an ocean might throw the hollows off your scent."

"I still don't understand," Noor said, beginning to sound a bit exasperated. "I never manifested any abilities until a few months ago. I didn't grow up able to do this."

Miss Avocet lowered her voice a touch and leaned forward on her desk. "Before you went, we gave you an experimental serum that would dramatically reduce your ability and delay its resurgence until young adulthood. You see, the hollows can smell us when we use our powers. So we thought that, in addition to hiding you in America, this would keep you safe for years to come." She smiled warmly. "I'm gratified to see that it did. What a remarkable young woman you've become, Miss Pradesh. I've often wondered about you. I was tempted to inquire after you, but I feared doing so might have tipped the wights off to your location."

Noor stared at the floor, kneading her temples with her thumbs.

"But I didn't grow up with an ymbryne or around other peculiar kids. I've been in foster homes ever since I could remember . . ."

"Who did you send her to America with?" I asked.

"It was one of your grandfather's associates," said Miss Avocet. "A woman named Velyana."

My mouth fell open.

Noor's head snapped up. "What did she look like? Has anyone got a picture of her?"

"I'm sure we've got one here somewhere," Miss Avocet said, waving at Francesca.

The ymbrynes-in-training leapt to action, and within a minute, a picture of the woman was located. "She's quite a bit younger in this photo than she would've been when she accompanied you," Miss Avocet said, and as she handed it over, I was able to glance at it.

It was V, all right—the same portrait of her that the diviners had shown us at their loop in Georgia.

Noor held it up. After a moment her hand began to shake. *"Mama,"* she whispered.

A chill went through me. Through all of us.

"She took care of me until I was six," Noor said. "And then she was killed."

◆　　◆　　◆

Noor paced back and forth in front of Miss Avocet's desk, turning the picture of V over and over in her hands. "They told me it was a robbery," she said. "Mama and I were walking at night when some men attacked us. I fell and hit my head. I still have a scar." She absently touched the hair above her right ear. "I woke up in a hospital. They told me she'd been killed."

"You can be sure it wasn't a robbery," said Miss Avocet. "And she wasn't killed. What you experienced was an attack by wights, probably accompanied by a hollowgast. She managed to fight them

off, it seems. But when you got hurt she realized she couldn't keep you safe anymore."

"So she gave me up," Noor said, her voice verging on tears. "And let me think she was dead."

Miss Avocet stood and came out from behind her desk. She clasped Noor's hands. "She had no choice. She knew you would only be safe amongst normals, and any contact with you would've put your life at risk."

"My God, that must have been so heartbreaking for her," said Emma.

"But *someone* must have looked in on her now and then," Hugh said. "Maybe it couldn't have been V, but . . ."

That gave me an idea.

I took Miss Avocet aside and asked her if she had any pictures of my grandfather in her archives. Within a short time one was located. It was a snapshot of Abe sitting on the porch of a house peering down the sight of a rifle, taken years ago, Miss Avocet explained, during a loop invasion preparedness drill. I showed it to Noor.

"He looks a lot younger here, but I think that's Mr. Gandy." She looked a bit confused. "Why? Did you know him?"

My heart skipped a beat.

Emma crowded in to look, then gasped. "Abe!"

Gandy had been Abe's alias.

"That's my grandfather," I said, and now Hugh and Horace were jostling to see the picture, too.

"He used to check in on me," Noor said. "I thought he worked for the foster agency!"

"Abe *was* checking up on you," Emma said. "But not for the foster agency."

"You've been part of our family all along, dear," Miss Avocet said to Noor. "You just didn't know it." And she stood up and wrapped Noor in her frail arms.

After the ymbryne let her go, Noor took a moment to collect herself, wiping a tear from her cheek.

"You okay?" I asked her. "This is a lot to process."

She nodded quickly and looked up, her eyes full of quiet determination. "She's alive," she said. "And I'm going to find her."

*   *   *

"*Ahem.*"

I spun around at the sound. Discovering nothing, I tossed a questioning look at my friends, who seemed equally startled. We'd all heard someone clear their throat—loudly—but when we turned to look, there didn't seem to be anyone there.

"Millard?" said Emma, realization dawning. "When did you get here?"

"More to the point," Miss Avocet said sharply, "*how* did you get here?"

"I've been here nearly the whole time," he said. "I came in a bit late, didn't want to interrupt."

"We have strict rules about invisibles sneaking around in the nude, Mr. Nullings."

"Yes, ma'am, my humblest apologies." Millard seemed to be walking toward the little knot of us standing beside Miss Avocet's desk. "I'm not sure whether Horace told you, but we're trying to make sense of not just this prophecy, but of a map, too—one that we believe leads to a loop where V currently resides."

Miss Avocet raised an eyebrow at Horace. "No," she said slowly. "Horace had not mentioned that."

"There was hardly time, ma'am," Horace said. "And besides, maps are Millard's expertise."

Miss Avocet merely sighed.

"So. What's the news?" Noor asked Millard, her face brightening. "Did you find something?"

"Not yet. Olive and Claire are still downstairs searching for any Midwest geographies that resemble your map fragment, but it's a bit of a needle-in-a-haystack situation. However, I think this fascinating new revelation could help us." He took a heavy step toward Noor. "You lived with V until you were six, yes?"

"Five and a half," Noor said, and then she was nodding, already seeming to know what he was about to ask. "You want to know if I remember anything about where we lived."

"Yes. If nothing else, it would give us an idea of her general stomping grounds."

"Why would V hide in the same area she was attacked?" I asked.

"If she's in some secret loop, it could be very close indeed; proximity doesn't really matter so long as the loop entrance is skillfully hidden. I just need some telling, concrete detail. The names of any towns where you lived would be ideal . . ."

Noor's brow scrunched. She shook her head. "I can't remember any. We moved around a lot, lived in a lot of different places. Never stayed anywhere for long."

"Surely you remember *something*," Millard said, a bit desperate. "Even the smallest fragment of a memory could prove essential."

Noor bit her lip, lost in thought. "Well, we lived in a city for a while, in a little apartment. I remember the radiator pinging all night long, and these big vents in the street that let out steam. And we used to take the bus, this old bus with green plastic seats that smelled like lemon oil."

"Oh, that sounds like it might be something!" Bronwyn said, sitting up.

Millard sighed a long-suffering sigh. "The map fragment is not urban," he said. "So, no, those memories are not terribly useful. Was there someplace else?"

"Lots of places," Noor said. "But none for very long." She

paused, thinking. "Except one. A little town. We used to go back a lot. But what I can remember of it is really hazy." She let out a sharp, frustrated breath. "*Weirdly* hazy. Almost like . . ."

"Someone took your memories?"

Francesca. I hadn't realized she'd been listening.

Noor looked at her strangely. "I didn't even realize that was possible!"

Francesca and Miss Avocet locked eyes. "Ma'am," said Francesca, "do you think Miss Pradesh could have been memory-wiped?"

Miss Avocet was nodding, kneading her hands together. "If she has other memories from that time, it's possible someone might have done only a partial wipe on her. To remove a specific batch of memories."

"Wait, *what*?" said Noor, her eyes getting wider. "You guys are serious about this?"

"Memory-wipes are quite common," said Bronwyn.

"On *normals*," Hugh said in an undertone.

Noor was not looking reassured.

Miss Avocet laid a steadying hand on Noor's arm. "It sounds as if it was only a small one, to keep you safe from harm, dear. If V worried for your safety, she might also have worried that you would one day try to return to where you once lived, out of nostalgia, or some pull for a place that felt like home."

Noor studied her shoes. She said nothing, but her heartbreak was clear.

"Imagine someone doing that to their own child," Emma said, her voice solemn.

"I had to do it to my own parents," I said with a heavy sigh. "It wasn't an easy choice."

Noor was shaking her head. "Maybe V wasn't trying to keep me safe at all," she said quietly. "Maybe she just didn't want me."

"Stuff and nonsense," Miss Avocet cried, standing upright so quickly she pinched a muscle in her back. She grabbed at the edge of her desk for support and, wincing, slowly eased herself back down. "Oh dear. Francesca, I may have snipped a bit of muscle again. Would you be a dear and fetch me my oils?"

"At once, ma'am," Francesca said, and hurried off.

Another loud throat-clearing. Millard.

"Apologies, Noor, but I'm afraid we don't have time for you to feel sorry for yourself," he said. I nearly shouted at him for being so unkind, but he cut me off.

"It's abundantly clear," he was saying, "that this V woman cared a great deal about you, otherwise she might've just handed you over to the wights. So might we please refocus the conversation?"

Noor scowled, but somehow she seemed a bit mollified. Soon her scowl eased into steely resolve.

"Very good," Miss Avocet said, still positioned awkwardly in her desk chair. "Miss Pradesh, would you submit yourself to a small procedure?"

"A procedure?" she asked, her eyebrows high.

"You see," Miss Avocet said, still wincing a little, "very occasionally we ymbrynes make a mistake"—it clearly pained her to admit it—"and we memory-wipe the wrong people or memory-wipe them a bit too much, and it becomes necessary to try to undo a bit of what we did. We have a man on staff, Mr. Reggie Breedlove, whose talent is the retrieval of some of those lost memories. Now, it's not science, this, and because it's been so long since your wipe, I can't guarantee we'll get much in the way of results."

"Oh," Noor said, a hopeful edge to her voice. "I think it would be worth a try,"

Miss Avocet smiled. "That's the spirit."

Fifteen minutes later, Breedlove arrived at Miss Avocet's office; Francesca had administered to the ymbryne the necessary oils for her injured back. Miss Avocet stood straight up, revived, and Breedlove stumbled in like a drunk, or at least like a man who'd just been roused from bed, his suit and tie put on hastily. He was tall and olive-skinned, and he had a wide face and even wider eyes that never seemed to blink.

Francesca led him toward us. He continued to stumble over a pile of books, catching himself just before falling.

"He looks a bit off balance," Emma said doubtfully.

"Have a little faith in your elders," snapped Miss Avocet.

Breedlove went to work right away. Noor, having been assured by Miss Avocet that this wouldn't hurt a bit and wouldn't erase any *more* of her memories, was seated in a straight-backed chair in front of the fireplace.

He stood behind Noor like a hairdresser might. "Stare into the flames," he instructed her. "Don't think about anything."

"I'll do my best."

Breedlove held his big palms out on either side of Noor's head. He closed his eyes. A fine, thin stream of smoke began to waft out of his nostrils.

Noor's eyes searched the fire, as if she were seeing something in the flames. Her hair—the strands that weren't gathered in a ponytail—rose and danced in the air.

I leaned toward her. *"Are you okay?"* I whispered.

"Please don't speak," Breedlove said.

I was about to argue, then thought better of it.

Millard paced the rug nervously. Emma and Bronwyn sat, each hugging herself on the couch, unintentionally mirroring the other.

Miss Avocet was completely still, her eyes shining.

I stood close to Noor, studying her face for any reaction—ready to put a stop to this if it seemed to be hurting her.

Thirty seconds ticked by.

"What are you doing?" I asked Breedlove.

Francesca held up a hand to me, but this time, Breedlove allowed the interruption. "Searching for blank spots," he explained.

I was about to ask a follow-up question when he suddenly stiffened.

"Yes, here," he said. "This section is full of little holes." His voluminous eyebrows shot up. "And one large one."

"Anything you can restore?" Miss Avocet asked.

"Perhaps." His hands drew closer to Noor's temples. The stream of smoke from his nose thickened, and his own hair began to stand up. "Perhaps a few things."

And then Noor started speaking. Slowly, as if half in a trance.

"I remember playing in a river. A deep, wide river. It had a really long name."

Miss Avocet cut her eyes toward Francesca. "Are you writing this down?"

Francesca held up her pad. So did two other ymbrynes-in-training standing behind her.

Noor said, "There was a big tree in the yard. An elm, Mama said. It had a swing. I fell once and twisted my ankle. She wouldn't let me go on it for a month after that and I was so upset."

"What else?" Breedlove asked her, his voice growing melodic. The smoke from his nostrils was fast becoming a problem, rising in dense tendrils toward the rafters above us.

Noor didn't seem to mind.

"Apples," she said. "Wild apples from the woods we used to pick in the fall. They were so sweet and delicious, and the juice would run down my arms. But then . . ." She was quiet for a moment, and so was the room but for the sound of pens scribbling on paper. Then she went on. "Itchy, so itchy. All over." She began to scratch her arms and her chest, as if feeling it again. "I got these little red bumps from playing in a briar patch. They looked like triangles," she said. "After that we didn't play in the woods much. Mama said they were dangerous. There were men with guns there. Men in bright orange jackets. We saw them once in the parking lot of the big store, and they had a big dead animal strapped to the roof of their truck. It was so sad. When I saw it, I cried."

"What was the name of the store?" I said, just above a whisper.

Breedlove glowered at me.

Noor's face tightened. Her eyes wandered the flames. Then she shook her head.

"I remember a bad smell. There was a factory, or something, and sometimes it smelled like rotten eggs."

The ymbrynes-in-training wrote furiously.

"Good," Millard said quietly. "What else?"

"The sound of a woodpecker early in the morning. He lived at the edge of the yard. He was so small. Sometimes he'd come sit on my windowsill. It looked like he was wearing a tiny red cap right on his head."

"Sounds like a downy woodpecker," Miss Avocet said.

Noor was talking faster and faster. The smoke was positively pouring from Breedlove's nose now.

"A long, long road. A mountain with no top on it. Lucky Charms soaked until the milk turned pink." She began to moan a little. Abruptly, Breedlove took his hands away.

"That's all," he said. "If I go any deeper, I could risk damaging her mind."

Noor's head dipped and she slumped in her chair, spent.

Millard, Bronwyn, and I darted over to her. I knelt down by her chair. "You okay?"

Noor looked up, surprised, as if coming out of a dream. "Yeah. Yeah, just . . ." She ran a hand down her face. "A little tired."

Breedlove pinched his nose closed, snorted once, and extinguished whatever fire had been smoldering in his head. Then he came around to face Noor, stumbling on the edge of the rug. "More snippets may return to you in the coming days," he said. "But only bits and pieces."

"Thank you," Noor said, smiling wearily at him. "That was"— she swallowed hard—"intense."

"I'm sure it was," Millard said.

Noor looked at him—or the place where his voice had come from. "Was any of that helpful?"

"I'm quite confident we can make something of it."

"We already have," said Francesca, and she turned to the ymbryne-in-training behind her, a shy girl nodding into her notebook.

"From just the species of flora and fauna you described," the girl said, "it seems certain the place you're describing is in the eastern half of United States, not the Midwest."

Noor looked struck. "What? Are you sure?"

"Are there tornadoes in those states?" I asked.

"Some," Millard said, nodding fast. "Not as many. But some."

Hugh sighed. "Even three or four US states is still an awfully big haystack."

"Granted," said Millard. "But it's a smaller one than we had before."

CHAPTER FIVE

*N*oor was a little unsteady on her feet for a few minutes, but would entertain no talk of resting, so we all headed downstairs to the Mapping Department. It was a baffling warren of tall library stacks and ladders on wheels, and the place was filled with bright white daylight, which came seemingly from the air itself. I assumed it was some peculiar trickery, as there were no windows and no lamps anywhere. Between the stacks were open areas with long flat tables atop which maps could be spread out, and we found Olive, Enoch, and Claire at one such table, half buried in a pile of giant atlases.

"We're nearly done with Oklahoma!" Olive announced when she saw us.

"Thank Hades," Enoch grumbled.

"Have you brought lunch?" asked Claire.

"This is no time for a break!" Millard said. "Clear all these away, it seems we've been barking up the wrong tree."

The three of them groaned.

The rest of us piled the now-useless Midwest maps on the floor and started over. Millard began giving orders like a drill sergeant, which under any other circumstances we would've resented. But this was his domain, and this task too important. So we obeyed with little complaint.

"Hugh," Millard barked, "climb up and get every atlas from that topmost shelf there, and be *very* careful with the big one, it's a real Map of Days and it's in delicate condition. Jacob, make a list of all the loops in Ohio, Pennsylvania, New Jersey, New York, and Maryland with long rivers immediately to the north and west of them. And Noor, I have a special task for you."

The atlases of those states were divided among us. We paged methodically through them, looking for long rivers with very long names, for topography and town layouts that matched the map fragment H had given us.

Soon we were lost in work.

◆   ◆   ◆

Hours passed.

The atlases piled up around us in stacks so tall they divided us like cubicle walls. Millard made occasional grunts of interest or surprise at some little detail or another he'd stumbled across. After an hour I asked Noor if she needed a break, but she shook her head. I slid a glass of water in front of her after another hour, and she drank it down in two gulps, then looked up at me, surprised and grateful, as if she'd forgotten she needed things like water to function, and dove right back into the atlas she'd been combing through. An hour after that, Claire whined, "Anyone want lunch *now*?" and held up a finger she'd bandaged to twice its width after sustaining a tiny papercut. "There's a stew restaurant at the bottom of Oozing Street that got two stars from the *Muckraker*'s food critic."

"Two stars out of how many?" Hugh asked.

"Five. Though it's the only establishment in the Acre to have been rated above one, so . . ."

"I guess we do need a break," Millard said with a sigh. "They say an army runs on its stomach."

"You guys should definitely get something to eat," Noor said, but her head didn't rise from the page.

"You're not coming?" I asked.

"You go ahead," said Noor. "I'm not hungry."

"That's the spirit," said Millard.

Hugh slammed a book down a bit too hard. "If you all had only cared this bloody much about finding Fiona," he said angrily, "we would've had her back by now."

Emma looked stung. "Oh, Hugh," she said, but he was already hurrying out, trying his best to hold back tears. A single bee buzzed in the spot where he'd been working.

"I'll talk to him," Emma said, and ran after him.

Noor looked at me. "What just happened?"

Millard said, "Our friend Fiona—who Hugh has long been in love with—went missing a while ago. She's presumed dead."

Bronwyn picked up the atlas Hugh had been leafing through. "Oh no," she said mournfully. "He was reading about Ireland." She held up the book for us to see.

"Enoch, you were supposed to be watching him!" Claire cried.

Enoch only rolled his eyes.

"Fiona is from Ireland," I explained to Noor.

"I'm so sorry," said Noor, shaking her head. "This must be so awful for him."

"You know, I had a dream about Fiona the other night," said Horace.

Our heads whipped in his direction.

"You did?" I asked. "Why didn't you say anything?"

"I didn't want to get his hopes up. Not all my dreams are prophetic, and it can take time to sort out which are which."

"What was the dream?" I asked.

Millard went back to his atlas. "I'm listening," he said. "But you know I don't put much stock in dreams."

"I *know*, Millard. You've only told me ten thousand times." Horace shook his head, but continued. "Anyway, in the dream Fiona was riding on a bus. There was a little boy with her, in a green tunic and a little hat with a feather in it. And she was frightened. I felt, very keenly, that she was in danger. It could mean nothing. But I wanted to tell someone."

"I think dreams contain lots of meaning," said Noor. "But that meaning doesn't have to be literally true."

Horace looked at her gratefully.

"Just please don't tell Hugh," said Millard. "He'll have us checking every bus in Britain, and when we find nothing, he'll be even more crushed than before."

◆　　◆　　◆

Emma and Hugh returned a while later with cups of takeout stew for everybody. Hugh apologized for his outburst, Emma rewarmed each of our stews with a quick dip of her pinkie into the brown liquid, and we ate while we worked.

"Don't any of you dare get stew on these atlases," Millard warned us. "The official penalty for damaging a book is thirty years' imprisonment—plus a hefty repair fee."

"*Oops,*" Hugh said under his breath, surreptitiously wiping at a page with his shirt.

After a few more hours, the seemingly sourceless light began to fade. We squinted and leaned closer to our work, determined to keep going, but then an officious boy appeared at the end of the stacks and bellowed, "The department is closing for the day! Kindly see your way out!"

"We'd better go," said Horace. "There are a few patients from the old asylum still loose in the building, and they're said to come out and roam around at night."

"Finally," Enoch muttered.

We were all exhausted.

As we walked out, Noor asked Millard what progress we'd made.

"Slow but steady," he said. "We're a great deal closer than we were this morning. But there are acres of proverbial weeds left to plow through"—he couldn't stifle a yawn—"unless you happen to remember a town name."

"I'll try." Noor sighed. "Sorry to wear you all out like this."

"Don't worry about it," I said. "Really."

"This concerns us all," Emma added.

Noor smiled meekly. "Thanks. It means a lot."

We emerged into the busy lobby, where all the ministries people were flooding out the doors and closing up for the day, when I overheard something that made me unreasonably happy:

"Don't you worry," Hugh said to Noor. "We'll find her."

And he patted her on the back.

◆　　◆　　◆

It was getting toward evening. Low on the horizon, a sickly yellow sun glinted at us through nets of factory smoke. Peculiars who'd been working all day were milling around in the streets and in the Acre's few public squares, blowing off steam. There was a lot of it to blow off, with the recent drama and the pall of tension hanging over the entire loop, and every conversation I overheard as we walked sounded heavy and full of dread.

Noor had slowed a little and fallen behind our group. I turned and saw her staring wistfully through the breaks in the tenement buildings, into the distance. So much had happened to her today. To us all, but to her especially. She'd hardly had a moment to process it.

I slowed my pace until she caught up to me. It took her a moment to notice, and then her head snapped up in my direction.

"Sorry to lag," she said. "Just lost in my own head."

"Anything you want to talk about?"

She shook her head. Looked down. For a moment our steps synchronized on the worn cobblestones. Finally, she said, "Do you ever think about running away? Picking some door in the

Panloopticon and just . . . going somewhere for a while? Get away from it all?"

"That's never really occurred to me," I said, frowning. "Though it does sound appealing."

"That's never even *occurred* to you?" She looked incredulous. "How is that possible? You have a thousand doors to a thousand places just waiting to be discovered. No airport, no passport, no customs—"

"Actually, that last part isn't true. We're getting special treatment these days only because things are so dire, but most peculiars need tickets for the Panloopticon. And they go through customs just like normals do."

Noor rolled her eyes. "You know what I mean. It's not the same thing at all."

I smiled. I did know what she meant.

"I don't know," I said finally. I looked out toward the blurring horizon. "Ever since the first time I came to Devil's Acre it's been nothing but drama and chaos and putting out fires. I'd love to explore one day, but it's not something I've had much time to think about . . . yet," I added, trying to put an optimistic spin on what had probably sounded a little hopeless.

"That's fair," she said. She looked to the horizon again. "If you had to pick another loop to live in right this second, which Panloopticon door would you choose?"

"Right this second?" I asked.

She nodded.

"Somewhere calm and beachy where nothing ever happens," I said right away. "I could use some more boring in my life."

I realized then that I was describing my hometown, the very place I'd wanted to escape my whole childhood. I wondered what the hell was happening to me.

"I'd go somewhere ancient," Noor said. "Hey, how far back can you go into the past?"

"As far back as loops have existed, I guess. Which has got to be a few thousand years. Millard used to have a big Map of Days with a lot of super-old, collapsed loops marked in it, and there were some from ancient Rome, ancient Greece, ancient China . . ."

"That sounds amazing," Noor said, a faraway look in her eyes. "That's what I'll do." She paused. "I mean, if I ever get the chance."

"I know you will," I said.

She laughed. "I like your optimism."

"One day we'll put all the fires out," I said. "And then we can explore as much as we like."

She looked over at me and smiled, and I realized I'd said *we* without even thinking about it. "We're falling behind," she said quietly. But she was still smiling when she said it.

Just as we caught up with our group, some peculiar girls passed us going the opposite way. They jumped and waved, giggling in bursts. "Can I have your autograph?" one said.

I felt my face go hot with embarrassment. Noor stifled a surprised laugh before raising an eyebrow at me, and I shook my head, refusing to meet Noor's eyes.

"Can I have a kiss?" another girl called out.

Now my skin was crawling, too. I kept my gaze straight ahead, waiting for the mortifying moment to pass.

"Oy, I'll spare you a kiss!" Enoch called after them, but the girls ignored him and kept walking.

Emma glared at them.

Finally, Noor nudged me with her elbow. "So. Does that happen a lot?"

"Once in a while."

"Must be rough," she joked, but her smile was genuine. Maybe there was a secret silver lining to all this strange attention. After all, I was not above hoping that Noor Pradesh would find me just a little bit impressive for being inconsequentially famous.

"Hurry up, you two!" Emma was glaring at *us* now.

We picked up our pace a little, but I wasn't ready for the conversation to be over. At least until Noor said, "Was it weird? Being with your grandpa's ex-girlfriend?"

I nearly jumped out of my skin, I was so surprised. "How—How'd you know we were . . . ?"

"It's pretty obvious. I see the way she looks at you."

I sighed. I was hoping I was the only one who saw those looks. "Well, we're not together anymore."

Noor asked me what happened. This, I *really* didn't want to go into.

She wasn't over him.

I might've shriveled up and died of embarrassment if those words left my mouth.

"I think in the end it was the age difference," I said, which was maybe 10 percent true. "We just couldn't . . . relate."

"Mm. I can see that."

I don't think she bought it. In fact, I'm sure she saw right through me. But she took pity on me anyway and let me change the subject, which was good enough for now.

◆　　◆　　◆

The ten of us stopped for a moment to watch a group of telekinetics have a tug-of-war with a rope—that none of them were touching. Noor was, naturally, fascinated, so we found uncomfortable seats on a low wall in Old Pye Square and stared out at the strangeness before us.

"So, what is there to do around here at night?" Noor asked.

"There's the Shrunken Head—the public house on Stabbing Street," said Emma. "But they mostly serve embalming fluids and mice wine. And it gets crowded."

"There's the aforementioned hanging," said Enoch. "Happens every night at six p.m. sharp by the docks."

"I *really* don't like hangings, Enoch," said Olive.

"Oh, *fine*. It's boring anyway once you've seen it a few times."

"The grimbear blood-sport ring got shut down after the wights were defeated, thank the birds," said Hugh, though I noticed Emma's and Horace's faces tighten at the word *defeated*. It had a false ring now.

"Most everything is shut down because of the stricter security rules," said Bronwyn. "Plus there's a new curfew that starts at sundown."

"Which is fine. I think civilized people should be in bed by dark, anyway," said Claire.

The security rules apparently included guards watching over everything. I could see them on roofs around the square, scanning the area.

Emma saw me looking and said, "That's the home guard. New recruits—most of the old ones got wiped out in the hollowgast raids."

"Poor buggers," Enoch muttered.

"The ymbrynes aren't taking any chances," said Bronwyn. "I think they're quite scared."

Just then a group of people started chanting and marching around in a circle in the middle of the square.

"What do we want?" shouted one of the marchers.

"Loop freedom!" the others replied.

"When do we want it?" said the lead marcher.

"Relatively soon!" the others bellowed angrily.

"Well, this is something," said Horace. "Look: democracy!"

Some of the marchers were carrying signs. WE WANT EQUAL TREATMENT! Another, echoing that morning's *Muckraker* headline, read: YMBRYNE INCOMPETENCE!

"These are the muddle-brains we were telling you about back in Florida," Enoch muttered to me. "Who want to stop living in loops and go join the real world."

"As if we wouldn't be burned at the stake," said Emma. "Didn't we all study the same peculiar history books?"

"Their movement is growing," said Millard. "If the ymbrynes don't handle their business and get the wights under control, they'll lose support amongst the rank and file."

"But ymbrynes are the reason we survived the twentieth century!" Claire said angrily. "Haven't they proven they know best? Without their loops we would all have been eaten by Caul's hollows!"

"Some are saying we could have been better prepared for the raids," said Millard. "And that we should have attacked their compound here in Devil's Acre long ago."

"Sounds like Monday-morning quarterbacking," said Noor.

"Thank you, exactly," said Millard. "What's a quarterback?"

"Ungrateful sods!" Enoch shouted at the marchers.

I felt a sudden coldness near me, and a smell like refrigerated compost wafted over us.

"We're meeting this Saturday," said a low voice. "We'd love to have you come and speak to everyone."

I turned to see seven feet of black robes. "You're all invited," Sharon said, teeth gleaming.

"You're associated with those fools?" said Enoch.

"But you work for the ymbrynes!" Claire barked at him.

"I have a right to my own political beliefs. And I happen to believe it's time the ymbrynes' long monopoly on power transitioned into something more equitable."

"They listen to regular peculiars' ideas," said Emma. "They have public forums!"

"They pretend to listen, nod their heads, then do whatever they think is best," said Sharon.

"Well, they're *ymbrynes*," said Bronwyn.

"See, that attitude is precisely the problem," Sharon replied.

"*You're* precisely the problem," Claire shot back.

Suddenly a loud, deep rumble shook the ground and rattled all the windows around the square. Someone in the crowd screamed, and several of the marchers dove to the ground.

"What was that?" Horace yelped. "Another jailbreak?"

"That's either a disaster or a breakthrough," Sharon said, a hand cupped to his hood, listening. "The new battery wasn't supposed to be fully charged until tonight . . ."

And he took off toward Bentham's house faster than a man that big should have been able to run.

◆　　◆　　◆

The curfew went into effect, and we went back to the house. Everyone was tired and wanted to unwind and get ready for bed. It had been a long day spent in close proximity to one another, and we'd all had our fill of conversation and excitement. Well, almost all of us.

Noor and I found ourselves alone in the upstairs common room.

I couldn't stop thinking about our earlier conversation. She'd been so surprised that I hadn't used the Panloopticon freely, and it made me wonder about myself. *Why hadn't I?* I'd heard my own answers out loud, of course, but I wondered, now, if they were the full truth. Worse, Noor had gotten the idea that I was uncurious, which I knew wasn't true at all.

But my quiet contemplation only inspired her to ask me more questions—*What's wrong? Something on your mind?*—and I realized then that there were lots of things I hadn't told her about myself. Things I wanted her to know. Things about my early days with the peculiars, about how I'd first met them, about what it was like to find out I was one of them. I told her the whole story: my coming to misty, mysterious Cairnholm with my dad; the clues I followed from my grandfather's last words and his old photographs; and their leading me to Miss Peregrine's ruined house and then into her loop. Meeting these kids who I had thought were now either very old or long dead, and my bafflement and shock that they were *still* kids. All the doubt I had wrestled with: Should I believe my eyes? Could I trust my own mind? Noor actually gasped when I got to the part where I realized I could see the hollows, too, and then again when I told her about the stranger on the island revealing himself to be my psychiatrist—and a wight.

I talked until my jaw hurt, but found myself leaving out small details, mostly about Emma and me. I didn't want to go into it—the role my feelings for her had played in my decision to abandon my normal life. But it felt good to talk. To connect with someone who seemed to feel the same things I once felt.

It made me feel less alone.

But eventually all my babble made me self-conscious.

"Okay, your turn," I said quickly. "I want to know more about *your* life."

"No way." She shook her head. "My life only got interesting like three months ago, and you know about that already. Now tell me what happened after you all left the island. I hate cliffhangers!"

"I'm sorry, but your life could not *possibly* have been more boring than mine was before all this."

"Just tell me this, and then if you insist on talking about my boring life, we can. Did you ever think about telling your parents?"

I almost laughed. "Yeah. I actually tried to, but my mom couldn't handle it and my dad basically disowned me. It got so bad Miss Peregrine had to wipe their memories, so they don't even re-member."

"Yeah, you mentioned that before," she said quietly. "I'm so sorry."

"They're on an extended vacation now. They think I'm home alone. I guess they'll start worrying when they come back and I'm not around."

"The part about your parents totally sucks. But the rest is . . . like destiny, or something. Your mom and dad didn't really feel like family to you. Believe me, I know what that's like. But in the end you found a new one." She smiled and brought her hands slowly together, forming a perfectly round ball of shadow between her palms. "It's amazing, how it happened." Then something changed behind her eyes, and a heavy cloud seemed to pass over her.

There was a small gap between us on the ratty couch, and I scooted toward her and closed it. "You're going to find her," I said, wrapping my hands around hers. "I know you are."

She shrugged, feigning indifference. "I guess we'll see," she said. "Who knows, maybe she won't even remember me."

"Of course she will. I'm sure she's still heartbroken over you. And I know she's going to be so happy to see you again."

She drew in a long breath and sighed. "Can we stay here and talk about our boring old lives for a while?"

"Yeah." I laughed. "That sounds nice."

And we did. We talked for hours—about her old life and mine and what happened after I left the island and a dozen other things. I could've talked to her all night and into the morning, and probably would have had Horace not padded downstairs, bleary-eyed, complaining that he could hear our voices through the floor. Only then did either of us realize how late it was or how bone-tired we really were, and we went, regretfully, to bed.

CHAPTER SIX

I woke up, for the second time in two days, to loud banging. This wasn't an explosion, though—it was someone pounding hard on a door.

It was still dark out.

"Jacob!" Emma shouted from downstairs.

I scrambled out of bed, barefoot and bedraggled, and raced into the hall. There was a thunder of feet on the stairs as we all rushed down.

Emma was standing at the front door, which was open.

"Miss Blackbird's here," she said, stepping aside to reveal the ymbryne standing there. "It's about Miss Peregrine."

"Where is she?" I said. "Is she here?"

Miss Blackbird skipped the greetings and got straight to the point. "Miss Peregrine is in America, in the loop where the peace talks are being held," she said, her three eyes staring at me. "We got the Panloopticon working an hour ago, and shortly after that we received an urgent message from her via parrot."

Miss Blackbird pushed into the house. She looked rattled. "There's a situation," she said cryptically. "She asked for you specifically."

"Me?" I said. "To come there?"

"Immediately," Miss Blackbird replied.

"Can you say what it's about?" asked Emma.

"If it's you she's asking for," Miss Blackbird said, "I'd imagine there's a hollowgast involved."

I swallowed hard. That old tightness in my chest again. "Just let me get dressed."

"There's no *way* we're letting him go alone," Noor said. She had slipped in beside me without my noticing, and when I glanced at her in surprise, she squeezed my hand.

"I would never have advised that Jacob go alone," said Miss Blackbird, "but you're much too inexperienced, Miss Pradesh. And besides, Leo Burnham and his men will be there, and seeing you would be like kicking a nest of angry hornets."

"I know that," Noor said, frowning. "I wasn't going to suggest *myself . . .*"

I was secretly glad; the idea of taking Noor anywhere near a hollowgast—voluntarily—made my stomach hurt.

"Choose two friends," said Miss Blackbird, ignoring Noor. "Get dressed and meet me outside in three minutes."

And then she swept outside in a dramatic flourish and slapped the door closed behind her.

I needed no time to think about it: I asked Emma and Enoch to come with me. Even though Enoch was a pain in the ass and things were a little tense with Emma at the moment, they were brave, resourceful, and good under pressure. I knew I could count on them.

"I'll get my things," Emma said, her face hardening with resolve, and she dashed up the creaky stairs.

Enoch grinned. "Oh, *fine*, I'll save your arse again . . . Let me get a few pickled hearts." And he ran after Emma.

Then we all went upstairs. I put on the new clothes and boots I'd gotten the day before and said goodbye to everyone. My friends filed past me in the hall, wishing me luck and whispering advice: *"Give 'em hell, Jacob,"* said Hugh; *"Watch your back!"* worried Horace; *"Do what Miss Peregrine tells you,"* said Claire. I pretended to be unafraid, but something icy was building in the pit of my stomach.

For a moment, Noor and I found ourselves alone.

"Are you really the only one who can do this?" she asked me. "Don't the ymbrynes have, like, adults who can handle things like this for them?"

"Not this kind of problem," I said, "if it's what I think it is."

"I know," she said. "Just had to ask." She was trying to put on a brave face, but couldn't hide her worry. I hoped I was hiding mine.

"I wish you could come, but I think Miss Blackbird is right."

"I have too much to do here, anyway." She paused, looking uncertain, then said, "I remembered something else last night. From when I was a little kid with Mama. It was a road sign I could see from our driveway. I don't know if it's a big deal or not. But I need to find out."

"It could be something," I said. "Are you sure you'll be okay here?"

"*You're* the one to worry about. I'll probably just be combing through old books with Millard and company."

It was sweet to hear her refer to my peculiar friends by name so easily. She was fast becoming one of us.

"I know you'll find her," I said. "And I'd really like to be there when it happens."

"I'd like that, too," Noor said.

She attacked me with a hug. "Take care of yourself," she said into my chest. "I need you in one piece."

We stood there holding each other for a long moment. I didn't want to move.

"I'll be fine. Promise."

"You better be."

"And I'll be back soon."

I kissed the top of her head. She smelled like shampoo and books, and the ice that had been forming in my stomach began, ever so slightly, to melt.

"*Ahem.*"

Enoch was standing on the stairs, arms folded.

And then there was a knock at the door and I heard Miss Blackbird shout, "That's three minutes, Mr. Portman!"

◆   ◆   ◆

Miss Blackbird was silent as she led Emma, Enoch, and me across the Acre. The sunrise had not quite broken yet, and home guard soldiers were still out enforcing the new curfew.

We reached Bentham's house. A few Temporal Affairs minions stood watch outside, and on the roof I could see more guards peering out into the distance. Everyone was on high alert.

We went inside and up the stairs, but instead of stopping at one of the usual floors, we kept climbing. The door to the loop where the conference was being held wasn't in the main Panloopticon hallway, but in Bentham's dusty attic, surrounded by his old, glass-encased curiosities.

At the far end of the room was a beautiful old elevator. This, Miss Blackbird told us, was the loop entrance. It was new, she explained, connected by the ymbrynes especially for the conference. She pressed a small brass button on the door and the elevator slid open. The interior was all rich, oiled wood. There was a panel on the rear wall with a large lever attached and three words stamped around it in art deco lettering: UP, DOWN, and LOOP.

"Please watch yourselves over there. America," she muttered, shaking her head, "is no place for children."

"Sounds like you're ready to start planning our funeral," Enoch said as we filed into the elevator.

"Not at all!" Miss Blackbird said, then tried to smile encouragingly. "Best of luck, hey?"

Here goes nothing, I thought, and threw the lever all the way to LOOP. The door slid closed by itself. The elevator car descended a foot, then jolted to a stop.

Enoch looked irritated and said, "What the devil—"

And then we began to free-fall.

My feet floated off the floor and my last meal threatened to come up.

"What . . . is . . . happening?" Emma managed to say, though I could hardly hear her over my popping ears.

And then everything went black, and we lurched suddenly and dramatically to the left and were thrown against the wall. A few seconds later, a pleasant chime sounded—*ding!*—and the lights flicked on again. We came to a shuddering stop.

I was swaying on my feet, battling nausea, when the door slid open to a wall of darkness. We were hit by a rush of hot, damp air, which felt like being bear-hugged by a big, sweaty man.

"Where are we?" said Enoch, and I felt a wave of dread pass over me.

Emma lit a flame in her hand as she took a tentative step out of the elevator, and the glow showed us a long, rugged tunnel hewn from rock, not much taller or wider than me.

I was slammed with a flood of awful sense memories, and my skin puckered despite the heat. The last time I was in a place like this, I was shot with a gun, and a giant tree-creature had nearly killed everyone I cared about.

Emma must have been feeling something similar. "Oh God," she said, "you don't think we got sent to the—"

"Don't be daft," Enoch said. "That place got flushed down the interdimensional loo."

"You're in a gold mine, a half mile underground."

It was Miss Peregrine's voice, doubling, tripling with echoes, and with it came an instant relief. This wasn't a nightmare. We hadn't been sent back to that hell-maze.

A gleam of light appeared and she came around a corner, a lantern shining in her hand.

"Miss P!" Emma cried. "Are you okay? What's happening?"

We rushed toward her and she toward us. Emma gave her a quick, hard embrace.

"I'm fine," she said quickly. "But you and Mr. O'Connor shouldn't have come. This is a dangerous place."

"Figured that," said Enoch. "Which is exactly why we came."

"Miss Blackbird told me to bring friends," I said in their defense, "and I asked them."

It was clear Miss Peregrine didn't approve, but she knew trying to send them back would be useless. It amazed me: After everything we'd all faced together, she was still underestimating her charges.

"All right," she said, shaking her head. "So long as you stay quiet, stay behind me, don't talk to Americans, and don't wander off on your own. Do you understand?"

"Yes, miss," they said in unison.

She nodded. "Welcome to Marrowbone, children. We have quite a mess on our hands."

＊　　◆　　◆

"Whose crackpot idea was it to hold the peace conference down a *mine*?"

Enoch had to shout his question at Miss Peregrine's back—she was walking so fast we were practically chasing her through the tunnels.

"This is just the entrance. The talks are being held in the town above us, at the surface. I wish you were costumed in era-appropriate clothes." She gestured to a sign pointing down another spur of the tunnel that read COSTUMING. "But there isn't time, and the normals in this loop have mostly been rounded up anyway."

"Rounded up?" I said.

She didn't answer me.

We came to another elevator, much more primitive and scary-looking than the last. We crowded into its wire cage and Miss

Peregrine pulled a lever on the floor. A giant engine roared to life somewhere, and the elevator began to screech upward. It was a claustrophobe's nightmare: All we saw for a while, on all sides of us, was passing rock.

"It's a long ride," Miss Peregrine said, her voice rising over the noise, "so now's a good time to tell you a few things. Besides which, it's hard to find a place in Marrowbone where an American spy isn't trying to overhear what you're saying."

I couldn't help but notice how tired Miss Peregrine seemed. Her hair was disheveled and her blouse was tucked in crookedly— the kinds of details she never overlooked.

"There was a kidnapping earlier today. The victim was an important peculiar in the Northern clan, and it appeared she was taken by someone from the Californio clan, so a posse of Northerners was assembled, and despite the ymbrynes' strident objections, they rode into the Californios' camp and took a prisoner. Fighting broke out, but thankfully we were able to stop it before anyone was killed."

"But that's not the whole story, I'm guessing," Emma said.

"No. The 'evidence' of the Californios' guilt is too perfectly obvious—almost constructed. It stinks of the wights. Not to mention it occurred only a few hours after the wights' prison break. I believe they snuck in and took the girl, and did it in a way that implicated the Californios—practically guaranteeing a conflict between clans that would destroy our attempts to make peace. It took an immense amount of persuasion on our part to prevent a battle in the middle of town today. I'm afraid we've only managed to delay one, unless we can prove beyond a doubt that wights were responsible."

"And you think a hollowgast might have been involved," I said. "And that's why you called for me."

"Yes," the ymbryne said.

"You want me to find evidence," I said. "Something only I can see."

"That's right."

"You want Jacob to prevent a war," said Enoch, twisting a finger in his ear as if he hadn't heard correctly. "By giving the Americans evidence *they can't see?*"

"You'll have to figure out a way to make them see it," Miss Peregrine said, and she laid her hand on my shoulder. "I'm sorry, my boy. But you're the best hope we have right now."

◆　　◆　　◆

We came out of that black hell into a cool bright day, and I could breathe for the first time in a while. Miss Peregrine led us quickly past three men with guns. One looked like a mountain man, decked in raggedy furs. The second was dressed like a cowboy in a wide-brimmed hat and a long leather duster coat. The third, in a suit and tie, had to be one of Leo Burnham's guys. They were staring one another down with such intensity that they barely registered our presence.

"One sentry from each of the American clans," Miss Peregrine said under her breath. "Best not to make eye contact."

And then we came to our ride. I'd been expecting something along the lines of a stagecoach. Instead, there was a horse-drawn, glass-enclosed hearse waiting for us.

"It was all they had on short notice," Miss Peregrine said by way of apology. "Climb in."

Enoch oohed. Emma made a sour face but made no comment. There was no time to debate.

The hearse's attendant held the back door open for us, and we climbed inside. There was just enough headroom to sit upright.

"How fancy!" said Enoch, running a hand over the black velvet curtains.

It was the second time in three days that I'd taken up space normally reserved for a dead body. It seemed like the universe was trying to tell me something, and not in a terribly subtle way.

Miss Peregrine said something to the driver, a long-bearded man with a flat aspect. He flicked the reins and we took off, leaving the attendant behind with the three armed men.

A landscape of forests and hills rolled by, and those hills not covered in trees were littered with mining machinery: narrow-gauge train cars heaped with excavated rock; machines belching steam and smoke into the air; heaps of slag. There were a few actual miners here and there, smoking, leaning tiredly on shovels—looped normals from the period, I assumed.

Miss Peregrine pointed out the clans' camps as we rode: That collection of buffalo-hide tents at the forest's edge was where the Northern delegation camped. The Californios' delegation occupied Poverty Flat, the shacks at the edge of town. And Leo's Five Boroughs clan stayed in the Eagle Pass Hotel, the best (and only) accommodations in Marrowbone.

"Where do the ymbrynes sleep, then?" I asked.

"In trees," she said simply.

We rode into town through Poverty Flat, a depressing collection of hovels that looked like they might blow away in a strong breeze.

A few blocks later, we were in the center of Marrowbone—and it was a proper Old West town, the first I'd seen with my own eyes. The streets were lined with the usual assortment of saddle shops, gunsmiths, and saloons I'd come to expect from watching cowboy movies. Only one thing seemed off: There was no one around.

The horses slowed, then stopped. Miss Peregrine called out to the driver and asked what the matter was.

"I ain't goin' one foot farther," he said. One of his horses let out a high, nervous whinny.

"Looks like this is our stop," Miss Peregrine said, and we climbed out.

"Where is everyone?" I asked.

Miss Peregrine gestured up the street. "Just ahead."

I squinted, then saw them—dozens of people standing in the shadows of awnings, crouched behind barrels and wagons, on opposite sides of the street. The Northerners on our left, facing the Californios on our right. As we walked toward them—yes, *toward* them—it became quickly apparent the two clans were in some kind of silent standoff, like the armed men at the mine entrance.

"Neutral party!" Miss Peregrine shouted as we approached. "Hold your fire!"

"Hold fire!" shouted someone on the Northerners' side of the street.

"Hold fire!" came the reply from the Californios' side.

Another ymbryne stole out of a storefront and hurried down the wooden sidewalk toward us. It was Miss Cuckoo, her metallic silver hair and dark skin vivid against Marrowbone's chalky, sun-bleached streets.

"Alma!" She was anxious, short of breath. Her eyes flicked toward me. "Good, you've got him. They are all waiting."

"Have there been any aggressions?" asked Miss Peregrine. "Any shots fired?"

"Not yet, by some miracle," said Miss Cuckoo.

We followed her quickly back the way she'd come, our shoes ringing hollowly against the wooden sidewalk. I couldn't imagine what Miss Cuckoo was talking about until I saw, among the Northerners, a sallow-faced woman armed with a giant log—a foot thick and twenty long, at least—held over her shoulder like a javelin she might toss. Not far from her stood a pair of men with dead birds hanging from their belts and shotguns in their hands, and near them was a young girl rolling a boulder from side to side on the ground in front of her, using just the tip of one finger to move it. On the Californio side, a boy in a cowboy hat was glaring across the street while kneading his hands, and I could see electric sparks coursing between his fingers. An even younger boy stood at fearless attention with a bandolier of bullets strapped across

his chest and a sombrero on his head so big it smooshed down his ears a little.

Both sides of the street bristled with people brandishing weapons—peculiar and conventional—and it was clear just one act of violence could set off a bloody battle.

Miss Peregrine stopped and turned to us. "We're about to meet the clan leaders," she said. "Don't speak unless you're spoken to." And then she turned and went through a doorway, and we followed her into what I gathered was a saloon—bar, tables, the sour smell of spilled beer.

There were maybe ten people inside, clustered around a couple of the tables near the bar, and as soon as we walked in, they all fell silent and turned to stare at us. Miss Cuckoo blocked our way and hissed, *"Wait,"* while Miss Peregrine approached a gentlemanly fellow in a wheelchair.

"That's Mr. Parkins," Miss Cuckoo whispered to us, *"leader of the Californio clan."* Across the room, a man in a voluminous buffalo coat was staring bullets at Parkins while rolling a coin between the knuckles of one hand. "Antoine LaMothe, head of the Northern clan," Miss Cuckoo added. Flanking the two leaders were men I took to be their personal guards—one was dressed like a fur trapper, the other like John Wayne—and a small, elegant older woman I recognized as Miss Wren was speaking to LaMothe in an undertone.

"And over there is Leo Burnham," said Miss Cuckoo, "who I believe you already know."

It was him, all right. Unmistakable in his pinstriped suit, cream-colored homburg, and purple tie, one elbow up on the bar, watching the proceedings with a vaguely amused look while sipping a drink. I resisted a powerful urge to go punch his ugly face.

Miss Peregrine went to join Miss Wren, who was still speaking quietly and urgently with LaMothe. After a bit more arguing between the two, it was Miss Peregrine's turn to talk. I tried reading

J. M. Parkins

her lips with little success. But it looked like Miss P wasn't finding much success, either. LaMothe was shaking his head angrily.

Parkins, leader of the Californio clan, had clearly been watching this exchange when he slapped the arm of his wheelchair. He seemed furious.

"Give it a goddamned *chance*, LaMothe," he shouted.

LaMothe spun around, his face turning red. "Give me back my goddamned earthworker!"

"We didn't *take* your goddamned earthworker!" Parkins exploded.

Their bodyguards tensed, readying to draw weapons should they need to.

"Sure you didn't!" LaMothe again. "You've only been talking about how badly you want one for the last fifty years!"

Parkins's chair rolled forward a few feet of its own accord. "We didn't take her, and that's that! Now, listen here, you people had better bring Ellery back to our camp by sundown—or there'll be hell to pay!"

I assumed Ellery was the name of the prisoner—the one taken as revenge. I frowned. This felt like a lot to keep track of. My head was ping-ponging back and forth as the two clan leaders traded threats and insults.

"Why wait until sundown?" LaMothe cried. "Come at us!" Two raccoons that had been hiding in the folds of LaMothe's coat rose up and hissed in Parkins's direction. They were attached to the lining of his coat by their tails.

Miss Peregrine and Miss Wren were pleading with the men to calm down, while Miss Cuckoo slowly shuttled Enoch, Emma, and me toward the door.

But we found it blocked from the other side by another of Leo's men.

Leo Burnham unleaned himself from the bar, stepped between LaMothe and Parkins, and bellowed, "SHUT UP, ALL OF YOU!"

And, amazingly, they did.

"Antoine, you really want to start a war with Parkins over something he maybe didn't do?"

"He *did* do it," LaMothe growled, which nearly started another shouting match.

"We let the birds drag us out to this hick loop so we could iron out our differences, no? So if they think Parkins didn't do this thing, at least let 'em make their case."

"My thinkin' exactly!" said Parkins.

"Thank you, Leo," Miss Wren said. "Well said."

"Fine," said LaMothe, glaring at Miss Peregrine. "Say your piece."

Leo cocked his thumb at us. "These your hotshot crime-scene investigators, Peregrine? The ones hiding behind Frenchie's skirt?"

"Nobody's hiding," I said, and stepped forward.

I saw Leo's face change. He finally recognized me.

"Wait a goddamn minute," he said. "*This* kid?" He was shaking his head. Almost laughing. "You got a lotta nerve, Peregrine."

"You know him?" said LaMothe.

"He's a troublemaker. And his grandfather was a criminal."

My lip twitched. I wanted to slap him. Miss Peregrine put a hand on my back, as if to say *I'll handle this*. "You're mistaken on both points. I assure you, Jacob is one of our best and brightest, and the most accomplished tracker of hollowgast in the world."

"There's more than one?" Leo said, narrowing his eyes at me.

"I can see them, sense them from a quarter mile away," I said.

I was about to continue and talk about how I could control them, when Miss Peregrine squeezed my shoulder and cut me off.

"His detection skills have saved our lives many times," she said quickly.

Leo seemed reluctant to accept this, but after a moment of internal struggle, he let it go. Miss Peregrine had clearly done a lot to earn his trust in the days since I'd last seen him, when he'd hardly been able to tolerate the sight of her.

"What makes you think a hollowgast had anything to do with it?" Leo asked, still eyeballing me.

"Experience and intuition," said Miss Peregrine. "I can't prove it—but I think Jacob can." She turned to face Parkins and LaMothe. "And if he doesn't find any compelling evidence, we won't stand in your way; settle this however you must."

"But I warn you," Miss Wren said, her face pallid and grave, "if you make war, the ymbrynes will not take sides, and the wider world's loops will be shut to you forever."

Leo laughed. "The rest of the world can go to hell."

"Let them look if they like," LaMothe said with disgust, his raccoons rising up to hiss venomously at Parkins. "I already know where the trail leads."

*　　◆　　◆

Where the trail began was the Northern clan's camp, a collection of large (and rather impressive) animal-skin tents outside of town. Some were elaborate, with doors and windows cut into them, and one was two stories tall—LaMothe's, I assumed. One was even suspended in the trees, high above our heads.

LaMothe showed us the tent from which the girl—Ellery was her name—had been taken. He showed us the backside of the tent, which faced empty woods, and where it had been ripped open. He showed us the bed where she'd been sleeping when she was taken.

It had happened earlier in the day.

There were clear signs that a struggle had occurred—a flipped cot, personal items strewn across the floor—but none of which I would consider the classic signs of a hollowgast attack. No python-shaped depressions in the grass from the whipping of tongues. No bite marks made with distinctively long razored teeth. And most disappointingly, no puddles of hollowgast residue—the stinking black goo that leaked incessantly from their eye sockets. But the clan leaders and ymbrynes were watching me search, and I knew there would be trouble if it looked like I was getting frustrated, so I pretended to examine Ellery's pillow very closely and feigned interest in the texture of the long tear in the tent wall.

Meanwhile, I could hear Emma outside the tent showing people the wights' mugshots, in the hopes one of them had been seen, but she was coming up empty.

I began to get worried. Worried about failing, and about how the hell we would get out of this loop if a war between two extremely well-armed peculiar clans broke out.

LaMothe himself was getting frustrated. He sensed I wasn't finding anything, and he called for one of his underlings to bring in the evidence *they* had collected.

"We found this pitched into the trees." He pulled a knife out of a bag and dangled it. "It's the one that was used to cut open this tent—you can tell by the serrated edge—and it's one of theirs." He pointed out a symbol carved into the knife's leather handle, which looked like a *C* inside a braided lariat.

"It's one of ours," Parkins admitted, "but we don't know how it got there."

"The hell you don't!"

"Could've been stolen from us!" Parkins said. "Planted by these wights!"

LaMothe's burly bodyguard stepped forward. "What about the drag marks?" he said. "They lead straight to your camp!"

"Coulda been faked!" Parkins shouted. "Hell, maybe *you* faked it so you could justify coming for one of *our* people!"

The emotional temperature was near boiling.

"Now, now, gentlemen!" Miss Wren said, putting herself between the two angry men. "I'm sure Jacob is about to prove our case!"

"Almost got something!" I lied, just trying to buy time. "Give me one more minute!"

Miss Peregrine rushed over to me. *"I hope you're not kidding,"* she whispered.

I winced.

Her face fell.

For a moment she looked hopeless, then distracted by something, and a spark of what seemed like inspiration lit up her face.

She turned to face the others. "Excuse me!" she said loudly. "Mr. Portman has had a breakthrough! Please follow us!"

She marched out of the tent, crooking a finger at me to follow.

"Just what I suspected!" she said, faking excitement. "A very clear trail of ocular residue!"

"Of *what*?" LaMothe said.

"Eye leakage. Every hollowgast weeps a constant stream of oily tears. Only Jacob can see it—and he *has*, and it leads this way!"

"Jacob, that's brilliant!" Emma said, color returning to her pale cheeks.

Enoch punched me lightly in the shoulder. "Knew you were good for something."

I was baffled, of course. What was Miss Peregrine up to?

"You're finding drips along the tree line," she hissed quickly in my ear.

Having no other choice, I played along and pretended I was following a trail. We walked along the forest's edge, Miss Peregrine at my side. When these pissed-off cowboys and mountain men inevitably realized I was making all this up, I was pretty sure one of them would shoot me. It wouldn't be long; the troops were getting restless.

LaMothe started grumbling.

"What's more likely?" he was saying. "That some invisible monster took my Ellery and set up Parkins and his people to look like they did it? Or that this Californio trash finally kidnapped her? Everyone knows how bad they need an earthworker; they're piss-poor farmers and can't get nothing to grow."

"Let me say something," said Leo, who'd been uncharacteristically quiet for some time. "I didn't want to say this, because it's not something I'm proud of. But we had a wight attack just a few days ago. Busted into my HQ with a hollowgast and stole a very promising feral right out from under me. From my *house*."

"You *saw* it?" Parkins said, turning around in his chair, which was floating a few inches above the rough ground as his bodyguard pushed it.

"No, John, the damned things are invisible. But I saw a man thrown across a room by it. And the stink is incredible . . ."

Oh my God, I thought. Burnham had thought H was a wight. It made a certain sense. H was in command of that hollow, like a wight would've been, and when they found his body he'd had no eyes—hence no pupils—to prove otherwise.

"It still doesn't make a lick of sense," LaMothe said. "Why take Ellery? There are easier peculiars to kidnap. Do the wights have crops to grow and fields to cultivate?"

"To cause chaos," Miss Wren said darkly. "When the rest of peculiardom is in chaos, they thrive. When we are distracted, they can get on with their real work."

"Which is . . . what?" asked LaMothe.

Miss Wren sighed. "Would that we knew."

All this time I'd been pretending to find more drips of eye goo. Miss Peregrine was looking up at the trees half the time, and twice she saw something there that made her nudge me in a slightly different direction.

Then I saw one. A *real* one. I almost couldn't believe it—

A footprint-sized patch of stamped grass, and in the center of it, a black stain. I stopped, suddenly, and bent down to examine it.

"What is it, boy?" Parkins said.

"Residue!" I replied, excited, before I could catch myself. "I mean, uh, an extra-big drip of it."

I pressed my finger into it. It squished a little, still wet, and the skin of my fingertip began to burn and throb.

Damn. The stuff was acidic. Before wiping it off, I brought the finger to my nose and sniffed, and nearly gagged at the unmistakable rotten-meat scent.

Definitely a hollowgast.

And not just any hollowgast, but the one I'd sprung from the blood-sport ring. The one that, until recently, had been powering the Panloopticon.

"I know this one," I said. "I recognize his smell."

"Like a blessed bloodhound," Leo marveled.

I looked at Miss Peregrine, amazed. *How did you know?*

She just smiled.

I followed the trail—a real one now—very quickly. The black drops were closer together in places where the hollow had slowed, and farther apart when it had moved fast. I didn't always have to see the spots with my eyes to know where they were; sometimes I could smell them. I found I could even smell them ten, fifteen feet away.

The trail followed the trees to the mine. But it skirted the entrance and curved around the side, and that's where I found a puddle of hollowgast slime nearly a foot in diameter. He'd been waiting here a long time.

I was bending to get a closer look when I heard LaMothe call out to his man, and they crouched down, examining something on the ground. Then they stood up and LaMothe extended his hand to Miss Peregrine. There was something small and white wriggling in his palm.

"What is that?" she said.

"It's one of Ellery's worms," LaMothe said. "They wriggle out through her eye patch sometimes, when she's upset."

"Then we know she was here. And so was the hollowgast."

"Well, that proves it!" Parkins said. "It was them wights and their hollow. They took her out of the loop."

"But someone would've seen 'em leave," said Leo. "We have guards posted."

"Not if they went out this way," said LaMothe, and he walked over to a large boulder that stood against the side of the hill. "Somebody help me push."

It took seven of us, but we were able to roll the boulder a few feet to one side. Behind it was a tunnel that led away into the dark.

"I'll be damned," Parkins said. "Is that a back way into the mine?"

"And out of the loop," said Leo.

"A hollow wouldn't have had any trouble moving that boulder," I pointed out.

"Well, I think that about clears things up, don't you?" Parkins said testily. "Now, LaMothe. Your people better return my girl, and double quick."

LaMothe laughed. "Oh, this doesn't end here. This ain't over until we get Ellery."

Parkins was practically vibrating with frustration. "Now, listen here, LaMothe—you don't see Burnham holding up the talks because the wights took a feral from *him* . . ."

"This is different. This was an act of war perpetrated upon me while we was supposed to be talking peace."

"Mr. LaMothe, be reasonable," Miss Wren pleaded.

He rounded on her. "Okay, try this on. You say these were the same wights who broke out of your jail. So either you can't keep your own house in order, or I'm left to assume you let 'em out on purpose."

"That's absurd!" Miss Wren cried.

"He makes a damn good point," said Leo. "You birds were supposed to have put the kibosh on these wights and their monsters months ago. And now they're out raising hell again? How can we trust anyone so incompetent?"

LaMothe turned his hissing raccoons on me. "So you're some famous hotshot tracker?" he said. "Well, you better be."

LaMothe stepped toward me and shoved a small card into my hands. It was a photograph of a girl wearing an eye patch and a giant black dress that swallowed her bottom half.

"No." Miss Peregrine snatched the photo away from me. "Jacob's not involved in this."

"You're the one dragged him into it," LaMothe said, his eyes burning like coals. "Clean up your mess, Peregrine. Get my girl back. Or you can forget about any peace accord."

CHAPTER SEVEN

I'm so sorry, Jacob. I so regret putting you in this situation."

Miss Peregrine, Emma, and Enoch were following me through tunnels as I tracked the trail of hollowgast residue. It was easy enough to follow down here, but what about on the other side of the loop?

"What if I can't do it?" I said. "I've never tracked a hollow like this before. I'm not like Addison, who can smell peculiars from a long way off . . ."

"What you can do is even better. You can sense them."

The trail led to the loop entrance the Americans used—yet another elevator—which led us up through a much gentler changeover and into the present. We walked out into a lobby full of tourists.

"Hope you folks had a great time!" A grinning tour guide slapped a sticker on my shirt that read *I saw the Olde Time Gold Mine and all I got was this lousy sticker!*

Soaked into the carpet by the exit, I saw a black spot. The hollow had come through this way, into the present.

The trail of hollowgast residue continued outside, down the sidewalk, around a corner—and I found it easier and easier to follow, so that after a while I hardly even had to look for it—my nose, and more than that, a sensation in my gut, was telling me where to go. I felt like an old cartoon character following the wafting scent of a pie cooling in a window.

We were passing through the crowded center of the downtown,

and I worried that my companions' old clothes might attract attention—until I looked more closely around me. There were people in Old West costumes, in full cowboy attire and dressed like old-timey madams, walking everywhere. A lot of the old buildings had been preserved. What had once been a lawless frontier town had become a kind of open-air Wild West theme park, and you could get your photo taken in Old West gear, buy chaps and ten gallon hats and replica buffalo bones at gift shops, and watch costumed reenactments of famous shootouts. One was happening in the town square right now, the duelists cheered on by a crowd of sunbaked tourists and their bratty, distracted kids. I couldn't help but be reminded of the very real armed standoff that was still happening inside the loop—and I realized that this town was the perfect cover for a loop entrance. The comings and goings of strange people in strange costumes would arouse no special interest at all.

"This is fun for normals?" Enoch said. "Watching people *pretend* to shoot one another?"

"Keep your eyes sharp," Emma hissed, scanning the faces of the crowd. "Murnau and the other wights could still be nearby. It would be best if we saw them before they saw us."

That brought me solidly back to reality. Right now we were hunting the wights, but if they ever realized it, they'd start hunting us right back. The idea jogged loose a question that had been burning in my mind earlier, but which I hadn't been able to ask in front of the Americans:

"Miss P, how did you find the place where the hollow residue started?"

Emma's head snapped toward me. "What's that?"

"There wasn't any residue in the tent," I said. "I made that up. The real trail started a thousand feet away—and somehow Miss P led me right to it." I looked at her expectantly.

She returned a sphinxlike smile. "As we inspected the scene, I realized the wights themselves never entered the Marrowbone loop.

They sent their hollowgast instead—along with someone else. Someone who wouldn't attract much attention. That was the person who snuck into the girl's tent and kidnapped her, dragging her to the spot where the hollowgast had apparently been waiting—where you discovered its residue trail."

"But how did you track *that* person?"

"Ymbrynely intuition," she said.

Enoch groaned. "Oh, come *on*."

"All right, then. I noticed light-but-unusual boot prints leading in and out of the torn tent-back—a tread pattern made by a high-traction sole, not the smooth-soled cowboy boots favored by the Californios or the moccasins most Northerners wear. It led out along the tree line."

"You never cease to amaze, miss," Emma said.

"So who's this other person?" asked Enoch.

"Based on the shoe size and, well, ymbrynely intuition, I suspect it's a girl of about the same physical age and build as Ellery. Just follow the hollowgast's scent and sense trail. These wights don't travel anywhere without hollows, and I doubt they'll suspect they're being tracked that way. You have the advantage—for now, at least."

"It's only an advantage if they always travel on *foot*," I said. "If they got into a car . . ."

I'd been expecting the trail to dry up at any moment—to deadend at a parking lot and an empty parking space.

"Stuffed into a car with a hollowgast," Enoch said. "What a disgusting scenario."

"Disgusting or not, there's no way I could track that. There wouldn't be any residue droplets to follow, and the scent trail would be way too faint." I sighed. "My tracking ability just isn't that developed."

Miss Peregrine raised an eyebrow at me. "I think you might surprise yourself, Mr. Portman. Look where you've led us."

I looked up. The trail was headed straight for a bus station.

"Are you kidding?" Emma said. "They took a hollowgast on a *bus*?"

"No way," I said.

We went inside. The waiting area was depressing and gray, and probably hadn't been cleaned since the 1970s. Bums occupied the corners; everyone else looked haggard and pissed off as they waited. I followed a light trail of hollow residue to the bus boarding area, where it suddenly disappeared.

Unbelievable—they *had* caught a bus.

I ran back to find my friends, and there was Emma, running toward me, eyes wide. "Somebody recognized one of them!" she said, waving the wights' mugshots at me, then grabbing my arm to pull me over to the ticket window.

"Yeah, I saw them," said the man behind the counter, bored. "Couple hours ago. They left on the five o'clock to Cleveland."

He returned his attention to a basketball game he was watching on his phone.

Miss Peregrine rapped on the window. "How many stops does that bus make between here and Cleveland?"

He sighed. Fished a paper out of a drawer and slapped it on the counter. "Here's the schedule."

She looked at it. "Five stops," she said. "In a journey of about one thousand miles." She rapped on the window again. "When does the next bus to Cleveland leave?"

"Forty-five minutes," he said without looking up.

She turned to me with a self-satisfied smile. "See, Mr. Portman? Just when you were about to lose hope."

"We'll stop at all the same stops they did," Emma said, "and you can check for hollow goo . . ." She was rubbing her hands together, getting excited just like she did whenever a plan came together, or an impossible problem began to seem solvable. It was one of the things I loved about her, and always would.

Enoch groaned again. "And here I was hoping we might spend tonight in our own beds."

"You still can," I said. "No one's making you come."

"He's coming," Emma said. "He just can't pass up a chance to complain."

◆   ◆   ◆

We found a deserted section of the waiting area and sat on a bench, a broken coin-operated TV bolted to the arm. My head felt like it weighed a million pounds, it was so full. I was vibrating with stress, but I also could've fallen asleep on the metal bench if I just lay down. Everything in our world was unsettled and breaking apart, and yet Emma and Enoch were joking about something they'd seen the normals in town wearing, and Miss Peregrine's expression was completely placid as she looked around, thinking whatever she was thinking. Maybe they were so used to living under the looming threat of multiple catastrophes that it didn't affect them much anymore— but I couldn't take it.

"Why are you guys so sure I can do this?" I said, struggling to hide my frustration.

"Because you're Jacob." Emma shrugged.

"I never said you could do it," Enoch said. "But it sounded more interesting than bookmarking atlases with Millard all day."

I turned to Miss Peregrine, our rock of sanity and wisdom. "What happens if I lose the trail and can't find them? What happens if we can't get the girl back?"

Tell me it won't be so bad. Tell me the world won't end if I fail at this.

"What will happen?" She sighed. "The Americans could lose faith in us, pull out of the conference, and go back to fighting one another. Or they may go to war right away, no matter what we do."

She said it so casually, my jaw almost dropped.

"Miss P, pardon me for saying so, but you don't sound like you care all that much," said Emma.

"I care a great deal," she replied, "and the other ymbrynes and I will do our level best to keep the negotiations afloat no matter what happens. But there's only so much we can control. The Americans have to want peace. We can't force that. And even if we forge an airtight peace accord, it's always possible that it could fall apart one day."

"Then why send us to do this?" said Enoch. "If it might not matter anyway, why bother rescuing this girl?"

Her placid expression vanished, and her eyes narrowed. "Because it's not the girl I care about," she said. "It's the wights."

Now Emma looked shocked. Miss Peregrine didn't usually speak so bluntly. But it seemed she had decided to treat us like adults. "This kidnapping wasn't a random act. I don't buy Miss Wren's theory—I think this abduction was about more than causing chaos and sabotaging the peace."

"Then what was it about?" I said.

"Follow the wights," she said. "Observe them. And we may yet find out."

"And the girl?" Enoch said.

"Get her back if you can. But don't take unnecessary risks. I could abide any number of personal failures, but I could not abide losing any of you."

"And what will you be doing while we're on this dangerous mission?" Enoch asked.

"I'll be watching."

Emma looked surprised. "You're not coming with us?"

"Not exactly," Miss Peregrine replied. "But I'll never be far away. Oh—and I want you to bring Hugh along."

Enoch cocked his head. "That's a bit random."

"Can he be here in half an hour?" I said, glancing at a wall clock.

"Should be here any minute," said Miss Peregrine. "I sent for him some time ago."

And just then Hugh walked into the building, escorted by Ulysses Critchley, and waved to us, grinning, from across the ticket hall.

"Why Hugh?" Enoch said under his breath. "If you thought we needed backup, why not—I dunno—Bronwyn?"

"Because he is capable and selfless," said Miss Peregrine. "And frankly, he needs a bit of adventure to take his mind off Fiona."

I couldn't argue with that. The poor guy spent every unoccupied moment worrying himself to death.

◆   ◆   ◆

The bus company's name and logo had been borrowed from a character in children's literature (he could fly, befriended fairies, and lived on an island where no one aged), and the cartoon image of him that was emblazoned on the bus, smiling in a jaunty feathered cap, clashed hilariously with the desperately gritty station.

Before I could follow my friends aboard, Miss Peregrine pulled me aside to speak to me alone.

"You've had dreams about him, haven't you. My brother."

I forgot, for a moment, to breathe.

"Yes."

"But they seemed like more than just dreams," she said. "Like he was inside your head."

I was nodding like a robot. "Yes. Yes."

"I've had them, too."

"Really?"

"He may be trying to reach out to us via our dreams. To torment us. The two people he hates the most in the world—who he blames for his downfall. But believe me, Jacob. Taunting us with visions is *all* he can do."

"Are you sure?" I said. "What if they're trying to bring him back?"

She shook her head firmly. "It's impossible. He's stuck down a very deep hole, and he's stuck there forever. That I promise you."

"But that won't necessarily stop them from trying," I said. "Do you think that's what they're doing? Trying to bring back Caul?"

"Please keep your voice down," she said, glancing around. "And don't let your imagination run away with you. Remember, Bob the Revelator also predicted many things that *never* came to pass. So let us just focus on the task before us, and don't make too much of this. And please, don't tell the others."

I nodded. "Okay."

"But the next time he appears to you in a dream—*tell me*."

The bus started its engine. My friends were waving to me from the windows.

And then I ran onto the bus.

◆　　◆　　◆

"I brought some gifties," said Hugh, digging into a small bag in his lap. We'd only been riding the bus for a few minutes and Enoch was already asleep, but now he roused himself. Emma and I leaned over our seats to look across the aisle. "When everyone found out I was coming, they gave me things to bring to you. Claire packed us stew-meat sandwiches." He pulled out several, wrapped in brown paper, and distributed them. "Spare underwear and socks, courtesy of Bronwyn. Oh, this is good—two peculiar sheep's wool sweaters from Horace."

"Yes!" said Enoch. "I was wondering what became of those."

"They got a bit moth-eaten, but Horace has been repairing them in his spare time."

"They can stop bullets, but not moths?" Emma said.

"Devil's Acre moths can eat through metal," Hugh explained.

"And flesh, I hear," said Enoch. "Wonderful species."

Hugh held up a dog-eared book. "Olive's copy of *Peculiar*

Planet: North America." He shook it and a map fell out from between the pages. "And Millard tucked in a recent map of American loops."

"And this one's for you," he said, and handed me a small box.

"Who from?" I asked.

He winked. "Guess."

There was a note on the top of it written in a neat, looping hand. It read:

The sunset you missed.

I opened it. A stream of amber light floated up and out of it, glistening and sparkling like dust motes caught in a sunbeam. They circled around me so that it was all I could see for a moment, before fading away. I was left with a pleasant tingling in my face.

"Wow," said Hugh. "That was beautiful."

"It actually was," said Enoch.

"Someone might have seen that," Emma said grumpily. But the other dozen or so passengers on the bus were staring at their phones or looking out the windows, and no one had.

"Don't be jealous," Enoch teased her. "It doesn't suit you."

"What? I'm n-not . . . ," she stuttered, frowning. "Oh, shut *up*."

She got up and went to sit in a different seat.

"Don't mind her," Enoch said. "She takes a long time to get over things. She moaned about Abe for half a century."

"Let me see that loop map," I said, anxious to change the subject.

I squeezed into Enoch and Hugh's seat and we opened it across our laps, and pretty soon we were absorbed in the strangeness of it.

I'd seen loop maps written in gold calligraphy, in leatherbound atlases that weighed a ton. I'd seen them scrawled on restaurant placemats, traced over other maps, routes drawn with pushpins and yarn. But I had never seen anything like this one. It was a real map, and a modern one, like something you'd buy at a gas station on a road trip. Strangest of all, there were ads running down the sides.

Ads for *loops*. They sounded like truck stops: gas, food, lodging . . . with a few peculiar perks.

Hot meals at all hours, read one. *Hotel-style accommodations.*

Another boasted: *Disaster-free loop day! Perfect weather, peaceful normals. Experience our hospitality!*

And another: *Armed peacekeepers ensure a relaxing stay.*

One even had a coupon: *Clip for a 10% discount!*

"What kind of bizarre country is this?" asked Hugh.

"One without ymbrynes," said Enoch.

Peculiardom was many things, but it had never struck me as particularly capitalistic. American peculiardom was a different animal from what I'd come to know in Europe. That had already been made obvious to me in a hundred ways since I'd first met H a few weeks earlier, but the realization kept hitting me.

"A hotel-style loop," Enoch said sleepily. "Sounds like heaven."

"Don't get your hopes up," I said. "I don't think these wights are interested in creature comforts."

"Well, they'll have to stop somewhere," Enoch said. "The kidnapped girl is loop-trapped. She'll age forward if they don't."

"You're assuming they need to keep her alive," Hugh said.

"They went to a lot of trouble to snatch her," said Enoch. "I'm sure their intention wasn't just to let her wither into a pile of dusty bones."

We rolled on. The sun began to sink. Enoch and Hugh joked around, messing with the other passengers using one of Hugh's bees. I could tell Enoch was doing his best to keep Hugh's spirits up, and it made me like Enoch a little more. He was sweet-natured despite his best efforts to be a jerk all the time.

I went back to my seat and fell asleep with one of Horace's sweaters balled between my head and the window. It was an uneasy sleep full of uneasy dreams I couldn't remember.

❖   ❖   ❖

I woke with a start. Someone had sat down next to me.

It was Emma.

Her hands were knotted in her lap and she looked tense. She checked over her shoulder to make sure Enoch and Hugh weren't listening to us. When she saw they were sleeping, she spoke.

"We need to talk about it," she said. "What happened between us."

That woke me up quick.

"Oh," I said, rubbing my face. "Okay. But I thought we had sort of . . ."

Agreed not to talk about it.

"I've been trying not to think about it," she said. "Tried ignoring it, pretending it isn't there. Pretending that we were only ever just friends. But it's not working."

"That's pretty obvious," I said.

Every time someone mentions Noor, you go dark.

"I just need to say I'm sorry one more time. I'm sorry for what I did. I shouldn't have called him."

A surge of complicated emotions rose in my chest. It sounded so small when she said it. I had ended things with her because of a phone call. Part of me still wondered if I had overreacted. If I had broken her heart over something petty.

"Had you been doing that a lot?" I asked her. "Calling Abe?"

"No. Only that one time, from the road. And that was just to say goodbye."

I didn't know if I believed her. Or if I cared. Suddenly, the way I'd felt that day flooded back; the sad certainty that she'd never really been mine, and never would be. That I had fooled myself because I loved the idea that someone like Emma could love me.

"In a way, I'm glad you did it," I said. "It made me face something I hadn't wanted to look at head-on."

"What's that?" she asked timidly.

"You said it yourself a few days ago. I'm not Abe, and I'm never going to be."

"Oh, Jacob. I'm sorry I said that. I was angry."

"I know. And that's why you let yourself be so honest. Because the truth is, you still love him."

She was quiet. And that was her answer.

It was simple.

She had been unable to stop herself from falling for me because I reminded her so much of him. And I hadn't broken her heart, because she had never really given it to me in the first place.

"I don't want you to hate me," she said.

She lowered her head. She looked so young in that moment, in that light. I felt sorry for her.

"I could never hate you."

Her head fell against my shoulder, and I let it stay there.

It was nearly dark now. I watched the last sliver of crimson sun slip behind some mountains beyond the road, the land around us fading to a sad late-evening blue.

"So what did he say?" I said. "What did you talk about when you called him?"

"He didn't say anything, really." She sighed. "He was angry. He said I shouldn't have called."

"You couldn't help yourself."

She said, so quietly I could hardly hear: *"He said I was interrupting dinner. And he hung up."* When she looked up, there were tears in her eyes. "I felt like such an idiot. And then I had to come back to the car where you were waiting and pretend nothing had happened."

A little stab of pain shot through me, and then a thought I hadn't anticipated flitted through my head: *Was my grandpa kind of a jerk?*

I put my arm around her and said, "I'm sorry, Em."

"Don't be," she said. "I needed to hear it. To let him go, finally."

Finally. But too late for us.

"I know we can't be close like that anymore," she said. "But we had a friendship, too, and it was real, and worth something."

"It still is," I said. And something unlocked in her, and her shoulders began to tremble.

I'd meant what I said.

I still believed that all the wonderful things I had felt about her were true. They just didn't make me in love with her anymore, not the way they once had.

"Thank you," she said, still sniffling. "So, how do we do this?"

"Like this," I said, closing my arm into a hug. "And now we should both get some sleep."

* ❖ ◆

A tap on my arm. Emma, whispering, *"We've stopped."*

I blinked. It was the middle of the night and we'd arrived at some bus station in Iowa.

"You go first," Enoch said, nudging me down the aisle toward the door.

I got out, surveying the ground around the bus parking area for hollow residue. Nothing. They hadn't stopped here.

We went into the station, which had a small, all-night food court. Enoch and Hugh got some rubbery hot dogs. Emma had a bean-and-cheese burrito. They were all aging day by day now—teenagers in growing teenage bodies for the first time in almost a century—and they were always hungry. But my stomach was in knots, and the thought of eating made me nauseous. It was odd, I thought, how sometimes my friends seemed ancient, but at other times I felt older than them.

We got back on the bus and rode on.

I was drifting in and out of an anxious sleep when, sometime before dawn, Emma shook me awake.

We were stopped on the highway, the bus snarled in a long traffic jam. Somewhere up ahead, we could see the lights of emergency vehicles flashing.

I started to get a bad feeling.

Three lanes of traffic were bottlenecked into one. Slowly the scene came into view: There had been a bad accident. There were police cars, ambulances, a fire truck, flares. Cops directing traffic. A circus of grim activity. My eyes couldn't help following a swirl of bold black tire marks, past a torchlight parade of flares, to the back of a wrecked bus.

"*Oh my God,*" Emma whispered, her face washed over by red and orange flashes.

"Could that be the same bus?" Hugh said. "The one *they* were on?"

"We'd better find out," I said.

Enoch said nothing, but he was nodding.

Traffic had come to a standstill. I led my friends off the bus, pushing through the door over the driver's grunted objections.

"There's no way the police are going to let us snoop around an accident scene," I said.

"You'd be surprised where you can go if you act like you belong there," said Emma.

There were a few paramedics still circling the wreck, but it seemed the accident was a few hours old already, and the injured had long since been taken away.

The bus lay on its side like a fallen giant, its bent and gashed frame flickering in the riot of lights. It looked like it had skidded off the road, tipped sideways, and dug a hole in the earth on its way to the edge of some woods. There were no other smashed vehicles that we could see. The bus appeared to have lost control and crashed on its own.

It didn't take me long to find the hollow's residue trail. It was splattered all around the bus, and it led from the wreckage into the woods. There were no police, no EMTs in the woods. Nothing at all but dark trees.

I followed the trail and my friends followed me. When we'd gotten twenty or thirty feet past the tree line, Emma sparked a flame in her hand to light our way.

We passed a pile of trash. A cluster of spiny brush. And then we found her, lying in a pile of leaves.

The girl. Ellery.

She was dying. Bleeding from a gash on her head. Her leg twisted unnaturally beneath her.

We rushed to her.

"Someone get help!" Emma shouted, and Hugh took off running, back toward the EMTs.

She was a slight, pale girl. She had only one eye, and the eye patch that normally covered the other one was gone. In its place was a black and puckered hole.

While we waited for help to arrive, we tried to find out what had happened. But Ellery was disoriented, fading in and out of consciousness.

"They wanted me to cry," she was saying. "The men with the blank eyes. They made me cry."

As she said it, a tiny white worm crawled out of her eye socket. It tumbled down her face and onto the ground, where I noticed a hundred more just like it, wriggling among the fallen leaves.

I nearly vomited. Emma and Enoch seemed unfazed.

"They stole her," she said, starting to cry. "They took her from me."

"Who?" said Emma.

"Maderwurm," she whispered, voice shaking. "She'll die now. She can't live outside."

Emma, Enoch, and I looked up, exchanged a look of dread.

"Where are the men now?" I said.

"Gone," she said. "Will you kill them?"

"Oh, definitely," Enoch said.

"But not the girl. She doesn't want to do the things she does. They make her."

"What girl?" I said.

"She did it. She stopped the bus."

"How?"

"With her ropes. And she gave me the most beautiful flowers . . ."

She began to convulse just as the EMTs arrived. Their flashlights lit everything up, and a moment later we were pulled away so they could work on her.

Ellery was writhing, groaning, and something else was happening, though she was blocked by the EMTs and I couldn't see what it was. I heard one of them swear as the group of them backed away from her.

Someone said, "What the hell is going on?"

And then suddenly I could see her again.

Ellery was in the grip of a violent convulsion, and there seemed to be a nest of silky threads growing around her.

"Jesus," Enoch said. "She's starting to age forward!"

It was hair, sprouting from her scalp at an exponential rate, blanching from brown to silver to ivory as it did.

And then a sudden wind bent the branches and blew the leaves around us, and we looked back to see a helicopter landing just beyond the woods. We crouched, watching, unsure what to do. Several figures jumped out of the helicopter and ran toward us.

It was the Americans. LaMothe and his bodyguard, running through the woods shouting Ellery's name. Miss Peregrine, Miss Wren, and Miss Cuckoo were right behind them and couldn't spare even a glance in our direction. The EMTs were shoved away—horrified, they had been about to run anyway—and as the Americans bent over Ellery, I saw the ymbrynes pouring something from a glass vial into her slack mouth.

It was clear they were trying to save her somehow, but the girl was aging fast nonetheless. They picked her up and I got a look as she was carried past—in the space of thirty seconds her skin had thinned to near translucence and her eye had clouded to milk.

The ymbrynes could do nothing more for her. The Americans took Ellery, and Miss Peregrine peeled off from them and came over to where we were huddled against a tree.

"Miss!" Emma cried, and hugged her. "Where'd you come from?"

"I told you I'd be watching!" she said, hair whipping in the helicopter's wind. "Good thing, too . . ."

"Will she die?" Enoch shouted.

"We gave her an emergency serum to slow the worst of her aging, but she may still succumb to it. Where is Hugh?"

"He went to get help," Emma said. "Hasn't come back."

A look of worry flashed across the ymbryne's face.

We ran to find Hugh and spotted him by the wrecked bus, which was crumpled and lying on its side surrounded by flares and police tape. The police who had been standing guard over the accident had left to investigate the helicopter, so for the moment, no one was there to stop us from running right up to the bus's exposed undercarriage.

As we approached, I saw that the tires were blown. The axles, broken. Hugh was standing beside one, pulling at what looked like a rope. Ropes had tangled around the axles, clogged up the wheel wells.

"Ellery said something about ropes," Emma said as we ran toward Hugh. "She said there was another girl, and she used ropes to stop the bus—"

"You were right," I said to Miss Peregrine. "There was a second person. A girl."

But when we got closer, we saw that what Hugh was holding wasn't a rope at all. It was a vine.

Vines were wrapped around the axles, around the wheels.

"What on earth . . . ," Emma said, picking one up. It was green and thorned, and here and there it had delicate purple flowers.

"Ellery also said something about flowers," I said. "That the girl gave her flowers."

Enoch picked one off the vine. "I recognize this . . . They used to grow all around our house on Cairnholm . . ."

Hugh still hadn't said anything. He took the flower from Enoch and held it up in the garish, dancing light of a flare.

"Miss?" he said, a haunted look stealing over his boyish features. "This is a dog rose."

Miss Peregrine turned to him. Locked eyes and nodded seriously. "Yes, Hugh."

I said, "I don't understand." But the others all seemed to.

"It was Fiona's flower," Emma said quietly. "She could grow them even without meaning to. Sometimes they'd sprout behind her as she walked."

I felt the air thin, my head go light. "Are you saying . . . ?"

Enoch looked at the vines. "Only Fee could have done something like this."

"Oh my God," Hugh cried, tears streaming down his cheeks. "She's *alive*."

Emma wrapped him in a hug, and he leaned into her. He was overjoyed and devastated all at once. "They have her. They *have* her. Oh my love. Oh my God."

"We'll get her back, Hugh," Miss Peregrine said. "Don't doubt it for a second."

CHAPTER EIGHT

*W*e would all be taking off in the Americans' chopper—it was big enough to fit everyone, and it was the quickest way out of there. We waited while the chopper was readied to leave. We were worn to the bone, our bedraggled bodies parked among the emergency vehicles. Miss Wren kept the police at bay somehow, I suspected with some wild story she had concocted or a few well-timed memory-wipes. LaMothe alone remained upright, pacing anxiously while Miss Cuckoo and Miss Peregrine ministered to Ellery, applying balm to her forehead and what were ostensibly medicinal drops to her remaining eye. The cavity once covered by Ellery's eye patch was now half obscured by long hair. A pale worm poked its head through the silvery strands; shuddering, I looked away, but the scene change didn't do much for the queasy feeling in my gut.

Hugh, I realized, was nearing hysteria. Emma and Enoch were trying to keep him calm, but he still seemed too stunned to be reasoned with. Worse: He was crying again. I stood up and started toward him, but Emma pulled him close, curving their bodies together as she whispered anxiously in his ear. I took another step forward and she stopped me with a single look—narrowing her eyes at me over his shoulder. *Let me handle this,* she mouthed.

So I gave them space.

I found myself briefly alone, feeling useless but simultaneously relieved to be useless. My deferred exhaustion now sank into me, muddling my mind despite my best efforts to remain vigilant. I leaned against a nearby police car, my propped elbow slipping with every passing second, watching Miss Cuckoo stalk down the roadside. Her manner was perfunctory as she memory-wiped any traffic-jammed normals who seemed too interested in what we were doing. I almost laughed. I felt light-headed.

And then, suddenly, I heard a voice.

Nice to see you again.

The fine hairs on the back of my neck stood on end and I stiffened. It was a teasing singsong of a voice, gentle but venomous—and strangely familiar. I turned to look around, but there were no strangers here.

I heard it again. *So. Are you excited?*

The words seemed to rise up from somewhere inside of me, almost a manufacture of my own mind. I was so tired I wondered whether I'd slipped into a waking dream. No, a nightmare.

Small, revolting little noises—lips smacking, vowels stretching—filled my head. They were sounds of exaggerated satisfaction, like someone snuggling into warm, clean sheets after a long day.

Mm-mmm, the voice whispered. *That's better. I could get used to this again . . .*

"Who's there?" I said, whipping around.

"Jacob, are you all right?" Emma was staring at me.

I blinked at her, startled, forgetting for a moment where I was. "Yeah," I said. "Sorry, I'm fine. I think I just . . . fell asleep." I frowned at the lie. "Maybe I should take a walk. Get some air. Clear my head."

Emma nodded distractedly, she and Enoch both too focused on their own task—calming Hugh—to question my strange behavior. So I walked. Not too far to be irresponsible, but just far enough to clear the voice from my head, and to convince myself of my own lies: that this was nothing. That I'd heard nothing.

I took long, determined steps toward nothing, wending my way through the maze of emergency vehicles. The night air pushed at my body, the once-welcome breeze growing aggressive. A sudden gust of wind wrapped around my legs so abruptly that I stumbled sideways, catching myself against the back doors of an ambulance.

I heard the voice again.

There's a new world coming, it whispered, *and it's going to be so beautiful—*

"Who are you?" I said, hissing into the darkness.

Just an old friend.

"And what does that mean?" I said, my head whipping back and forth and my heart racing.

The voice laughed. It was a dark sound, rough and throaty. And then, familiar words:

Ev'ry land on earth will sink, and reek and wallow in stench and stink, of rotted trunks of beast and man, and vegetation crisped on land . . .

A lock rattled.

The back doors of the ambulance swung open, nearly knocking me off my feet. By now I was thoroughly freaked out and yet— somehow, I found myself drawing nearer the darkened interior. I didn't know why. I didn't even know I was searching for something until I saw it, until it seemed obvious what I might find here.

A body. Unmoving beneath a sheet.

My every instinct was screaming at me to run, to call for help, to catch a flight back to my boring, predictable life in Florida.

I shut it out. Told it to die.

And then I steeled myself and clambered into the ambulance. My heart beating out of my chest, I lifted a corner of the sheet. I saw the face of a young man, dead, half his head caved in.

Jesus.

"Just an old friend," the voice said, and now it was coming from the body, from the dead young man's bloodied mouth. "But I'll be back soon . . ."

I let the sheet fall, my body now shaking uncontrollably.

A song began to play from the radio in the cab, and play loud. It was "With a Little Help from My Friends."

Chills ricocheted down my spine. I felt wild, out of control. I ran out of the ambulance—and into Enoch. He grabbed me, eyes wide.

"Where'd you go?" He shouted over a noise I hadn't noticed before: the chopper's engine. "Come on," he said, "we're leaving!"

And he pulled me away toward the waiting helicopter.

◆　　◆　　◆

Two minutes later we were in the air, strapped into seats, headsets muffling the roar of the blades. Ellery was laid across the laps of LaMothe and his bodyguard in the front row, and the rest of us were squeezed into the back. Miss Wren and Miss Cuckoo had had to assume bird form so we'd all fit, and they were perched near the pilot, scanning the dawning skies ahead. The ymbrynes had done all they could to stabilize Ellery, but getting her back into a loop was her only real chance of avoiding death—so we were headed for the nearest one, some backwater town called Locust Gap.

I was still shaken by what had happened on the ground a moment ago. Was it a vision? A hallucination?

It was Caul's voice I'd heard.

Caul's voice quoting the most apocalyptic parts of the prophecy to me. Which meant—what?

Which meant I was losing my mind, probably. Either that, or Caul was just finding new and creative ways to torment me.

Hugh was having a meltdown. Despite Emma's and Enoch's best efforts, he was doing worse.

"They've got Fiona right now," he was saying through his headset mic for all to hear, "and the longer we take, the harder it will be to get her back. We need to search every loop within two—no, three hundred miles of here. And we've got to do it now—"

Emma put a hand on his arm. "Hugh, that just won't work—"

"Sure it will! We've got a helicopter!"

LaMothe turned around and glared. "This is my helicopter, boy, and the only place it's going is the nearest loop, so we can save this girl's life." His glare shifted to Miss Peregrine. "Get your ward under control."

"Please, Hugh, you must calm down," Miss Peregrine said. "We need to choose our next move very carefully. We're all upset about this. We're all worried about Miss Frauenfeld. But this critical moment is the worst time to flail about blindly with no plan."

"Fiona's loop-bound, too," Hugh muttered. "She'll age forward, too."

"Oh God," Emma said, going a bit pale. "I forgot."

I had forgotten, too. Because Fiona wasn't at the Library of Souls with us when it collapsed, she hadn't had her internal clock reset like the others. Which meant she could age forward.

"It's likely they took Fiona prisoner after Miss Wren's loop collapse, months and months ago," Miss Peregrine said. "She was seen leaping from the cliff's edge. We can only surmise that she survived the fall and was collected from the woods below."

Hugh's eyes fell shut as he imagined it. "What have they been doing with her? And what do they want with her?"

"We don't yet know," said Miss Peregrine, "but you can be sure they didn't keep her alive all this time just to let her age forward in the middle of"—Miss Peregrine glanced out the window—"Iowa."

"Yeah," Hugh said miserably. "I suppose."

"After we make this one stop," Miss Peregrine said, "we'll return to Devil's Acre, gather all our people and intelligence, and make a proper plan. And we will get her back."

He nodded. "If you say so, miss."

◆　　◆　　◆

We touched down in a field next to an old barn, trees and bushes whipping in the downwash. The ymbrynes and the Americans were out of the helicopter before the rotors even began to slow. Miss Wren and Miss Cuckoo winged into the barn in bird form, and by the time the rest of us had caught up to them, they were in their human shape and somehow fully dressed again, not a hair out of place.

We helped LaMothe and his bodyguard carry Ellery up a ladder to the barn loft where the loop entrance was, and after a quick changeover that left my stomach jittery, we carried her down again and out into a warm, foggy morning.

"Hold it right there!" someone said, and then I saw a man pointing a gun at us.

He was seated casually in a wooden chair, and he wore a top hat and an odd, mustachioed mask. "Name and clan affiliation!" he barked.

"Don't you know who I am?" LaMothe thundered back.

"Don't much care, so long as you're not a Yankee and you got fifty bucks for entry." Then he tipped his head, sat forward, and muttered, "Wait a dadburn second . . ."

"That's right," said LaMothe's bodyguard. "This is Antoine LaMothe. And if you don't want to find yourself in front of a firing squad—"

Instantly the man tossed away his gun and threw himself on the ground. "Sorry, Mr. LaMothe, sir, I didn't recognize, I mean, didn't expect you—"

Miss Wren stepped forward and pulled the man to his feet. "We need a bed for this poor girl," she said. "Somewhere we can make her comfortable while we apply a few poultices."

"Of course, of course," the man said, laughing nervously, "there's an establishment just this way, very accommodating, and no doubt they'll waive the cost for distinguished persons like yourselves . . ."

We followed him as he led the way, bowing and scraping,

toward a cluster of clapboard buildings. The largest had an awning that read RESTOURANT, spelled just like that. There were three people loafing at the entrance—a waiter in a white jacket and two cooks in matching aprons. The masked man shouted at them to prepare a room, and they straightened and disappeared inside.

The ymbrynes left us outside. "We won't be long," Miss Peregrine said to us. "We just have to make sure the girl is stable, and then we'll go."

Hugh was a bundle of nervous energy. He was struggling to keep his freak-out contained, and it was making a vein on his temple throb. I couldn't blame him. The love of his life was in the hands of Caul's most notorious lieutenants, and God knew what was happening—or had happened already—to her.

But there was nothing any of us could do about it right then, so I looked around the bleak little town for something that might distract him.

"Wanna know why Karl wears a mask? Bet you do," trilled a little voice, and then a young girl emerged from around the corner of the restaurant. She couldn't have been more than six. Her clothes were simple, brown hair cut into a short bob.

"Why?" Enoch said boredly. "Ambrosia addict?"

"It's for anonymonimity," she said, tripping over the word, then trying it again several times without success. "Whoever's guarding the entrance always wears a mask. Just in case they have to kill anyone? So people don't go revengin' on 'em?"

"You don't say," said Enoch, more interested now.

"I'm Elsie, and you're new. You all here with those demi-ymbrynes to change the loop clock's gears? They been getting stuck lately, causing trouble." She spoke in rapid singsong, her face intense with curiosity.

"Those weren't demi-ymbrynes," Emma said. "They were real ones."

"Ha!" she said. "You folks are funnnnn-y!"

"We're not joking," I said.

"And the furry guy with them was the leader of the Northern clan," Enoch said.

"Serious?" Elsie said, her eyes going wide. "What're y'all doing here?"

"Can't talk about it," said Enoch. "Top secret."

"And we're not staying long," Hugh added pointedly, and then his eyebrow shot up. "Unless . . . you didn't happen to see four men come through here with a girl earlier today, did you?"

"Nope. Nobody's come through in months."

Hugh's face fell.

"Except ol' hangy there." She pointed to a desiccated corpse hung from a gallows across the street. "He was a highwayman tried to rob us? So we shot him and hung him up there as a warning? We take a real dim view of thievin' ever since Brother Ted's sparkstone got stole." She eyed us hopefully. "You're not here about *that*, are you?"

"About what?" Enoch said.

"Brother Ted's sparkstone. I was hopin' maybe if such important folks were here it's 'cause the man who stole it been caught, and you all's come to return it."

"I'm sorry," Emma said, with a note of genuine regret. "We don't know anything about that."

"Oh." Her unsinkable spirits deflated a little. "You want to meet Brother Ted anyhow? I know it'd cheer him. He ain't been the same."

"We really shouldn't," Emma said.

Elsie's head hung. "Aww, I understand," she said, then glanced over at a little house not far away. "Though he lives just over yonder . . ."

"Why not," I said. "If it's close."

I met eyes with Emma and nodded at Hugh, and she got the message.

"Yeah, let's meet him," she said, hooking her arm around Hugh's.

"Twenty-three skidoo!" the girl yipped.

Hugh came reluctantly, and we all walked over to the little house while Elsie talked a mile a minute. "It's been slow, slow, *slow* lately, nobody around at all. Just some salesman and the loop keeper. Teacher's supposed to come and give me lessons soon. Other than that, it's awful boring here. Where do you come from?"

"London," Emma said.

"Oh. I always wanted to go somewhere big like that. Is it nice?"

Enoch laughed. "Not particularly."

"That's okay, I still want to see it. What time are you from? I mean, when were you born?"

"You ask a lot of questions," Hugh said.

"Yeah, that's what I'm famous for. Brother Ted calls me the interrogatrix. Will you take me with you when you go home?"

Emma looked surprised. "You don't like it here?"

"I just want to see someplace besides Locust Gap. I was born in Cincinnati, by the way. But I been here since I was four."

"That's not so long," I said.

She nodded. "Yeah. I reckon not. I'm only forty-four."

We entered the little house.

It was like stepping into an oven. There was a huge fireplace roaring with flames, a pile of heavy blankets in front of it.

"Hi, Brother," said Elsie, and the blanket pile turned slightly in our direction. There was a kid in there, cocooned in the middle of all that.

"Good Lord," said Hugh. "He'll be roasted alive!"

"Don't touch him," Elsie warned. "You'll get frostbite. He's got a temperature of minus fifty."

"H-h-h-hello there," the boy said, shivering the words out. His skin was blue, his eyes red-rimmed.

"*Poor thing,*" Emma whispered.

Sweat was already beading on my forehead, but as I approached the boy I could feel waves of cold emanating from him, beating back the heat and the sweat.

I turned to Elsie. "You said someone stole his—what now?"

"His *sparkstone*," she said, and gave the boy a mournful smile. "He'd tell you himself, but it's hard for him to talk, his tongue gets so stiff with cold."

"Maybe I can help," said Emma, "if just for a little while," and she summoned flames in both her hands, stoked them until they were bright, and stood with them held above the boy.

"That's n-n-nice," he chattered. "Th-th-thank you, m-ma'am."

The temperature was getting unbearable. The hotter it became, the more I began to notice a strange, acrid smell. Like someone cooking trash. But I tried to forget about it and focus; the boy was warming just enough to form sentences now.

"I have this c-condition," Ted said, his skin a shade or two less blue. "Only thing that ever helped me live normal was the sparkstone. A little green stone that was always aflame and never went out, which my ymbryne gave to me long ago." He looked sad and wistful. "This was back when we had ymbrynes. She'd brought it from far away, she said, 'c-cross the sea. She said if I kept it in my s-stomach it would keep me warm always. And it did for a long, long time."

The smell was starting to become even more oppressive than the heat. I pinched my nose closed against it. Strangely, it didn't seem to be bothering anyone else.

"And then that man came to town," the boy went on, his words flowing easily now. "He said he was a doctor. I was always a little cold, never could go without a coat and a sweater—and he said he could fix that for me. If I just coughed up the sparkstone and let him tinker with it."

I was listening so intently that I didn't realize I had been walking toward the corner of the room until I was halfway there. Something was drawing me. The smell. And a queasy feeling.

"He took it from me," said the boy. "And when I tried to chase him and get it back, something stopped me. Something strong that I couldn't see." He was shaking his head, blinking back tears. "It pinned me to the wall. Stuffed my mouth so I couldn't scream. I passed out . . ."

There, in the corner, was a spot on the floor that had been stained black. The source of the smell.

"Jacob," Emma said quickly, "that sounds like—"

"A hollowgast," I said. "And there's a drop of its residue right here."

The boy nodded. "That's where it held me."

"When was this?" I asked.

"Five, six months ago," said Elsie.

"What did the man look like?"

"Like anybody," he said, blinking. "Like . . . nobody."

"He had glasses, didn't he, Ted?" Elsie said. "Dark glasses that he never took off."

There was a loud knock on the door, and it opened. Miss Peregrine came into the room and then drew in a sharp breath, overwhelmed by the heat.

"We're going," she said.

Hugh and Enoch said quick goodbyes and ran after Miss Peregrine.

Elsie looked at me, pleading. "Ain't there something you can do? You know fancy people . . ."

"We have a lot on our plate right now," I said, "but we won't forget you."

Elsie nodded. Bit her lip.

"Thank you," Ted said. "It's always nice to see friendly faces. Don't get much of that around here."

"I'm so sorry," Emma said to him. "I wish we could stay longer."

"It's okay," he said, sighing, and he turned his gaze heavily back toward the fireplace.

Elsie did, too, and for a moment in the strong light of the fire she looked both young and ancient, and lost.

Emma slowly closed her hands. She seemed so sad and sorry. We barely knew these people, but her heart was, as I already knew, bigger than France.

By the time we got to the door, the boy had already started to turn blue again.

CHAPTER NINE

*W*e left Ellery in Locust Gap with LaMothe's body-guard. I wanted to see how she was doing, but the ymbrynes insisted that she needed rest and quiet, not visitors. Our fast action had saved her life, but what kind it would be remained to be seen; she had aged most of a normal lifetime in a single evening, and the effect that had on one's brain was often dramatic. Still, LaMothe seemed grateful for what we'd done. He didn't say as much, but I could tell. He was quiet on the helicopter ride back to Marrowbone, less quick to snap and grumble, and his raccoons had finally stopped whining and writhing.

The rest of us didn't talk much. Enoch fell asleep. Emma talked quietly with Hugh for most of the ride, massaging his balled fists back into open hands.

I thought about Noor. I'd been doing that a lot, lately, pretty much whenever I wasn't being distracted by someone less interesting or something life-threatening. In quiet moments, I only had to picture her face and I'd feel 10, 20 percent less stressed. The tension that cleaved my chest nearly all the time would slacken—and some-times, if I pictured being close to her, if I imagined kissing her, that tension would shift into something else, a clench of pure wanting, of desire.

If I was being honest, it was something I'd never felt about Emma. What we'd had was so chaste, so Victorian. What I felt for Noor was different. More chemical. More visceral.

But tender, too.

She was so brand-new to this world. I wondered how she was feeling, whether she was adjusting. Was she okay? Were they making any progress with Millard's maps, coming any closer to finding V's loop? What would that be like, if—no, *when*—Noor found her?

Which reminded me: What about finding Fiona?

Since Ellery and LaMothe's bodyguards weren't along for this ride, Miss Wren and Miss Cuckoo had the space to stay in human form, and they talked low and serious with Miss Peregrine for most of the trip. I hoped they were hatching ideas about where the wights had taken Fiona—for Fiona's sake and for Hugh's—but I couldn't be sure. Before all this had happened, Hugh had actually begun to have moments of peace and fun and levity, but now the wound had been ripped open again, and it was twice as wide. I knew him well enough to know he wouldn't rest until she was back among us and safe again, and that if, bird forbid, something happened to her, it would absolutely kill him.

I shoved that thought away, and in its place a question popped into my head that I'd been dying to ask Miss Peregrine. I couldn't do it over the headset mic, though. It wasn't something I wanted LaMothe to hear.

He seemed to be asleep, his bald head smooshed against the window, but still.

I couldn't wait, either.

"I have to know something." I leaned over her seat, whispering, and she turned away from the other ymbrynes. "Back in Marrowbone, in the camp, when you found the start of the hollowgast's trail? It wasn't just the boot print, was it?"

Miss Peregrine shook her head. "No."

Hugh was listening intently now.

"I found this outside the tent, amongst the trees." And she drew from her blouse a pressed purple flower. A dog rose.

Hugh reached out and touched it, turned it over in his hand. "She was there?"

"Yes. And the wights never were." Miss Peregrine got so quiet I was half reading her lips. "It was Fiona who brought the girl to the hollowgast, which had hidden itself a safe distance from the Northern clan's camp, waiting."

"I don't understand." Hugh's brow was scrunched, his eyes darting around. "She was helping them?"

"Not willingly. I've been conferring with Misses Wren and Cuckoo about this, and we believe she was—and likely still is—mind controlled. The bus accident was the result of a lapse in that control. Fiona tried to escape. Perhaps even to kill her captors."

Emma gasped. Hugh said nothing; his jaw was clenched so tight I feared for his teeth.

"Damn, they probably want to kill her," Enoch muttered, then clapped a hand over his mouth. Emma shot him a poisonous look.

"No," Miss Peregrine said. "The wights are too focused, too practical. They've kept her alive, and gone to all the trouble of bringing her here from Wales, for a reason. Whatever that reason is, it's not yet been fulfilled. They won't kill her."

"Not yet," Hugh said. "Not until they're done with her."

LaMothe was stirring. There was nothing else to say.

We rode the rest of the way to Marrowbone in tense silence.

❖　　❖　　❖

We were standing on the street in present-day Marrowbone, just outside the mining museum loop entrance, when a tourist paused to snap a picture of us. LaMothe barked at him to keep moving, and the tourist scurried off.

Miss Peregrine smiled tightly. "We'll be gone from the conference a few days, at least," she said. "We've got a more pressing matter at hand."

LaMothe nodded. "I hope you find your girl," he said, and he actually reached out and shook Miss Peregrine's hand.

"Thank you," Miss Peregrine said. "We'll do all we can for Ellery, once she's well enough to travel. We have a wonderful healer in Devil's Acre, if you'd entrust her to us for a little while."

He nodded appreciatively, then turned and spoke directly to me for the first time. "I'm sorry I doubted you, boy. You've got a rare talent." And he slapped me on the back so hard I nearly fell over.

He started to go, but Miss Wren caught him by the raccoon tail. "If you could try not to start a war while we're gone," she said.

"If one breaks out, it won't be us who fired the first shot." He tipped his top hat and went.

◆   ◆   ◆

A few minutes later we were reentering Bentham's attic via the Panlooticon, and the elevator door opened to a strange sound: applause.

The attic was filled with people—ymbrynes, friends, ministry workers, random peculiars I knew only in passing—and they were all clapping, their faces bright and smiling. For me.

I felt a friendly nudge from behind as Miss Peregrine pushed me out of the elevator.

"They know what you did," she whispered. *"And they're all very proud of you."*

There was Horace, beaming and shouting. Brownyn, carrying both Olive and Claire on her shoulders so they could see over the crowd, all of them cheering. Miss Blackbird and Miss Babax were congratulating me; even Sharon was there to give me a pat on the back. It was strange, what it did to me to see them all gathered like that, their smiling faces pointed in my direction. It stunned me. It filled me with joy. I felt buoyant, flooded with dopamine. I was reminded of my purpose, of all that we'd been fighting for. Here it was:

My truest friends, my truest home.

I loved my peculiar family, and I knew then that I would fight with them—and for them—for the rest of my life.

I felt Miss Peregrine's hand on my shoulder. I turned and caught her in a rare moment of tenderness, her eyes shining with emotion.

"You did fine work, Mr. Portman," she said softly. "Fine work."

I stood there, grinning like an idiot, trying to figure out how to hug each one of my friends individually, when suddenly the crowd seemed to hush; the moment I caught sight of her, all else faded. The whispers, the questions, the curious eyes—none of it mattered. My mind felt paralyzed. Because there—right there—pushing through a knot of Sharon's broad-shouldered cousins—there she was. Out of breath and rushing forward as fast as she could, her face at once desperate and beaming with happiness.

Noor.

"Jacob," she said, gasping a little as she pushed through a wall of bodies, somehow oblivious to the spotlight pointed in her direction. "You're back . . . I only just heard . . . I was in the library with Millard . . . I was so worried . . ."

I formed a wedge with my hands and parted the crowd, closing the gap between us. I didn't even say hi—I just kissed her, right there in front of everybody. Her surprise melted, changed as her body sank against mine. The rest of the world fell silent as a shower of sparks erupted in my chest, my head.

We broke apart, finally, though only because we'd both become aware of how much the room had quieted—and how many people were staring at us.

I also realized I needed to breathe.

"Hi," I said, grinning stupidly, my face hot and probably beet red.

"Hi," she said, grinning, too.

And then we laughed. Laughed as relief and joy and nervousness flooded our bodies. We both seemed to have realized that we'd crossed a line of no return, rushing headlong into new territory. Past friendship. Straight into—

I wasn't sure what.

But I felt breathless at the thought of it, of what we might be. And then I felt surprised. Surprised by my ability to feel so much— joy, terror, fear, grief—all at the same time. My smile faded and the real world returned in a rush, the room coming back into focus with an abrupt, sobering shudder. Still, the harsh edges of reality seemed softer now. A strange miracle.

Nearby, I could hear Miss Peregrine talking to someone in a somber tone about Fiona. Sharon seemed to be heading in our direction. Noor and I still stood near each other, no longer touching, not even looking at each other, but something had changed in the air between us. Then someone started tapping me on the shoulder, and I turned, already frowning, ready to tell Sharon to back off, that I didn't want to talk about loop freedom right now.

But it was Horace.

"Jacob," he said anxiously, "I know you've only just arrived, but we have a lot to discuss. Noor and Millard and I made some startling discoveries during your absence."

I looked to Noor. She bit her lip. "Yeah, I didn't have a chance to mention that part," she said sheepishly. "But Horace is right. We have a lot to talk about. It's been crazy here."

"You've had a breakthrough?" I asked, that familiar hope building in my chest.

"Actually, we did," she said, and laughed. "That sign I remembered seeing across the street from our house? Turns out it was an ad for a store that only had branches in Ohio and Pennsylvania. So we've narrowed it down to just two states!"

"That's amazing!" I said. "You're so close!"

"Not *that* close—Millard says finding a secret loop in a territory that big could still take weeks. And it's been going slow today because Millard's been working on something else."

"Something else?" I frowned. "What could be more important than this?"

Noor shrugged.

I looked to Horace.

Horace shrugged, too, and then toyed absently with his cravat. "Who knows? It's hard to pin him down long enough to ask," he said. "Especially when he insists on wandering around naked, like an uncivilized animal."

"Some animals wear clothes," I pointed out, thinking of Addison.

"I said *uncivilized* animals."

I was about to refocus the conversation when Enoch pinballed through the crowd and grabbed Horace by the shoulder. "Did you hear about Fiona?" he cried. "She's still out there, mate! She bloody well survived!"

Horace jumped like he'd touched a live wire. "What!"

Clearly, he hadn't heard. None of them had.

"Who said what about Fiona?" Bronwyn shouted, shoving Ulysses Critchley out of the way to reach us. "She's alive?"

"Oh my goodness!" Olive cried, so excited she floated off Bronwyn's shoulder and got lodged in the rafters.

"That's—that's—" Claire stammered, and then she passed out and tumbled off Bronwyn's shoulder into her waiting arms. "Astounding," she moaned.

"Well. Where is she?" Bronwyn said, head pivoting. "This calls for a celebration!"

"She's a prisoner of the wights," Emma said, and tossed a rope up to Olive. She glanced, very briefly, at Noor and me, then quickly looked away.

"Oh," said Horace, looking stricken. "Hell."

"We'll go and get her!" Bronwyn said, her mood ever unsinkable. "We'll put together a rescue team today—this minute! Where have they got her?"

"We don't know," I said. "That's the problem."

"Hell," Bronwyn said, her shoulders sagging.

I turned around to look for Hugh. He was still by the elevators, in serious conversation with Miss Blackbird and Miss Peregrine.

"I don't understand why Miss Peregrine insisted he come with us," Enoch said, "when she knew that if we *did* find Fiona she could be in dire shape. Mind controlled at the very least. Maybe even—" He stopped himself before saying it. *Dead.* "That would've crushed him flat."

"My goodness, Enoch," said Horace, "have you grown a heart?"

Enoch glowered at him. "Seems a bit cruel, that's all."

"No," Emma said firmly. "Leaving him out of it wouldn't have been doing Hugh any favors. If we'd found Fiona without him, and he ever found out Miss Peregrine knew we were on her trail, *that* would have crushed him," said Emma. "He deserved to be there, no matter what."

"How's he holding up?" Noor asked.

"As well as can be expected," said Emma. "He's a strong kid. But he's angry, and he's worried."

"We all are," I said. I turned back to Noor and Horace. "So. You have news."

"It isn't for public consumption," Horace said. "Let's go somewhere we can talk that's a few decibels quieter. And rather more private."

"So long as there's food," said Enoch. "I'm starving."

◆　　◆　　◆

It was still early, hours before curfew and the sun still middling in the Acre's putrid sky, and the Shrunken Head wasn't crowded yet.

"I don't generally approve of public houses," Miss Peregrine said, dubiously regarding the tanned and wrinkled head that hung above its door, "but as our cupboards are currently bare, and you've all had a trying few days, I'll make an exception."

"Go to Hades, you pompous old crone!" the head croaked in reply—and either Miss Peregrine didn't hear, or she didn't want to give it the satisfaction of reacting.

We scored two tables in a nook near the back of the place and shoved them together to make a passable private area for ourselves. All my friends were there but Millard, who had welcomed us when we'd returned to the Panlooticon, but then quickly raced off again to attend to whatever it was he was up to without saying goodbye.

I took the chair beside Noor. Horace was on my other side. Miss Peregrine, Enoch, and Emma were directly across the splintered wooden table, which had initials and epithets of every variety carved into it, and Bronwyn sat at the end with Olive and Claire.

I was dying to hear the others' news, especially after Horace had teased us, but he and Noor made us tell them all about what we'd seen and done first. Emma, Enoch, and I took turns telling it while Hugh brooded at the end of the table, nursing a pint of cloudy ale. The camp, the accident, Ellery and her torn-out worm, Brother Ted and his stolen sparkstone. When we'd finished, it struck me how many odd things coalesced around a single question: What did the wights want?

"As it happens," Horace said, scooting his chair closer to mine, "we have an idea about that."

Which was right when our food arrived. Of course.

Bowls of potato-and-fish soup were distributed. We didn't have the courage to ask what kind of fish it was and the barman who brought it didn't bother to specify.

"Miss Avocet and her team have been digging more deeply into the *Apocryphon*," Horace said. "While Francesca has been working overtime translating a new section of the prophecy that we hadn't understood before."

We all leaned in.

"And?" Emma said.

"There's more to the prophecy than we realized."

Miss Peregrine slapped down her soup spoon with a loud clack. "You should've told me the moment we got back," she said angrily. "Now—what is it?"

"In a footnote we only just discovered," Horace said, "before the part about the coming time of darkness, et cetera, the prophecy talks about the rise of a group it calls 'the betrayers'—who it describes as 'pitiless men who tried to pervert the soul of nature, and who were cursed in return.'"

"Sounds a lot like the wights," Emma said, and Bronwyn and Olive nodded grimly.

"That's what Miss Avocet thought, too," Horace said. "But the next bit gets stranger. And worse. It appears to mention Caul himself—and the Library of Souls."

I felt my throat tighten.

"I've never seen a prophecy reference another prophecy before, but this appears to be a quote from the Book of Revelation in the Bible: 'And they had a king over them, which is the angel of the bottomless pit, whose name is Abadon.' It goes on to say the betrayers will resurrect him from said pit."

Enoch nearly choked on his soup. "Resurrect him?"

"And when he returns, he'll be imbued with terrible power."

"What power?" Bronwyn said, rigid in her chair.

My vision had gone black at the edges, and my whole body was cold. The corpse under the sheet. Caul's voice quoting the prophecy back to me.

"The power from the pit of ancient spirits," I said, the empty sound of my own voice surprising me. "Which has to be the Library of Souls."

Noor was watching me with concern, but I couldn't meet her eyes. I didn't want to betray my fear, not yet, so I did what I often do when I'm afraid: I looked to Miss Peregrine. But our ymbryne's expression was stone; she was clearly still processing. Everyone looked panicked, and Horace was taking sip after sip of water, as if unburdening himself of these horrors had turned his mouth dry.

Only Enoch seemed unfazed.

"What a bunch of tossers," he said, and took a loud slurp of his soup.

"It isn't funny, Enoch," Emma said with a withering glare.

"Sure it is. It all makes sense now—why they wanted Fiona. And that American girl's *Maderwurm*." He shook his head and laughed quietly.

"What are you talking about?" I said, anger starting to rise in place of horror.

"It's plain as day," he said. "The wights are following a recipe." He dinged his spoon against the bowl. "Making resurrection soup, like a coven of witches. Double, double, toil and trouble!"

Like she was speaking to a child, Bronwyn said, "That's *awful*, Enoch."

He sighed. Put down his spoon. "Am I the only one who listens to Miss Peregrine anymore? Caul's trapped in a collapsed loop. Forever. There's no coming back from forever."

"Unless there is," Olive said.

"Millard said he was trapped, too," Claire chimed in.

Enoch was shaking his head. "The wights are clearly desperate. Grasping at straws. They had no better options other than to slink permanently into the shadows and accept defeat with something like grace, which wouldn't exactly be in character for them. So they're trying something mad because it's the only thing they could think of. But it's impossible." He pointed his dripping soup spoon at Miss Peregrine. "You said so yourself!"

The longer he went on, the more desperate he sounded for confirmation.

Now we turned to Miss Peregrine, our hopes hanging on her next words. She looked pensive. "I suppose I did say that, didn't I."

Something in Miss Peregrine's voice made Enoch stop eating. His spoon was frozen halfway to his mouth. "You suppose?"

"It's possible they're just desperate, as Enoch says, and would try anything. But it wouldn't be like them to spend so much effort on a fool's errand—especially not Murnau. I suspect he may be getting direct orders from Caul himself, perhaps via dreams." She glanced meaningfully at me. "Mr. Portman's had a few. So have I."

Horace let out a little whimper. "Uh-oh."

I snapped my head to look at him.

"What's uh-oh?" said Enoch.

"Something wrong with the soup?" the barman said over my shoulder. "Needs more eel powder?"

"NOT NOW!" Enoch shouted at him, and after the man had slunk away, Enoch turned to Horace again. "*What's. Uh-oh.*"

"I've had dreams about him, too," said Horace, staring into his now-empty glass.

"You have?" I said.

"Remember those wake-up-screaming nightmares I was experiencing when Jacob first came to us? With boiling seas of blood and fire raining from the sky? Yes?" He waited for looks of comprehension from the group, then nodded. Swallowed. "Well, last night I had another one. Only Caul was there."

"Why didn't you say anything?" Bronwyn said, hurt. "You always come to me when you have nightmares."

"I dismissed it as a manifestation of my own fears rather than a prophetic dream," Horace said uneasily. "But if Caul's been visiting Jacob and Miss Peregrine in their dreams, too . . ." He dragged a shaky hand down his face, steadied himself, and said, "I've never seen Caul in a dream before, prophetic or otherwise. But I saw him very clearly, floating in the sky, directing the apocalypse like an orchestra conductor." He looked up at me. "I think it's him, and his resurrection, that ushers in this epoch of darkness and strife."

"Which I'm supposed to help end, somehow," Noor said heavily. " 'Emancipate' us from. With six others."

"Wait a second," I said, "we're getting way ahead of ourselves. First things first. Why do the wights think they can resurrect him? Because they read the prophecy, too? Did they assume it was about them, and about Caul, like we did?"

"It *is* about them and Caul," Horace said.

Miss Peregrine held up her hands, a plea for calm and reason. "For the sake of argument, let's say Horace is correct, that it is about them. How are they doing it? If they're following a recipe for 'resurrection soup,' as you say, whose recipe is it? What does it contain? And where did they get it? I think—"

"From your brother, miss. From Myron Bentham."

It was Millard. He was out of breath, having just skidded up beside Miss Peregrine at the head of the table. The headmistress, who wasn't in the habit of asking questions she didn't already know the answer to, was dumbstruck.

"I've just come from Bentham's secret office," said Millard, "and I think you'd better come back there with me now."

◆   ◆   ◆

Bentham's secret office was directly above his regular office, accessible via a ladder hidden in the ceiling. The ladder was concealed behind a large portrait of himself, one of many that covered the ceiling (but not, oddly, the walls). At the top of the ladder we discovered a cell fit for an ascetic monk: There were bookshelves crammed with books, a rolltop desk, and a single hard chair.

Bentham's old manservant, Nim, was waiting nervously in a corner as, one by one, we all climbed up.

"I've never seen this room before," Miss Peregrine said, turning slowly to look around. "Goodness, I asked Miss Blackbird and her people to search every inch of this house . . ."

"Nim knew about this place," said Millard, and the strange little man began to nod. "And so, apparently, did the wights."

"Mr. Bentham kept all his most sensitive papers and books here," Nim said, "away from peekers and sneakers, but he trusted old Nim, that's right." Nim was worrying his hands, picking away the skin of his fingertips while his eyes darted around the room. "It was Nim's job to dust, straighten, alphabetize, catalogue-ize . . ."

"Can you please get to the part about the wights resurrecting Caul?" Emma said.

"And what any of this has to do with Fiona?" Hugh growled.

Millard cleared his throat. "Yes—so. Everyone's always said it's impossible to escape a collapsed loop. All the experts who've studied it agree: Either it kills you, turns you into a hollowgast while flattening everything for hundreds of miles—as happened at the Tunguska Event of 1908—or, if you've just happened to imbue yourself with the soul of one of the most powerful ancient ones, as Caul did just before we collapsed the Library of Souls, then you're trapped forever in phenomenon we call esoteric sequestration—"

"Get to the point, Mr. Nullings," Miss Peregrine said.

"Everyone agreed it was impossible. Or nearly everyone. But apparently Bentham did not." Millard nodded at Nim. "Go on. Tell them."

Nim shuffled forward, still picking at his hands. "Mr. Bentham didn't want to do it. But Mr. Caul forced him to."

"Forced him to what?" Miss Peregrine said.

"Find a way for someone to escape a collapsed loop." He glanced up furtively, as if expecting to be slapped, then looked down again. "Mr. Caul hounded Mr. Bentham about it for years. I remembers. I hears things. Nim was always listening. Nim's my name."

"And did he?" I said. "Find a way?"

"Nat'rally he did! Mr. Bentham's a genius. But he lied to Mr. Caul about it. Told him it couldn't be done. But he wrote down the secret formula he'd found and put it in a book, because 'discovery is discovery,' he said, and he gave it to old Nim to hide, and told me not to ever tell him where I'd stashed it so it couldn't be tortured out of him, if it ever came to that."

"Let me guess," Enoch said. "You did a crap job of hiding it."

"No, sir, no, no, no, I didn't—but they found it anyway."

Millard stepped in. "After the wights broke out of prison, but before they left Devil's Acre, they came here—to this room—and they stole a single book. The one with Bentham's formula in it."

Nim pointed out an empty space on a shelf. "Thievin' bastards."

Emma tossed up her hands. "That's terrible. Awful. But how does any of this help us to stop them—"

"Or find Fiona?" Hugh said. He seemed ready to tear his hair out.

Miss Peregrine had seemed oddly calm through all this, and now she glided across the floor to Nim and laid her hands gently upon his shoulders. He flinched.

"Nim," she said, smiling like people do at children. "Did you happen to make a copy of Bentham's formula?"

He looked at her hand on his shoulder, then at her. "Mr. Bentham himself did, yes," he said. "Asked me to hide both of them."

The smile grew wider. "And do you still have that copy?"

"Oh yes, ma'am." He blinked, confused. "Would you—would you like to see it?"

"Yes, Nim, I would."

Nim went to the rolltop desk and unlocked it. It was crammed with disorganized papers. As he riffled through them, Noor raised a hand and said, in a tone that seemed calculated not to offend, "Can I just ask something?"

We all looked at her.

"Why are we so sure his formula would actually do anything? Just because the wights are desperate enough to try it doesn't necessarily mean it will work. Was this guy, like, some kind of wizard?"

Enoch rolled his eyes. "There's no such thing as a wizard."

Noor seemed ready to argue the point when Millard jumped in.

"It's a fair question," he said. "Understandable, too, given you never knew him."

"Bentham was like . . . the architect," I said, and Noor crooked an eyebrow at me.

"Loop science was his area of speciality," Millard explained. "He designed the Panloopticon, for example. And he was responsible, we now know, for the collapse that turned Caul and his followers into hollowgast—and the one that trapped both himself and Caul in the Library of Souls . . ."

"Okay, I get it," Noor said, holding up her hands. "He knew his stuff."

"Quite," Miss Peregrine said, but she was looking a bit green, and she was staring at Nim.

Nim extracted a single wrinkled piece of paper from the desk and was now waving it in the air. "Here, here, here!"

Miss Peregrine took it from him and began to read.

Her brow furrowed almost immediately. "Is this a joke?"

Horace leaned over to peek at it. "Quail eggs . . . jellied eels . . . cabbages . . ."

"Oh no, that's a grocery list," Nim said, hands fluttering as he reached for the paper and turned it over in the ymbryne's hands. "Other side."

She began to scan it. Her expression became unreadable.

Bronwyn turned to Millard and whispered, *"Seems an odd place to write something important."*

He shushed her.

Miss Peregrine's eyes were scanning the paper.

You could've heard a pin drop.

Then she exhaled. Some of the color had left her face. "Yes," she said quietly. "This explains a great deal, indeed."

And then she collapsed to the floor.

Everyone rushed to help: Bronwyn lifted Miss Peregrine into her arms, Millard fanned her with a book, Emma snapped a small flame before her eyes, and Horace ran to find her a glass of water. In a few seconds she was blinking and talking again, asking what time it was and whether the tea had been boiled; when she realized what had happened, she got embarrassed and chastised us to put her down immediately. The moment we did she nearly fell over again.

"It was the soup, that's all," she said as Bronwyn and Noor steadied her. "I had a bad reaction to that awful soup."

No one, not even Claire, believed her.

She had shown us she was afraid and now she was overcompensating, because her fear had made us all afraid.

After she'd had some water and a minute to regain her composure, she sat down at Bentham's desk. We were dying to know what was on the back of Bentham's grocery list. She flattened it before her—it was wrinkled and stained with something that looked like coffee—and she said, "I don't want to keep you in undue suspense—so sit and listen."

We sat around her in a circle on the floor, like kindergartners at the most stressful story time imaginable. Noor sat close to me, her proximity a balm even as she clenched and unclenched a nervous fist through the air in front of her, collapsing and reviving the light.

"The top line is written in Latin," said Miss Peregrine. And then she read it—in Latin. Noor and I exchanged a look, but no one else seemed bothered.

I raised a hand before Miss P moved on.

She peered at me.

"Um." I cleared my throat. "Can you translate, please?"

Even now, in the middle of all of this, Miss Peregrine found the time to pause long enough to look disappointed in me. "Really, Mr. Portman," she said, shaking her head. And then:

"It says, 'To summon a soul from deep in the pit, you will need, well, all of it.'"

"Your brother was no poet," said Millard.

"And with that, the list begins." She cut her eyes at me. "In English. There are only six items."

What followed was not so unlike the list of groceries written on the reverse, only these ingredients were more esoteric and disturbing.

"One: castings of the uberworm."

"Uberworm." My head snapped toward Emma and Enoch, who were already looking over at me. "What was it Ellery said they took from her?"

"Her *Maderwurm*," said Enoch. "Which I can only guess is—"

"A big, nasty worm," said Emma.

Bronwyn blew out her breath. "So, that's one ingredient they have."

"Shall I read on?" Miss Peregrine said.

"Two: tongue of the seedsprout, freshly harvested."

"What's a seedsprout?" asked Olive.

Miss Peregrine looked pained. "Fiona," she said. "It's an archaic term for her type of peculiar."

Hugh's face fell into his hands.

"Harvested fresh," Millard said. "Which must be why they're keeping her alive—"

"Millard, *please*," Miss Peregrine hissed. "I'm sorry, Hugh—"

"Go on, keep reading," he said. He uncovered his face, eyes red. Bronwyn wrapped an arm tight around him, and kept it there.

"Three: an indestructible flame."

We traded murmurs, trying to figure it out.

"Could that mean Emma?" Horace guessed.

Enoch let out an audible gasp.

"Perhaps if I were immortal." Emma shook her head. "But I'm not indestructible, so how could my flame be?"

And then it came to me. "The boy in the blankets, in Locust Gap."

Emma's eyes lit up. "Yes! He was horribly cold and used to have a thing that kept him warm—a flaming rock in his stomach . . ."

"The sparkstone," Miss Peregrine said, cocking her head at Emma curiously. "There is only one in the world."

"And some wight stole it months ago," Emma said.

We hadn't told Miss Peregrine about the boy, but she understood immediately and nodded in resignation. "That's three they have." She returned to the list. "Four: death beetles of the Underground Hittites."

Nim's hands clapped over his mouth. "Oh."

We all turned toward him.

"What is it?" Millard said sharply.

Nim's cheeks had gone pink. "They were under glass in Mr. Bentham's collection. Until the other night."

"When they were stolen by Murnau and his cronies," I guessed.

"Well, um, given the timing of their disappearance," he stammered, "yes, yes, I'm afraid so . . ."

Groans and murmurs went up. Enoch swore. Noor had gone very still and quiet. Millard was muttering to himself that this was worse, much worse, than he'd thought, and Miss Peregrine pinched the bridge of her nose and squeezed her eyes shut, as if chasing away a bad headache.

"My God," Horace said, panic rising in his voice. "They've collected nearly everything on the list! What's left?"

"Please, everyone, we mustn't lose our heads," said Miss Peregrine. "There are two items remaining."

The room went silent. She flattened the paper on the desk again and squinted at it uncertainly, like she couldn't quite decipher Bentham's handwriting.

Then she said: "Five: the Alphaskull of the Well of Hope (powdered, five to ten milligrams)."

Everyone was frozen, watching the others. Waiting for bad news. Waiting for someone to say that the wights already had the Alphaskull, or that alphaskulls were so common they practically grew on trees, or that alphaskull (powdered, 5–10 mg), was so easy to find it was sold in bulk at Costco, and the only thing standing in between the wights and the resurrection of Caul was a Costco Club membership card.

But no one was saying anything.

"What's the Well of Hope?" Noor ventured finally.

We all looked to Miss Peregrine. "I've no idea." She turned to Enoch. "Mr. O'Connor—you're our expert in all matters thanatotic. Ever heard of an alphaskull?"

Enoch shook his head blankly.

Miss Peregrine shrugged. "One left, then. Six: beating heart of the mother of birds." There were audible gasps. She looked up quickly. "And before you jump to any—"

"That means you, miss!" cried Claire.

"They're going to come for you!" Horace wailed.

"Horace, Claire—stop that!" Miss Peregrine snapped. "It does appear to reference an ymbryne, but I'm not the eldest, nor even the maternal figure amongst us. If anyone, that's Miss Avocet."

"But you're *our* mother, or close as we've got," said Emma.

"And Fiona's," said Hugh, "and she's on the list, too."

"And you're Caul's sister," Millard pointed out. "His actual flesh and blood. It makes a terrible kind of sense that he'd need part of you to come back."

I waited for her to argue. For her to tell Millard how mistaken he was.

But she was quiet. Her eyes searched a blank wall. Then she said, "Yes. Yes, I suppose that does make sense."

There was a long, heavy moment, when it felt like we were slipping over the edge. Giving up, giving in to fear.

And then Hugh spoke.

"It doesn't matter," he said. "We'll never let them take you."

And there was such iron in his voice, such unpanicked firmness, that it seemed to pull the rest of us back from the brink.

"That's right!" said Olive.

"Never," agreed Bronwyn.

"And if they haven't come for you yet," said Millard, "it's because you're the hardest bit, and they're saving you for last. So far as we know, they haven't got this other piece yet—the alphaskull."

"Whatever the hell that is," said Enoch.

Miss Peregrine stood up from the desk, steady on her feet now. "Then we will find out what the hell it is," she said, "and we will stop the wights from getting it."

"And get Fiona back," said Bronwyn.

"And decorate Devil's Acre with their heads!" cried Hugh, and a cheer went up.

For the first time in days, I saw him crack a wavering smile.

CHAPTER TEN

*W*e were now in the frustrating position of having a clear goal—find this skull and the Well of Hope before the wights did—but no clear way to achieve it. Tracking the wights via hollow residue had become nearly impossible; they had fled the scene of the bus accident in a car, presumably, and there was no way of knowing which way they'd gone. Nobody had ever heard of either the skull or the well, and until we had some idea about the location of at least one of them, we were effectively paralyzed. True to form, Miss Peregrine wanted the ymbrynes to handle the entire problem and told us to go back to the house and stay there while she conferred with them. "You must all get some rest," she said. "We have a fight ahead of us, and I need you in top shape." And in a great featherburst she assumed bird form and winged off.

Rest be damned.

It was unthinkable, anyway, with all this hanging over our heads—so we splintered apart and went to work.

Millard rushed off to the mapping archive to search American loop atlases for any mention of the Well of Hope. Horace, for whom sleep and work were often the same thing, actually did go back to the house to rest—his plan was to down a dram of "sleeping solution" and put himself into a trancelike slumber, where he hoped to dream the answer we needed. Hugh had been muttering darkly about interrogating the wights who were still imprisoned—"They know something," he'd said—and threatened to "sting it out of 'em if they won't talk." But cooler heads prevailed, arguing that not only would that break a number of ymbryne code laws, but revealing anything about what we knew to wights, even jailed ones, could jeopardize everything.

Then Claire said she'd worked with some peculiars in the Department of Arcane Fauna who had lived in America years before and ran away to ask them if they'd ever heard of an alphaskull or the Well.

At which point something obvious occurred to me: "If we think this thing is in America," I said, "why don't we just ask the Americans? LaMothe owes me a favor . . ."

So we made our way to Bentham's attic and the Marrowbone loop entrance—only to find the elevator blocked by a black-clad wall of Temporal Affairs minions.

"Oh, no you don't," Ulysses Critchley said, holding up the flat of his hand like a school crossing guard. "Miss Peregrine just left and gave us strict instructions not to admit you or anyone else. Miss Wren and Miss Cuckoo have been apprised of the situation, and they're with the Americans now."

I was about to start arguing with him when Olive pointed out that Hugh and Enoch were gone. We spun around to look, and she was right.

Emma was so mad she nearly lit her own shirtsleeve aflame. "I know just where they went," she growled. "Come on, Bronwyn, let's stop them before they do something monumentally stupid."

Which left Noor, Olive, and me to our own devices. It was clear we weren't getting into Marrowbone, and anyway, two ymbrynes were more than capable of getting information out of the Americans (if there was any to be gotten). We spent an hour wandering the Acre, feeling helpless.

We were so close, and yet . . .

Eventually, we all found our way back to the house. Nobody had come up with anything useful. Millard hadn't found anything in the ymbrynes' collection of American loop maps—and he was abundantly familiar with them now, after days of combing them for V's loop. Horace, despite his best efforts to force a revelation, had, much to his embarrassment, only dreamed of pizza. No one else had anything to show for their efforts, and Miss Peregrine hadn't returned.

We were a sad group.

I took in my friends' gaunt faces—Hugh's devastation, Emma's exhaustion, Noor's anxiety, even Enoch's lethargy—and I made a decision.

None of us were going to get any sleep tonight, anyway.

"All right." I clapped my hands together. "We tried, right? We tried to find more information while following the rules, didn't we? Gave it our best shot?" No one answered and still I nodded, mostly to myself. "Well, the night is young. I think there's enough time to try one last thing."

One by one, my friends looked up at me, eyes blinking, confusion mounting.

"I don't understand," Claire said, both mouths yawning.

"Nor I," said Olive, yawning, too.

"I do," Hugh said, his shoulders straightening. "I understand you clearly, Jacob, and I'm inclined to agree with you."

"And me," Noor said, smiling. That smile pierced me straight through the heart, messed up my insides. I loved it.

I smiled back at her. Big. Stupid.

And then, remembering myself—I smiled at the others, too.

Bronwyn had narrowed her eyes at me, her mind clearly at work. And then, suddenly, she turned.

"Olive," she said, tossing the words over her shoulder, "would you be a dear and take Claire to bed, please? It's well past your bedtime, and you know how Miss Peregrine likes you both to be asleep at eight o'clock on the button."

"All right," Olive said, stifling another yawn. "Come along, Claire," she said, taking the other girl by the hand.

They were already halfway up the stairs, Olive's metal boots clomping on the wood, when I heard Claire's voice, soft and echoing—

"But we read that one last time," she was saying. "You promised that tonight we'd read *The Terrible Tale of the Grimbear and the Nine Nosy Normals*. Or, oh, maybe we can read *The Witch That Wouldn't Burn*, that one is my favorite . . ."

Only when the littlest ones were safely off to bed did the others turn to face me. Enoch, Bronwyn, Emma, Horace, Hugh, Noor. Millard.

Six pairs of eyes blinking at me. A seventh pair, invisible.

"All right then," I said. "Who wants to help me break into the Marrowbone loop?"

Six hands shot up into the air. "My hand is raised, too!" Millard said.

I smiled so wide my face hurt.

◆   ◆   ◆

The sun had long since sunk beneath the grimy horizon, and in the absence of light, Devil's Acre became particularly gruesome. We had no youthful interest in breaking curfew to wander the streets at this hour; we simply had no choice. In order to make our way back to Bentham's attic and the Marrowbone loop entrance, and to reduce our chances of being spotted by the home guard along the way, we had to cross through the sketchiest part of town, which meant dealing with the dirtiest scraps of people—the ambrosia addicts, the wiliest thieves, all the unimaginable horrors lurking in the muck. Emma lit a small flame to keep us from being plunged too fully into the thick of it, but Millard snapped at her to shut it off, lest we be rounded up by the authorities.

"*The steep fines notwithstanding,*" he shout-whispered, "*I've no interest in sleeping naked on the cold floor of a prison, thank you very much.*"

"Then maybe you should start wearing clothes," Horace said archly. "I've offered dozens of times to dress you, and yet—"

Millard groaned.

"Quiet, both of you," Emma said. "We've got to keep our wits about us, and there's no chance of that with the two of you sniping at each other."

Bronwyn sighed. "Bentham's house seems much farther away in the dark, doesn't it? Are you sure we haven't passed it?"

"We're not far now," Hugh said quietly. I heard the buzz of his bees, who were helping guide us in the darkness. "We turn left at the lamp, and it should be just up the street from there."

Since there was only one streetlamp currently lit, it was easy to spot. But it was still at least a thousand feet away. A thousand feet of creeping, slithering night.

Something actually seemed to hiss in the distance.

We pressed onward, this time silently, the seven of us hemmed in by the dark. And by fear, too. By fear perhaps most of all.

Just then I felt a strange, warm breeze against my hand.

I looked down, startled, to find an isolated dot of light illuminating my palm. I stopped in place, lifting my palm upward, inspecting the tiny glow. And I was just about to say something about it to the group when Noor came up beside me.

I felt it, right away. I knew it was her without the visual confirmation. I could feel the sparks in my head signaling her nearness.

"I was just trying to find you," she said softly, taking my hand to draw me nearer. The glow slipped away between our linked fingers. She whispered as we walked. *"I hope I didn't freak you out."*

My spine felt like a live wire.

I shook my head no, forgetting she probably couldn't see me do it. But I felt kind of dazed. I don't know why this felt different, more extraordinary. In my limited experience, holding hands with a girl had never been particularly memorable. But tonight my nerves were unusually sensitive. I couldn't see anything but the blurred gaslight humming in the distance, and with one sense gone, the others had awakened.

Noor's grip on my hand was making me lose my grip on everything else. I wanted to tell her to let go, to give me my head back.

I wanted to hold on forever.

I took a single, shaky breath to clear my thoughts when three things happened at once:

Millard said, "Nearly there!"

Hugh—no, Horace—screamed.

And Emma caught fire.

That last one happened only for a second, and Emma was clearly embarrassed by it, because she couldn't put it out fully. She was flustered, muttering about how Horace had startled her, and why had he screamed anyway, everything was fine, wasn't it, but the flames kept jumping from her arm to her leg to the top of her head and then, finally, to the tips of her fingers—ten birthday candles that refused to extinguish.

She was still shaking her hands—the vigorous motion only making the flames worse—when Horace explained.

"I just remembered," he said. "I just remembered!"

"Remembered what?" Emma said, irritated, as she began to snuff out her little fires.

"The lamplight—I was staring at it and it reminded me of my dream, of a detail I'd overlooked. Do you remember when I said that I saw Caul was floating in the sky, directing the apocalypse—"

"—like an orchestra conductor, yes, we heard," Millard muttered.

"Don't you pay him any mind, Horace," Hugh said. "Go on."

"Well, he was floating in the sky—but the sky was above a hill. The sun was blazing—the lamplight triggered that bit—and I remember now that there were graves nearby. Inscriptions on said graves. I'm seeing it now. Seeing it clearly. The name of an American city. Something new."

"A new city, you mean?" Millard again. "But new compared to what? Anything can seem new depending on the historical context."

"Good point," Enoch said, sounding annoyed. And then he yawned loudly. "Can we get going? I'm freezing and hungry and I thought we'd be having more fun by now."

"You're only being unkind to hide your fear," Bronwyn said to him. "And that's not fair to the rest of us. We're all scared, you know."

"I'm not scared," Enoch snapped.

"Wait," said Noor. "Wait, wait." And I heard the frown in her voice when she said, "You said it was a 'new' American city. Do you mean new, like New York?"

Horace gasped.

"Yes," said two people at once.

The first was an exhilarated Horace.

The second—

Emma struck a new flame, the light of which illuminated both her fear and our ymbryne's anger.

Miss Peregrine.

Not just her, either. A flock of ymbrynes had descended upon us—Miss Peregrine, Miss Wren, Miss Cuckoo, Miss Blackbird.

The ymbrynes had come back from Marrowbone.

"Back to bed, all of you," Miss P said angrily. "Now. This instant."

"But, miss, we were only—"

"Enough," she said, breathing hard. "Breaking curfew? Deliberately disobeying my orders? I am more than shocked, Miss Bruntley, I am extremely disappointed. Now turn around and head home at once."

"But, miss," Hugh tried, "do you—Was there any news?"

A beat of silence. "Yes."

"Does it have to do with New York?" Horace asked.

Miss Peregrine sighed. The fight seemed to leave her. "Very

well," she said. "We can talk about it back at the house. I'm sorry for shouting, children. It's been a very tiring evening."

"It's all right, miss," Emma said. "You've been dealing with so much. We'll go back home and Horace will make you a nice cup of chocolate. Won't you, Horace?"

"I'd be delighted!"

"Brownnosers," Enoch muttered.

"What was that, Mr. O'Connor?"

"Nothing, miss."

"Indeed." Miss P took a sharp breath. "Ymbrynes? Shall we meet back at the house?"

A violent shuddering of wings was the only response.

◆　　◆　　◆

We were all of us—children and ymbrynes—settled in the living room clutching hot cups of chocolate when Miss Peregrine finally broke the news. Well, Miss Peregrine allowed Miss Wren to break the news.

Regardless, we were on tenterhooks.

Miss Wren took a step forward from the gaggle of ymbrynes. "The Americans finally gave us some information we believe we can act on. There is, in the upper portion of the American state of New York, a town called Hopewell. And in that town there is a loop of deadrisers."

"New York!" Horace shouted. "That's what I saw on the stone in my dream!" He and Noor shared an awkward, but enthusiastic, high five.

"And Hopewell!" Bronwyn cried. "Well of Hope!"

"Why wouldn't Bentham's list just say that, then?" Emma said.

"My brother loved puzzles," Miss Peregrine said. "And I'm sure he was trying to frustrate Caul by encoding his list a bit, in case it was discovered."

"And the alphaskull?" Millard said.

"If we're looking for a special skull, a loop of deadrisers isn't a bad place to start," said Enoch. "What do you know about them?"

"Not much," said Miss Cuckoo. "Only that they are quite isolated, and don't welcome visitors."

"Sounds like my kind of people."

Hugh banged his hand on a table suddenly. "We've got to raise an army and storm this place! Come in with guns blazing!"

"Not so fast," said Miss Peregrine. "I understand passions are running high, but we don't know what we'll find in this loop. Whether or not the wights have been there already. What kind of peculiars we'll be dealing with. We need to tread carefully—but prepare ourselves for a conflict."

"The wights could be waiting with an army," Bronwyn said.

"They don't have an army," Enoch said dismissively. "It's just a handful of fugitives."

"And a hollowgast," said Olive.

"Maybe more than one," I added.

"It wouldn't be wise to underestimate them," Miss Peregrine said. "That's why we've already begun to assemble an elite team of our very best peculiars for this mission."

Emma crossed her arms and frowned. "Who?"

Miss Peregrine smiled. "You, of course."

"You're the ones who liberated Devil's Acre," said Miss Wren. "There's no one with better experience or preparation than you all."

We were all grinning now. Beaming with pride.

"You'll have backup, of course," Miss Peregrine hastened to add. "A support team."

"Us," said Miss Cuckoo. "And a few other peculiars hand-picked for their special skills."

"I've got some grimbears who've been itching for a little exercise," said Miss Wren. "And a detachment of the home guard is already making preparations."

"But you'll be the vanguard," said Miss Peregrine.

"If you're willing to give it a go, that is," said Miss Cuckoo.

"Are you serious?" Bronwyn said. "We'd have gone even if you forbade it."

"And chained us in a dungeon," added Hugh.

"I know," Miss Peregrine said proudly. "Well, we have a great deal ahead of us, don't we?"

"Let's go murder some wights!" Hugh shouted, and the room exploded into cheers.

"Yes, yes, but first—sleep." Miss Peregrine stood up. "Off to bed, children. And don't forget to brush your teeth."

Everyone groaned.

◆　◆　◆

The house was a buzzing hive in the morning, everyone running around, squeezing past one another on the stairs, gathering whatever small items they thought might be needed for a dangerous mission. Food. Extra clothes. A favorite knife. Whatever could fit in a pocket or a small bag. None of us had much, anyway.

I was scrounging in the boys' common dresser for some fresh socks. Noor went to splash some water on her face. "I'd kill for another shower," she said, "but you can't have it all."

I ran after her. "Hey," I said, "can we talk for a second?"

She finished drying her face, looked at me, and frowned. "I know what you're going to say," she said. "The answer is, forget it."

"What was I going to say?"

She pulled me into an empty room.

"That I don't have to do this. That maybe I should just stay here, where it's safe. But I can handle myself."

"I know you can. But this isn't your fight. Or, it doesn't have to be."

She was shaking her head, starting to get angry.

"If you'd rather just focus on finding V," I said, "I would understand—"

"Were you serious when you said I was one of you guys?" she said. "Or was that just some line?"

"Of course you're one of us."

"Then this affects me just as much as it does you. Actually, more, because if we don't shut these assholes down now before they resurrect their devil king or whoever, it sounds like it's me who's going to be dealing with the mess they make. I'd rather get on that before they start the apocalypse."

"Okay," I said. "Good point."

"I *will* find V when this is over. Right now, this is my fight. And I'm not going anywhere. So no more of this it's-cool-if-you-stay-behind-and-twiddle-your-thumbs-while-we-risk-our-lives stuff, okay? We're in this together."

"Okay," I said. "We're a team."

She beamed. "We're a team."

"Yep. And just in case there is an apocalypse? There's no way in hell I'm letting you handle it without me."

She broke into a smile. "Okay," she said. "But let's try to avoid that."

"Okay." I laughed.

Enoch came into the hall. "Come on, lovebirds. We're leaving."

CHAPTER ELEVEN

*A*n hour later, we were flying down an American high-way in a small convoy of SUVs. It was night, and it was raining. There was a heavyset man from Temporal Affairs at the wheel. Miss Peregrine was beside him in the passenger seat, knitting something in her lap. Noor and Millard and I were on the bench in the middle row; Enoch, Emma, and Bronwyn were in the back. The rest of our friends and the other ymbrynes were in another SUV behind us, the backup they'd promised was in an SUV behind that, and somewhere in the slashing rain was an American escort.

It was the Americans who'd lent us the cars. We had taken the Panloopticon door to New York, where Leo promised us safe passage. The ymbrynes had told him that Noor had been tracked down by me and was staying with us now, though they allowed Leo continue believing it was a wight who had used a hollowgast to break Noor out of his loop, rather than H. Astoundingly, he agreed to let the whole matter drop, and as part of the Americans' deal with the ymbrynes, he promised never again to send his men after Noor. Noor and I could hardly believe it. Miss Wren refused to say what the ymbrynes had promised in return for all this, but it must have been something good.

As we drove, my friends' excited fervor had settled into a tense quiet. No one had spoken in minutes. Noor's left hand was on my knee, fingers laced through mine. With her right hand she played with the headlights of passing cars, scooping the light up and letting it seep out of her fist, scooping it up, letting it out. I found it hypnotic and calming.

"There's something I've been wondering," Emma said, her sudden words in the silence startling me.

"What's that?" Noor said.

"Why was Caul so obsessed with finding a way out of a collapsed loop?"

"Hm," Millard said. His thinking noise.

"Was he *expecting* to get trapped in a collapsed loop one day?"

"No one expects to get trapped in a collapsed loop," Bronwyn said. "Maybe it was just a precaution."

"If so, it was a very specific one," Millard said.

"He clearly knew about the prophecy," Noor said, bending the light between her fingers. "If he thought that angel-of-the-pit stuff was about him, maybe he assumed it was his fate to get trapped."

"What if it was part of his plan?" Millard seemed to be testing out a theory. "To be buried in the Library of Souls . . ."

"That's ridiculous," I said. "He didn't want that to happen. He was furious."

"Maybe that's exactly what he wanted us to think."

"Oh, hell," Enoch said. "You lot have gone around the bend."

"Think about it." Millard's tone was heavy, serious. "He was always talking about the old powerful peculiars, how they were the most pure expression of peculiarhood, et cetera. That's why he wanted the Library, to mine it for its powers. But maybe the only way he could really do that was if he was buried in it—then resurrected from it with all the powers of the library at his fingertips."

"*Born again,*" Emma whispered loudly. "*As a god.*"

I got chills.

Miss Peregrine clacked her needles together. "My brother was a power-hungry madman with a poisoned soul. But he was not, and will never be, a god."

"But he's been preparing for this," Emma said. "They all have."

"Even if he has, he isn't back yet, and we're not going to let him come back. So there's no need to spin out terrifying speculations and work ourselves into a lather."

"Yes, ma'am."

"Swenson, why don't you turn on the radio?"

The driver snapped on the radio. A pop song began to play. Something about a breakup. I heard Emma sigh.

Noor pressed her hand to her lips and exhaled a ghostly light against the window, where it spread like rolling fog, evanescent, before dissolving back into the air.

◆　　◆　　◆

Hopewell had been something once, but in the present day it was hardly a town anymore. We passed the broken-down ruins of an industrial plant, then street after street of empty lots and falling-down houses. It was a Rust Belt town that had died with the industry that made it; there were probably a hundred towns like it within a day's drive.

I kept my senses sharp for hollowgast, and we all kept an eye out for any sign of wights or cars they might have driven here and then stashed before going into the loop entrance, or anything strange at all. We didn't know whether the wights were here, or had already been here and left, or if the Americans' tip about Hopewell was worthless. So far, we'd found nothing, just piles of wreck and trash, thickets of brush—all easy places to hide vehicles, and much more than we had time to search.

To my surprise, the entrance to the deadrisers' loop was not in a cemetery or a funeral home, as one might expect. It was in a little park in the middle of the town, the only well-lit and well-maintained place we'd seen. There was a stone obelisk at the center of it. Behind a door hidden in its base was the loop entrance.

The rain began to slacken. Our convoy of SUVs parked within sight of the park, idling while the ymbrynes conferred with one another.

It was decided we should all go in together, so we wouldn't get separated.

We ran across the wet grass to the obelisk in a big group. Bronwyn yanked open the door. It was dark inside. Inscribed on the face of the obelisk were rows and rows of names.

LEST WE FORGET

The interior was tiny. There was room only for two.

I went first, to feel out for hollows. Noor came with me.

"When you get to the other side, stay put," Miss Peregrine said. "We'll see you in thirty seconds."

The door swung closed. We were briefly engulfed by darkness, then felt a light rushing sensation. We came out to find the world changed utterly. Now it was day—a cheerful summer morning. The formerly decrepit streets were stocked with cute, pocket-sized houses on small lots, and the stone obelisk we had stepped into was not what we stepped out of—instead we exited from one of the houses and emerged onto its front step, edged with blooming flowers.

"Not what you'd expect," Noor remarked, surveying our utterly pleasant surroundings.

We waited. Looked around. The yard was staked with little American flags, and the houses across the street were decorated with red, white, and blue bunting. It looked like the town was getting ready for a Fourth of July parade. Or it had been, on the day the loop was made. Cars from the 1940s and 50s were parked in driveways up and down the block. A dog came trotting out of a bright red doghouse to bark at us.

"Where is everybody?" Noor said, peering down the street.

But for the noisy dog, it was eerily quiet. It had all the trappings of a lively and populated little town, but it was as if all the people had been kidnapped in the night.

Thirty seconds passed. Then a minute.

No one else came through the door.

"This is weird," I said, trying not to let my mounting anxiety show.

Noor tried the door. It was locked.

I peered through its little pane of glass. Black inside.

"Just give it another minute," Noor said with studied calm. But it was clear we were both getting nervous.

What else could we do? We waited yet another minute for our friends to arrive through the loop. Noor started, very quietly, to hum. The same song, same melody I'd heard her humming before.

But no one came.

"This is bad," I finally admitted. "I think this is probably really bad."

We circled around to the back of the house. There were no other doors or windows anywhere. Just blank walls, like a locked box.

I was starting to get really freaked out. "They must've been locked out somehow."

"Or we got locked in," Noor said.

We traded an apprehensive look.

I was starting to feel a little sick.

No—not sick. The little pinprick I felt in my gut was something else.

Somewhere in this loop was a hollowgast.

＊　　＊　　＊

"I figured we weren't alone," Noor said when I told her about the hollow. She didn't seem frightened; things that panicked me tended to focus her. "Can you track it?"

"Not yet, unfortunately," I said. "My sense of it isn't strong enough."

Either that, or something was interfering with the directional perception that usually pointed me toward hollows. It seemed to be blanked out, wavering uselessly like a compass needle touching a magnet.

Noor and I decided we couldn't just wait for the loop entrance to open again. We were exposed, sitting ducks. And the sooner I found this hollow, the sooner we'd find our wights.

And, hopefully, Fiona.

We walked to the end of the block, turned a corner. There was no one around still—not even looped normals. In the distance was a hill, obscured by some trees, and it seemed to be the origin of a long, industrial-sounding whine, high and distant. It faded up and down, then went silent.

"It's probably the old plant we passed coming into town," I said.

We'd gone halfway down another block when we heard voices coming from one of the nearby houses: a man and woman having an animated conversation.

We rushed to the house and knocked on the door.

Nobody answered.

We were way beyond courtesy at this point.

I tried the door. It was unlocked, and swung open on a well-oiled hinge.

I called out hello and stepped into a normal-seeming suburban house from the middle of the last century. Right away, the source of the voices became obvious: a television set. Some old movie was playing. The TV sat on a hutch next to an artificial Christmas tree, oddly out of season, and a rocking chair with a doily pinned to the back. There was something ghostly and mournful about the scene, as if it were the man and woman in the television who lived here, trapped forever in the screen's black-and-white world.

I pushed the TV's knob and the screen went dark, and suddenly all was quiet. Noor tiptoed down a hallway toward the back of the house.

She stopped at a doorway. "Hello?" she said, then turned to me. "Jacob, there's somebody here!"

I rushed down the hall. There was a teenage girl asleep in a bed, covers pulled up to her chin. The walls were plastered with pictures from magazines.

"Hello?" I said. "Excuse me . . ."

She didn't stir. I took a few steps into the room. I glanced at the walls again. Every single photo was of Elvis Presley.

Noor came in, put her hand on the edge of the bed, and shook it a little.

We leaned over the girl.

"Is she even breathing?" I asked, trying to see whether her chest was rising and falling under the sheet.

A noise came from the front room. We froze.

"*That was the door,*" I whispered.

If a hollowgast had been that close, my gut would've felt it. But it was still just the minor, directionless pinpricks I'd felt earlier.

We went out of the room and back down the hall. "You've got visitors," I called out, not wanting to surprise anyone.

A white boy in high-waisted pants and suspenders stood in the open front doorway, watching us with cold detachment.

"Hi," Noor said, "we were just—"

"If you have any weapons, drop them now," he said, calm but firm.

"We don't mean you any harm," I said. "We just want to talk to you."

We heard footsteps behind us. I turned to look.

The girl was out of bed.

Her eyes were open but glassy, unfocused. She wore a night-gown. In one hand, she held a meat cleaver.

"No talking," the boy said. "Now, come with me."

"Please," Noor said, "just listen to—"

"BE QUIET!" the boy thundered.

He made two clicks with his tongue.

Someone on the porch opened the door. Outside, I could see a small crowd of people on the lawn. They stood very still, staring in at us.

They were all holding cleavers.

"Come with me," the boy repeated. "No sudden moves."

This time we didn't argue.

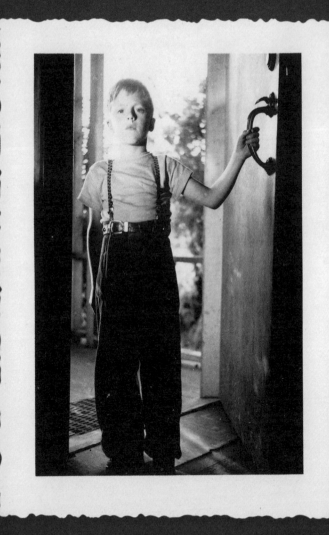

We were surrounded by dead-eyed, cleaver-wielding suburban-ites. They were herding us silently down the street, guided by the strange boy in the suspenders. He would click his tongue and they'd move left or turn right. If we spoke, they would raise their blades. If we moved in a way they didn't like, they would growl at us like animals.

The whining sound from the hill wound down, and then there was a loud but distant boom.

No one reacted.

"What was that?" I asked.

A fatherly man in pajamas behind me grunted and raised his cleaver.

After another few minutes we came to a big Victorian house, older and grander than anything else we'd seen in town. It had a tower and a turret and a wraparound porch with decorative railings. It reminded me of Miss Peregrine's house, and even in these dire cir-cumstances I felt a pang of nostalgia for that lost place.

We were made to stand in the middle of the lawn; the pajama people circled around us while the boy in suspenders went up to the house. The front door opened a crack and he had a discussion with someone on the other side, too quiet for us to hear.

I could see faces peering at us from the windows of the house. All of them kids.

The front door opened a bit wider. Someone young shouted through it: "What are your names?"

We told him.

"Who you with?"

"The ymbrynes from London," I shouted back.

I didn't want to shout that they were waiting just outside the loop entrance or that we were here to stop the wights, should any wights be listening.

Suspenders boy came back to the lawn. He said something I couldn't understand. All the cleaver-wielding pajama people lay down in the grass.

"Come inside," he said. "Josep will meet with you."

Noor and I exchanged a look.

It was progress, at least.

The boy in suspenders led us up to the porch and then inside, where we were greeted by another boy. He was physically no more than eight, and wore a double-breasted coat with a matching cap. He looked like the kind of child grandmothers call "my little man" and love to fawn over. He advanced toward us carefully, his face arranged in what seemed a permanent scowl.

"My name is Josep. I'm in charge here. What are you doing snooping around our loop?" His voice was lower and more adult-sounding than I'd expected from a person his size, and for a single, dislocating moment, I imagined he was lip-synching.

"We're looking for some dangerous people," Noor said. "Wights. We think they came here."

"And they have a hollowgast with them," I said. "They're very dangerous."

"Yes," he sniffed. "I know what a hollowgast is."

"I can see them," I added. "And hunt them."

Josep's eyebrows rose slightly, though I wasn't sure if he was skeptical or impressed.

"The wights are looking for a skull. A special skull," said Noor. "Do you have anything like that here?"

His eyebrows rose a little further. "We're deadrisers. We have many skulls."

I said, "Well, we have a team of people waiting just outside your loop entrance. Friends and ymbrynes. We've dealt with these wights before, and we know how to stop them."

"You've just got to let our friends in," Noor said. "Before the wights get the—the skull. The alphaskull."

Josep coughed dryly, cleared his throat. "Last night, a troop of angry strangers burst in here making demands and threats. Brought with them a monster, which is now terrorizing our peaceful streets. Now you've come, telling bizarre stories and having led a small army to our doorstep. I would be mad to let you in. Were I following protocol, I would have you both killed right now."

He glanced at the boy in suspenders, as if considering it.

"But I think we should have a lemonade first."

* * *

Josep led us through the house at a plodding pace. It was a place of low ceilings, heavy shadows, murmuring voices, black wood. In every room there were alien-looking plants flowering in near darkness. And standing in the corners, adult men and women: unmoving, quiet as cats.

"The strangers started arriving late last night," Josep said. "We sent our deadrisen foot soldiers to kill them, but their creature chewed them all to bits. They went straight up to Gravehill, and we hoped that might be the end of it. But then yesterday they came and snatched Saadi, our most promising student, and dragged him up the hill with them." A steady stream of children had begun forming a group behind us, following our steps from a safe distance, whispering all the while.

"That's when the noises began," Josep was saying. "Screeches, loud booms. They're excavating graves."

"The alphaskull," I tried again. "Does that word mean anything to you?"

"Yes. Gravehill is just what the name implies—a mound of ancient graves. Long before we came along—long before Europeans settled in America, in fact—this area was a settlement for peculiars. They buried their most vaunted leaders deep in that hill, including a very famous chieftain. If any bones up there are imbued with a

peculiar power, it would be his. But the graves are old and unmarked, so finding a particular skull would be very difficult."

"Then that must be what they're doing," I said. "Searching for it."

We passed through a pantry stocked with glass jars filled with organs and formaldehyde. The smell was enough to make you light-headed, and it reminded me of Enoch's old basement laboratory. We came to a sitting room with a bank of windows that looked out on a steeply sloping street. We were at the bottom of the hill.

There were chairs all around us, but Josep stood. The gaggle of children stayed outside the door, out of respect for their leader, it seemed.

Josep was starting to look and sound worried, but he hadn't yet decided what to do with us. I was thinking about our friends waiting outside and the wights up on the hill—but right now it was best not to push this guy too hard.

Josep snapped his fingers. "Man, fetch our guests a lemonade."

A man who'd been standing in the corner, who I only just noticed, straightened and shuffled out of the room.

"Is that mind control?" asked Noor.

"Oh no. He's dead."

Noor looked a little ill. I probably did, too.

"All the adults in this loop are dead," Josep said. "Only we children are alive."

We were astonished.

This seemed to upset him.

"You've never heard of Hopewell?" he asked, his chin rising a little higher. "This is a conservatory for the very talented. The young come here to hone their craft and practice the most arcane and so-phisticated deadrising there is—not to conduct séances, or answer to the beck and call of every bereaved nincompoop who wants to ask dead uncle Harry where he hid the family gold."

While he spoke, the reanimated manservant shuffled back into the room balancing a tray of crystal glasses. Josep glanced at a side table and did something with his face—it resembled an involuntary facial tic—and the man pivoted toward the table, bent at the waist, and set down the tray.

"When most people think of the reanimated, they picture decaying zombies. But not here! Our dead smell good and are dressed neatly. With the right guidance they can do nearly anything a living body can do."

The manservant stumbled as he walked, and a flicker of irritation crossed Josep's face. Josep lifted two glasses from the tray and offered them to us. "Lemonade?"

We accepted the glasses but kept them far from our mouths. Still, it seemed clear to me that this boy wanted us to flatter him, so I played along.

"This all sounds amazing," I said. "How do you keep them so fresh? Do they sleep in refrigerators?"

I looked at Noor and forced a laugh. She got the idea and manufactured a chuckle.

"Ha-ha. Oh no." Josep's mood was improving. "They're part of the loop, and their bodies reset along with it. They all died peacefully in their beds in the night, and the loop was made the next morning."

"They *all* did?" I said. "How?"

"There was an accident at the chemical plant. A deadly compound went airborne and the town's entire population suffocated in their sleep. The adults, anyway; the kids were mostly away at camp . . ."

"Oh my God," I breathed. I was sure I'd gone pale.

"A tragedy, yes," he said. "But thanks to one quick-witted ymbryne and an enterprising deadriser, a wonderful learning laboratory was born. Not only do the townspeople allow us innumerable opportunities to practice our craft, but we've made them useful in other ways, as you can see. They wait on us. Cook, clean, serve as bodyguards." He smiled, the first time I'd seen him do that. "Look at me, getting carried away. We don't receive many visitors other than our own kind, and I admit I'm rather proud of what we've built here. This is the future, as I see it. The world's dead vastly outnumber its living. Why not harness their power?"

"You have a lot to be proud of." I set down my untouched lemonade. "You've worked hard to create this place. But the wights will destroy it if you let them."

Josep sighed. He was about to say something when a little girl poked her head through the doorway.

"Excuse me, Josep."

We turned to see two more kids enter the room: a cute little girl in a blood-splattered apron and rubber boots who looked about ten, and a boy in a wheelchair, not much older. The chair was being pushed by a stooped woman in a bright yellow housedress, her mouth slack and her eyes rolled back in her head.

Josep frowned at them. "Eugenia, Lyle, I told you to stay in your rooms until this was over."

"Are they really here to make the strangers leave?" the little boy said hopefully.

"We are," Noor said.

"And their monster?" the girl added, tears springing to her eyes. "It was outside my room last night. I think it could smell me."

Josep was about to snap at them, but then his face changed, and he turned to me.

"I'm not about to let anyone destroy this place," he said. "But I'm also not going to allow more unknowns in on your word alone."

"All right, then," I said. "What can I do to prove I'm telling the truth?"

"The strangers brought two hollowgast with them. One stays with them up on Gravehill, to guard them while they're working. The other patrols the town, to make sure we don't cause them any trouble." He took a step toward me. His gaze intensified. "I'll let your people in on one condition."

"Name it," I said, a prickle of dread awakening in my gut.

"Prove you are who you say." His eyes flashed quickly to the little girl. "If you really have a special talent for hunting these monsters, dispose of this one. Then I'll allow your people to enter."

A charge of fear went through me, but there was hope there, too. Hope that I might be stronger than I thought. Better. Braver.

Noor grabbed my hand.

"You've got this," she whispered.

I said, "Take me to the place you last saw it."

◆　　◆　　◆

Thirty-two of Hopewell's dead were gathered on the front lawn, in what I hoped would look—to a hollowgast, anyway—like a sort of garden party. Josep had agreed to lend us a hand, and he and three other deadriser kids were controlling the dead: Lyle and Eugenia, peeping from the windows of the big Victorian house; and Josep and suspenders boy, from the small house across the street. Noor and I were hidden down the block, sunk low in the front seat of the biggest car I could find, a 1940-something Dodge Deluxe that had a front end like a battering ram.

The hollow that patrolled the town made predictable rounds, Josep had said, and the heavy trails of hollow residue I found in the street outside his big Victorian house confirmed that he had been up and down this particular block many times. I had also realized that my inner compass was confused because there were two hollows in this loop: one who felt familiar to me and the other new. When I imagined them as distinct, it became easier to resolve each of their signals. If these were the same wights who had escaped from Devil's Acre, they were probably still traveling with the hollow they had taken from the Panlooptican basement; that, I hoped, was the familiar signal. He felt distant. Probably up on Gravehill with the wights. The hollow patrolling the town was close—and getting closer.

Noor, as expected, could not be persuaded to let me handle this alone, and truth be told, I didn't want to face this without her. So I hadn't fought her on it.

We sat together in the Dodge, slouched just high enough to see over its yachtlike steering wheel, our eyes fixed on the far end of the street. Waiting. The dead milled about, staggering around the grass in lazy circles.

Every so often we heard another deep faraway boom as the wights continued their excavations.

My stomach was turning knots.

"They must be losing their minds out there," Noor said. "Our friends, I mean." She had scraped a stripe of light from the air and was squeezing it from one fist to the other.

She started humming. The same melody again.

"Does it have words?" I asked.

She nodded. "It's something I learned as a kid," she said. And then she looked up, slightly surprised, as if she'd just realized something. "It was Mama who taught it to me."

"Really?"

" 'Sing it when you're troubled,' " she said. " 'It'll make you feel better.' " She looked at me. "It almost always does."

And then, a few seconds before I saw it, I felt it. I stiffened, leaning forward until my chin was resting against the wheel.

Noor stopped humming. "You see it?"

And then I did—he lumbered from behind a house and into view, way down the block.

"There. See his shadow? Damn, he's an ugly one."

That didn't quite do him justice. This was maybe the biggest, foulest hollowgast I'd ever laid eyes on: He was easily nine feet tall, two feet of which were just his gaping black mouth. His sharp, pointed teeth were so long they were visible even from this distance, and his three tongues, fat as jungle pythons, were pinwheeling in the air around him. And this hollow, unlike others I'd seen, had hair—long, stringy, black, hanging down in matted patches from his scabbed head. He looked like chaos walking, a nightmare come to life. Which was the point; his job was to keep the deadrisers terrified and pacified. While they couldn't see it like I could, the unmistakable, thrashing shadow it cast, like a sea monster grafted onto a giant ape, was nearly as terrible as the beast itself.

I watched it weave from one side of the street to the other, tear a mailbox from the ground with its tongues, and fling it through the window of a house.

"What's it doing?" Noor said.

"Walking toward us. Trying to be scary."

"Is it working?"

Goose bumps rose along my arms. "Yeah. It's working."

I stuck the key I'd found under the visor in the ignition. The car started with a rumble. The hollowgast froze in the middle of the road—turning its tongues at me like three periscopes—and then walked fast in our direction.

I slid the gearshift into drive, but kept my foot planted on the brake.

The hollowgast was three houses away from the garden party of the damned, and now it was speeding up, using its tongues to propel itself farther, faster.

He continued toward us.

Two houses away.

I honked the horn three times. Inside the houses, the deadrisers would now be mumbling and whispering and clicking their tongues, just as we'd planned.

The dead stopped circling the lawn and turned toward the street. All at once they reached into their waistbands and bent down to the grass to retrieve knives and cleavers. One guy, still in his fuzzy slippers, picked up a garden hoe. They swayed and wobbled on dead feet for a few seconds, then flooded into the street to intercept the hollowgast.

I didn't expect them to kill it. They were just the first wave.

The hollow tried to sweep the dead away with its tongues, but there were too many. They fell upon it with their knives, hacking and slicing blindly. The hollow screeched, but it seemed more irritated than wounded, and it set to dispatching its antagonists one or two at a time: One was bitten in half; another had his neck snapped; a third was hurled onto, and impaled by, a picket fence.

"My God," Noor said, laughing nervously. "He's destroying them."

"Now it's my turn," I said. I lifted my foot off the brake and stomped down on the accelerator. The wheels let out a squeal as the car fishtailed, then found its grip and shot forward. We were thrown back in our seats. The road ahead was strewn with bodies and gore, but the hollow was still stumbling around, trying to peel off the last clinging few.

"Hold on!" I shouted.

We braced for impact.

The sound it made was loud and wet, a multipart crunch. One of the dead bounced off the windshield, spider-cracking it, and two more went flying in the air. The hollow roared with pain and surprise—we'd hit it while its back was turned—and it was thrown forward onto the pavement. A moment later it got caught under the fender of the car, its horrible body dragging along the ground.

The front-right tire blew. I slammed on the brakes. The car swerved wildly, spun around, and the back window shattered before we came to a full stop.

Noor turned to stare at me, afraid.

"You okay?" she said, her eyes quickly searching me for cuts and bruises.

I nodded, quickly scanning her. "You?"

"Do you think it's—"

A sudden smack rocked the car. The Dodge's nose lifted a few feet off the ground, then fell back with a terrific jolt.

"Time to get out!" I said, and we both opened our doors and flung ourselves onto the asphalt as the car lifted, then slammed down a second time. The hollow had gotten stuck beneath the rear wheels, and it was writhing and wriggling, trying to free itself. I shouted at Noor to get clear of its tongues, and thankfully, this time, she listened to me and backed off to the sidewalk.

I stood in the middle of the street, staring down the beast.

Lie still, I tried saying in hollowspeak.

The words came out in a jumble—not quite English, not quite Hollow. The creature paid me no attention.

Stop, I tried again. *Lie still.*

Better—all hollowspeak that time. But the creature was too busy bench-pressing the Dodge with its tongues; it hadn't even bothered to scrape off the last dead townie that clung to it, a weaponless man in bloodied pajamas who clawed at it uselessly with his hands.

I repeated myself a few more times while walking slowly toward it.

"Please be careful!" I heard someone cry out—Eugenia, from the window of that house.

The hollow finally succeeded in flipping the car, and it came crashing down on its roof with a fantastic glass-and-metal crunch.

Stay down, I tried. *Stay down.*

It sat up.

Don't move.

It peeled the clawing dead man from its torso and pitched him headfirst into a telephone pole. And then the hollow stood. It had a crushed leg and broken teeth and was weeping black blood from dozens of small wounds, but all that seemed to have only made it angry. It had only two tongues to fight with—the third it was using as a crutch for a mangled leg—but that was twice the number it needed to kill me, and I was well within their grasp.

I wished, wished, wished that this had been the hollow I knew, that'd I'd already controlled, the one from the Panloopticon and the blood-sport ring. I could practically snap my fingers and that hollow would fall into line behind me. But no, of course not. Nothing could ever be easy.

Stop. Sit. Sit down, I chanted.

There was a flicker of hesitation in its body language, but no more than that. It shot one of its tongues at me. It wrapped twice around my waist and chest, knocking the air from my lungs.

"Jacob!" Noor screamed.

"Stay back!" I tried to say, but the tongue was squeezing out my breath. Noor was coming toward me, and so were two of the deadriser kids, out of their houses now, trailed by a few more dead.

"No," I tried to shout, but it came out as a cough. "Don't get close!"

The hollow was pulling me toward it, my feet dragging along the ground. Maybe this hollow was different from others I'd fought and tamed? Bigger, stronger, its mind armored. Maybe the wights had learned something from their encounters with me in Devil's Acre and—I don't know—updated the hollows' brain firmware somehow?

"Let him go, you bastard!" I heard Noor shout.

That got its attention. The hollow paused, then turned, and that's when I saw what she'd made: a churning pool of darkness that spanned the street from sidewalk to sidewalk, in the middle of a sunny day. Her voice had come from somewhere inside the blackness. It was large enough to create a visual screen—and strange enough to confuse a hollowgast.

It whipped its free tongue into the darkness, toward Noor's voice. My heart nearly burst—but the tongue came back, having connected with nothing.

"Not even close!" Noor taunted, her voice slightly to the right now.

The hollow struck again, and again hit nothing.

"Missed again! You suck!"

The hollow was annoyed and distracted enough that it loosened its grip on me ever so slightly, and I was able to speak again, and start whispering at it in hollowspeak.

Let me go, sit down, stop.

The hollow struck again, this time swinging its tongue horizontally through the darkness like a baseball bat, and again my chest constricted in sudden fear for her life—but Noor must have thrown herself to the ground.

I heard her shout, "We want a batter, not a broken ladder!"

It struck once more, fast, and this time there was the sickening noise of impact, and a woman's voice going *ughhhh*.

My chest tightened and I screamed, "STOP!" in English, but it didn't help—the hollow reeled in its catch from the shadow.

But it wasn't Noor.

It was the dead girl from the house—the Elvis Presley fan—and as the hollow hoisted her up to get a better look, she started singing some old Elvis song in a scratchy, tuneless voice.

The hollow roared in anger, and the girl, without drama or expression, took out a knife she'd been hiding in her pocket and plunged it into the hollow's right eye.

It screamed, the noise loud enough to echo. And then the hollow bit off her head and tossed her flopping body onto a roof.

Let me go, I shouted in the stunned silence that followed. The hollow's spine stiffened. It cocked its head toward me like a dog hearing its master whistle.

Let me go, I said again—and this time it set me down on the street and unwrapped its tongue from around my waist.

Thank. God.

The knife in its eye seemed to have weakened it, in both body and mind. I wasn't about to let the opportunity pass.

Close your mouth.

It slurped its three tongues back into its mouth and snapped its jaws shut, and without its crutch it began to wobble, then fell into a sitting position.

The darkness suddenly evaporated, and there was Noor, picking herself up from the pavement where she'd been lying facedown, and relief flooded through me.

"That was way too close," she said, her eyes searching me. "Jesus, are you okay? Can you breathe?"

"I will be," I said, and coughed. "Don't come any closer."

She didn't.

Put your hands on your head.

The hollow did as it was told.

"Can you make him roll over and beg for treats?" asked Lyle, wheeling cautiously through the doorway of the house.

"I think he's had all the snacks he can handle," Eugenia said.

I felt the hollow go limp. He'd stopped resisting me.

"It's safe," I said. "He's under my control now."

Noor dashed into the street, leaping over strewn bodies, to throw her arms around me. "You were amazing," she said. "Amazing."

"You were," I whispered. *"If you hadn't done what you did . . ."*

"I didn't even think. I just did it."

"You scared the hell out of me, though. Please don't tease hollows." I almost—*almost*—laughed. "They really hate it."

The deadriser kids had come out of their houses and closed some of the gap between us, but stayed at a cautious distance.

There were more deadrisers, too, watching from the windows of the houses nearby, but only the ones we'd already met were willing to step into the street.

Josep ventured into the midst of the massacre. He looked deeply impressed.

"I'd heard the hollow-hunters were no more, so when you said you were one of them, I assumed you were lying. But you appear to be the genuine article."

"Now will you let the others in?" I said.

"I've already unsealed the door."

And from the street behind us I heard a welcome sound. My name, as shouted by Bronwyn Bruntley.

CHAPTER TWELVE

*O*ur reunion was joyful but short, and somewhat over-shadowed by the horrifying scene of bodies strewn across the street, which I quickly explained. The ymbrynes had spent a long time trying to break through the sealed loop entrance, which was on lockdown after the wights invaded, and only allowed Noor and me inside by some fluke. After an hour, Miss Peregrine and Miss Wren had been about to give up and fly off to fetch some other, more extreme method of breaking and entering, when the door opened on its own. The waiting had left my friends frazzled with worry and frustration, and Hugh shaking with anger. Everyone was furious with the deadrisers—but at the moment there were more important things to deal with.

Like the wights on the hill. Yes, they were up there. The presence of hollows had confirmed that for me, even before the deadrisers had told us their story. Yes, the wights were here for the skull on Bentham's list, and given that they'd been searching Gravehill for it since the previous night, they were probably not far from finding it. Each new bit of bad news made my friends' faces constrict a bit tighter.

"Did they have a girl with them when they came in?" Hugh asked Lyle, making a concerted effort not to attack the boy, and he described her.

"I saw a girl like that," said Eugenia. "They had her in leg irons."

Hugh's face went stony, and Bronwyn had to physically restrain him from running toward the hill that very moment.

We all wanted to go on the attack. But first we had to make a plan.

"Do you suppose they know we're here?" asked Emma, gazing up at the hill in the distance.

"If they don't yet, they will soon," Miss Peregrine said. "They'll expect this one to report back to them, and when he doesn't . . ." She glanced at the injured hollow. She couldn't see him, of course, but he was covered in human blood, which gave him a kind of visible outline. "That means if we want the element of surprise—assuming we still have it—we need to move now."

"I'm sorry, miss," said Millard, his voice coming out of the air. "But you're not coming with us."

"Of course I am!" she said hoarsely. She was starting to look very worn-out.

"But you're the final ingredient," Horace said. "If they manage to get the alphaskull and then you, too . . ."

Miss Peregrine tried to argue, but thankfully, Miss Cuckoo and Miss Wren intervened.

Miss Wren patted her arm. "They're right, Alma. We're all mothers to our wards, but you're also Caul's sister. If that infernal list refers to any of us, it is almost certainly you."

"You must keep to the rear," Miss Cuckoo said, "hard as we know that will be for you."

Miss Peregrine reluctantly assented. "I'll stay back, but I won't stay out of it."

That would have to do.

We stood in the deadrisers' grassy yard by a low white fence, beside the massacre, planning what might easily become another one. We would ascend the hill together, staying hidden for as long as we could, and try to be ready for anything. For days, Hugh had quietly been amassing new bees, and his stomach hummed audibly with them. Emma had preheated her hands; when she held them out they rippled the air. Claire had sharpened the teeth in her backmouth, and gnashed them in the air by way of demonstration. Enoch had stuffed a backpack full of pickled hearts and had already begun installing them in the chewed and fallen dead—"I can fix more of 'em," he said to Josep, "if you've got some spare parts handy."

"Remember, the wights favor guns," Miss Cuckoo said. "It's best not to run directly at them, unless you're quite close."

"And Hugh . . . ," Miss Peregrine said, delicately, pressing the palms of her hands together. "Should we encounter Fiona, please remember that she may still be under their control. So approach her with caution."

He shook his head slowly, looking away. Then said, almost too quietly to hear, "All right."

It was time to go.

Josep told us how to find a hidden path that led up to the top of the hill. After a confusing list of turns and landmarks, he waved his hand and said, "Never mind, I'll show you the way myself."

"Are you sure?" Eugenia said. "It could be dangerous."

"These people are ready to risk their lives to liberate our home," he said. "It's only fair I risk mine to help them."

❖   ❖   ❖

I considered leaving the hollowgast behind, but without me there to babysit, my control over it would gradually fade, and I'd have to tame the thing all over again. I knew it might be useful, having a hollow along as I went to face another one, even one this injured. So we trudged up the hill with the big, limping hollow, and though it was fairly docile now, I made sure to keep it far to one side of us.

There were houses at the bottom of the hill, but as the ground sloped upward, it became a vast cemetery.

"Just like in my dream," Horace said, looking around in wonder.

There was a paved road that snaked up the middle of the hill, from which the tree-shaded path we walked was more or less hidden.

Miss Peregrine stayed to the rear—as she'd promised to, and Miss Wren stayed with her—though I started to worry that if she fell too far behind she'd become easy to pick off from our group. Maybe she shouldn't have come at all.

Another bang shook the earth.

"They're getting louder," Bronwyn fretted.

We could hear the wights, but we still couldn't see them. I hoped that meant they hadn't seen us, either. Thankfully, they seemed to have placed total faith in the big, nasty hollowgast to guard their operations atop the hill. Emma had warned everyone to expect a patrol guard or two waiting along the climb, but so far there had been none.

"Maybe we really will be able to surprise them," Horace said cheerfully.

Horace, who was wearing a cravat into battle. Horace, who had stayed up all the previous night repairing the rest of the peculiar sheep's wool sweaters, which many of us were now wearing as a protective layer under our clothes despite the warm day. When this was over, I was going to tell him just how much I loved him.

A few of Enoch's twice-risen dead, looking much the worse for wear, limped and shuffled up the path behind us. I didn't know what good they would do; you could've knocked them over with a flick.

After a long, gentle climb the graveyard flattened, and I thought we'd reached the top—but then we cleared the trees and saw a second hill, steep and almost perfectly round, rising from the center of the plateau. Every side of it was stippled with headstones and monuments.

We stopped near the end of the tree line. Past the point where we stood, there was little visual cover. Noor scraped a thin layer of light away from the place where we were kneeling. "Not enough to look strange and draw the eye," she explained. "Just enough to make someone who was looking for us look somewhere else."

We knelt behind the screen she'd made and looked up. Josep

told us there was a second plateau at the top of the hill, about a hundred yards across. The oldest part of the cemetery. I could feel the other hollowgast there.

There was another ground-shaking blast, and then a fine rain of pulverized earth came down.

"Won't they destroy the grave they're trying to dig up?" asked Olive.

"There was once a peculiar in Devil's Acre," said Miss Cuckoo, "who lived in holes, and could burrow deep into the ground like a mole, and would blast the dirt out behind him with great force. I wonder if they haven't taken him hostage."

"I knew that bloke," said Enoch. "He was an ambro addict. They probably didn't have to mind control him at all."

"There!" Emma hissed. *"Look!"*

Two figures were now visible at the edge of the hill.

"Sentries," Miss Peregrine said. "Everyone keep still."

"And hope we haven't been seen," added Bronwyn.

I peered at them through a thin screen of branches. We were too far to make out their faces, but had we been closer, I suspected we would've recognized one or both of them from their mugshots. The figures turned slowly. Nothing in their body language betrayed alarm, or suggested we'd been spotted, and after a long moment the two figures withdrew and disappeared.

"We need to get to the top of that hill," said Hugh. He had begun to channel his anger into laserlike focus. "Battle strategy one-oh-one: Never engage the enemy from lower ground. They'll have all the advantage."

We agreed there was no way we could ascend the hill as a group and stay hidden, even with Noor's light-stealing abilities, so we split into two groups. One would flank to the right while the other went left, and with any luck, we would reach the top undetected and surround them. Maybe then—and when they saw I had their hollowgast—they would give up without firing a shot.

My brain, as ever, was a hope-making machine.

Bronwyn was going from person to person, giving pats on the back and rubbing shoulders. "Don't stop until the top," she said to Horace. "If anyone gets near you, don't be afraid to draw blood!" she encouraged Claire.

I reminded them that the wights also had a hollow—and that it could sense our abilities when we used them. "Try not to use your peculiarities until we get close."

"Until you see the wights of their eyes," Enoch said, and looked irritated when no one acknowledged his joke.

"Remember your sweaters," Horace said, moving aside his cravat to show his. "If you absolutely must get shot, try to keep it below the neck and above the waist."

"While you're at it, try not to get shot at all," said Noor. "I just met you guys; no one's allowed to die, okay?"

"Okay, Miss Noor," Olive said, and gave her a hug around the hips (which was as high on tall Noor as little Olive's arms reached).

We split up.

Our group was me, Noor, Hugh, and Bronwyn, and the other was Horace, Millard, Emma, Enoch, and Claire. I instructed my hollow to trail us at a distance, far enough to the rear that if it fell or grunted or crunched leaves too loudly, the noise wouldn't give away our position. Enoch left his battalion of limping dead behind in the woods. "A second attack wave if we need one," he called them, and someone had snickered. Millard, who had shed his clothes, would act as a messenger between the two groups, if one was required, and Olive had let Miss Peregrine badger her into staying behind with her and Miss Cuckoo and Josep.

Miss Peregrine would not be going with us. Before we left, she gathered us for a quick goodbye.

"There's no time for speeches, and even if there were I'm not sure I could summon the words needed to express the deep and abiding regard I have for you all. We are about to go forth into extraordinary dangers. One never knows when the end is coming, or if we may all be assembled together as a whole and complete family again. And so I want you to know that I regret every day that my full attention has been called away from you, and if these talks, and the rebuilding of our loops at home, have caused me to shirk my responsibility to you, I am sorry. In the end I am your mistress and your servant. You mean more to me than all the birds in the sky and the heavens above them. If you love me, I hope I have deserved it." She wiped quickly at her eyes. "Thank you."

Miss Peregrine wasn't the only one tearing up. I felt a flutter in my own chest, too. She raised a hand in a silent goodbye, and with heavy hearts we set off.

◆　　◆　　◆

My group flanked to the right, and the other went left. I didn't get really nervous until we lost sight of one another around the curve of the hill.

We used the graves as cover, scurrying between stones and monuments large enough to hide all four of us. Luckily, the hill was thickly forested with them, and after working our way to the side for a while, we started to ascend.

We quickly made it halfway to the top. I began to wonder where the sentries were; we'd been watching for them, but hadn't seen their heads poke out from the summit since that first time. What were they doing?

I started to worry that they knew we were here and were just waiting for us to get close enough to make a slaughter easy.

We dashed across a patch of open ground and ducked behind a mausoleum veined with mildew. "You know, maybe they're *letting* us get close," I said—but I'd hardly finished the sentence when there came a rattle of gunfire.

We froze. Waited. Another few shots rang out in quick succession.

They weren't aiming at us. They were shooting at our friends on the other side of the hill.

"Wait here!" I hissed, and before the others could stop me I ran back the way we'd come to see what was happening.

I came to rest behind a stone cross. I could just make out the other group, far across the sloping graveyard. They were huddled behind a massive marble angel. I could see chips flying off its wings, which were being chewed up by bullets.

I heard footsteps approaching but saw no one. I realized I didn't have a weapon—and then Millard nearly collided with me.

"I was coming to tell you *not* to come!" he wheezed. "Emma says keep going!"

"But they're pinned down!" I said.

"They have good cover, and they're providing a perfect opportunity for you fellows to take the other side of the hill."

"Fine," I said, "but I'm sending my hollow up there."

"No! You'll need it yourself!"

But I had already summoned it close and was grunting further instructions in hollowspeak. I'd gotten my hooks deep enough into its pea brain that I trusted it to function at least partially on autopilot.

Kill wights, I said. *Not peculiars.*

It crouched like a sprinter before the starting gun, then sprung into a one-legged, three-tongued lope across the graveyard, running like some freakish horse.

"Go!" Millard said, physically pushing me—and before I turned I saw Emma pop out from behind the marble angel and lob a firebomb up the hill toward the wights.

When I got back to my group, Noor and Bronwyn grabbed me and pulled me to safety. "That wasn't the plan!" Noor said, livid and terrified. "You can't just run off like that!"

I apologized, then told them what I'd seen. The message Millard had passed along. And then I looked around and said, "Where's Hugh?"

Noor and Bronwyn spun.

"He was just here!" Bronwyn said.

But he wasn't here anymore.

"Oh my God," said Noor, pointing to something on the ground, ten feet away. "Look."

It was a trail of purple flowers meandering away among the headstones.

Oh, Hugh. You idiot.

We ran, following the trail of flowers, not even bothering to hide behind the graves now.

The vine wound around a monument to Civil War soldiers, past a tomb decorated with empty flower vases, to a circle of graves.

There in the middle of it all stood Fiona, in a flowing white gown, ringed by deep beds of purple flowering vines. She was facing away from us, and Hugh was approaching her carefully from behind, repeating her name, his hand outstretched.

"Hugh!" Bronwyn shouted. "Don't!"

Fiona turned around. Her eyes were rolled back in her head. Hugh stopped moving forward for some reason. He looked down and then back at Fiona again, and I heard him say, "Sweetheart, no . . ."

And then something wrapped around my ankles, and I lost my balance and fell, and Noor and Bronwyn fell beside me. The carpet of vines beneath our feet had come to life, and was quickly swaddling us, mummifying us so that we could hardly move a muscle.

We struggled to free ourselves, but within a few seconds we were completely immobilized.

Helpless.

And then I felt its approach: the second hollowgast.

I grunted a warning to my friends just as it appeared above us on the hill—and then called out for my hollow, the giant one I had tamed earlier.

Emma and the others would have to do without its protection for a little while.

"Fiona!" Hugh shouted. "Please, love, don't do this!"

The vines around us tightened.

The other hollow had been heading right for me, but when it sensed the approach of mine, it stopped in its tracks, confused for a moment, and then seemed to gird itself for a fight.

Just before they collided, I saw two wights appear atop the hill, to watch.

The hollows charged across the slanting ground toward one another, leaping over headstones like hurdlers. They collided with a smack, the impact so hard it sent them both up into the air. Then they were on the ground, grappling, tongues whipping so furiously I couldn't tell which belonged to which. I tried issuing some commands to my giant hollow—*Choke! Bite! Gouge!*—but they seemed redundant given how hard he was already fighting.

Now the creature was fighting not just for me, but for its own life.

It was like watching a battle between two shrieking sea monsters. I saw that my hollow's hobbled leg wasn't much of a disadvantage; at such close range, the winner would be decided by their knifelike teeth and strangling tongues. Honestly, I never thought I'd see anything like this; it was mesmerizing to watch.

Noor fought uselessly against her restraints. "What's happening?" she said.

I tried to narrate, but it was happening so quickly I couldn't keep up.

The wights' hollow got mine in a nasty choke-hold, both of its arms and its remaining tongue wrapped around mine's neck—and I felt the life force of my hollow begin to falter. They were locked together, and neither could move; the wights' hollow could not afford to let go even for a second or the gnashing jaws of mine would sever its last tongue—and then their hollow reached behind itself, yanked a gravestone from the ground, and bashed my hollow in the head with it.

I felt its consciousness blink out.

Dead.

As we would be soon, no doubt.

The two wights descended toward us, and their hollow limped to meet them.

I began to whisper at their hollow, the same one I'd controlled in the blood-sport ring and the battery chamber, but it didn't respond. I'd have to be closer, and speak louder, to reestablish my connection to it. But how was I going to do that with these vines pinning me to the ground?

The wights were dressed in unremarkable business casual clothes, designed to help them disappear into modern life. I recognized them from the ymbrynes' mugshots. One was thick-necked and freckled—*Murnau*. He had a leather bag strapped across his back. The other wight was thin and wore round glasses on the end of a beaklike nose. There was a third man behind him. His face was a ruin of melted flesh.

I could hear gunfire continue to ring out from the other side of the hill. Our friends were still fighting. So there was hope yet.

The wights were standing among us. Arrogant, strutting. The hollow stood behind them, moaning a little and leaking from various wounds. The man with the ruined face was whispering to Fiona, and Murnau was talking to me.

"A valiant effort, boy. Truly impressive. If only your talents weren't wasted on the birds, we could do some real damage together. Oh, well."

"Maybe we can work something out," I said.

"You've had plenty of opportunities to join us and always refused. It's far too late. And you're too late to stop this, too." He reached into his bag and pulled out a skull, brown with age, the jaw missing. "Unless you're here for some other reason. Visiting the Catskills?"

He put the skull back, muttering something about *the master will be so pleased with me*, but I wasn't listening—instead I was trying desperately, under my breath, to gain a little control over Murnau's hollowgast again.

There was a loud buzzing sound, and everyone looked to Hugh. His mouth was open, and bees were starting to pour out.

Murnau shouted something at the man with the ruined face. The man with the ruined face then shouted something at Fiona. Fiona jerked, and a rope of vines clasped around Hugh's mouth.

His eyes widened pitifully. *"Mmmmf!"* Just a few bees had escaped. The skinny wight slapped at the air and killed one.

The man with the ruined face was the one controlling Fiona's mind. He wasn't a wight—he was an ambro addict, most of whom had long ago pledged their allegiance to the wights. Mind control must have been his peculiar ability.

I was still trying to gain control over the hollow's mind, but it was resisting me.

"Let us go now," Bronwyn said, "and we'll spare your lives when this is over."

Murnau just laughed.

"And you," Murnau said, kneeling down in front of Noor. "How's the search for Mommy going? Think she's just dying to see you again? Is that why she abandoned you—because *she wuves her wittew baby so much*?"

Noor was staring past him, her jaw set.

"Go die, asshole," I spat.

"The boy rushes to her defense. How romantic." He sighed. "Well, enough of this. I'm getting bored—and we have a plane to catch."

He stood up, reached into his jacket, and pulled out a gun. "Who wants to die first?"

Just then I heard a noise like a sheet flapping in the wind, and something let out a higher-pitch screech and collided with Murnau's head.

Miss Peregrine.

As he was thrown to the ground, the gun fell from his grip, and he swatted at the bird with his bare hands. She flapped her powerful wings, talons tearing at his face.

"Auuugh!!! Get it offa me!"

The skinny wight leapt into the fray.

"Jacob!" It was Noor. She turned her head toward me and opened her mouth a little. Bright light glowed from inside her throat. "I've been saving this. One shot. Where do I aim it?"

Miss Peregrine was on top of Murnau. So I indicated the ambro addict.

She made a sound like she was choking, then coughing, and then hocked a hot, spinning orb of pure light across the grass just above the ground. It wrapped around the ambro addict's shins and he began to scream—this one must have been searing hot—and he toppled to the ground.

Then I heard a screech. Miss Peregrine. The hollowgast had torn her away from Murnau and was swinging her around in the air with its tongue.

They had her. Which meant now they had everything. I felt suddenly blind with rage, with fear. I had to do something, and soon.

Murnau was starting to regain his footing.

And then I heard a gasp—Fiona. Her eyes were rolled forward again, and I felt the vines around us begin to loosen. The addict's control over her had wavered.

Murnau bellowed something unintelligible and ran at him, a vial in his hand—and he threw himself atop the man and upended the stuff into the addict's eyes.

The vines were slackening—but slowly. It was enough to get an arm free now, and one leg. And for Hugh to loose his bees. They streamed into the air and began to find their targets—the wights, the hollow.

Twin cones of light shot out of the addict's eyes. He screamed, flipped over. Murnau ignored the bees stinging him—his face was already running with blood from Miss Peregrine's talons—and he shoved the man so that he was facing Fiona.

Fiona went rigid again. The vines began to tighten.

I yanked my leg hard before their grip was complete, and it came free. Bronwyn and Noor were still caught.

Murnau hadn't seen—yet.

I ran for the hollow. It was holding our thrashing ymbryne above its open, smacking mouth like a bonbon treat, taunting her with death.

I slammed into the hollow. Bear-hugged it around its neck. I could feel its shock, the surprise at having been physically tackled by a such a weak creature—and that bought me a moment to act.

I gripped it around the sides of its face.

LISTEN TO ME, I screamed, pressing my head to its head. I stared into its black, weeping eyes. *You're mine, you're mine, you are mine.*

And then it was.

Hello, old friend.

Drop her.

It dropped Miss Peregrine—and then I felt a sharp pain in my back. The skinny wight had struck me with something.

I clung to the hollow. I wasn't letting go.

Kill.

The hollow whipped out its only remaining tongue. The wight was dead the next instant.

I heard Noor scream. Bronwyn, too.

Turn.

The hollow turned. The addict was yelling at Fiona, the light from his eyes smoking, the skin around them melting—and everywhere the vines were moving like nests of snakes. The girls and Hugh were struggling against the vines, which were constricting tighter and tighter around them.

Kill, kill, kill.

The hollow's tongue ripped off the addict's head. The lights from his eyes spun as it tumbled down the hill.

The vines loosened, unwound, slunk back into the earth. My friends collapsed to the ground, finally able to breathe. Fiona looked at them and moaned in horror at what she'd done.

Turn.

Miss Peregrine was alive—thank God—and turning human again, which meant she wasn't gravely injured.

I looked for Murnau—and saw him running away. I ordered the hollowgast to chase him down, but the hollow and I hadn't even gone ten steps when a hail of bullets pockmarked the ground and the headstones around me. Someone was covering Murnau's escape. The hollow was hit in the leg, and stumbled.

"Let him go!" Miss Peregrine shouted after me. "Take the others and get to safety!"

We surrounded Fiona. Hugh scooped her into his arms and she fell limply across him. He would accept no help and carried her by himself, his face rigid but streaming with tears.

I forced Miss Peregrine to come with us, though I knew her instinct was to chase down Murnau—but that was probably just what he hoped she would do.

We ran back around the hill, just in time to witness something astounding. My friends were no longer hiding behind the stone angel but charging up the hill toward the other retreating wights. Bringing up the rear was a very eclectic battalion: Miss Wren riding a grimbear; Enoch's limping dead, a dozen strong; and a surprising number of Americans. A Northern woman barreling headlong uphill with a medium-sized tree under her arm, branches and all. A Californio man, rolling a boulder along before him. A boy with lightning sparking between his hands. And several cowboy types with rifles, in firing positions, laying down a blanket of bullets to clear the way.

They took the hill, and in no time our forces had killed or caught six wights and several of their ambro-addicted turncoats.

Murnau was gone.

Somehow he had slipped away and taken with him a bag of resurrection ingredients. The ymbrynes dispatched a search party, but they didn't seem hopeful.

But Miss Peregrine was safe, and we had Fiona back.

Fiona.

God, it was good to see her again. We gathered among the excavations atop Gravehill—a wrecked place of holes and bones and piled-up earth—to take stock.

Hugh had not let her go for a moment since the vines had released him, but he was finally persuaded to let the ymbrynes examine her.

We all circled around anxiously to watch. The ymbrynes spoke softly to her. Asked her questions. She seemed dazed, but no longer hypnotized. Her eyes were normal, if red-rimmed and bloodshot, and there were bruises purpling on her arms and face.

"Are those from the bus accident?" Miss Peregrine asked her.

She nodded.

"Did they hurt you in any other way?"

She blinked several times, then looked away.

"Love?" said Hugh, grasping her hand. "Did they hurt you?"

She closed her eyes.

"Please talk to me," he begged her. "Tell me what they did to you."

She opened her eyes again. Looked at him, and slowly nodded her head.

Then she opened her mouth. Blood spilled out. It ran down her chin onto her white dress.

Tongue of the seedsprout. Freshly harvested.

Murnau had gotten what he needed from her, after all.

CHAPTER THIRTEEN

*W*e brought Fiona back to Devil's Acre and straight to Rafael the bone-mender to begin her recovery. Hugh never left her side. Neither did the rest of us. We crowded her room, talking to her, telling her stories about all she'd missed, and just hanging out in the hope it might make her feel like she was home again, even though the home she'd left behind—Miss Peregrine's—was gone forever.

We thought some feigned cheer might buoy her spirits.

Enoch got the first smile out of her, telling a story about falling into the Ditch and coming out with one of the wrinkled old bridge heads having bitten hold of his trouser leg. And pretty soon our fake cheer began to feel real.

She was alive.

Fiona was alive and back among us. Yes, she was hurt. And yes, Murnau was out there somewhere with Fiona's tongue and the alphaskull and all the other ingredients on Bentham's infernal resurrection shopping list. But he hadn't gotten Miss Peregrine—and he never would.

We told ourselves we had won. We had crushed the wights. Killed or captured all but one of them—and their hollows. I had brought the last one back to the Acre, returning it to the place where I had originally tamed it, the old grimbear enclosure in the bloodsport ring. Only Murnau remained, so far as we knew, and if it really was important that Fiona's tongue be "freshly harvested," well—the clock was certainly ticking on that.

It seemed we had beaten them.

The wights who'd been captured in the deadrisers' loop had a glum, defeated air about them that I'd never seen in wights before. Noor and I caught sight of them slouching through the Acre in chains the day after we returned, while they were being transferred out of an interrogation room in Bentham's house. I had every intention of keeping my distance, but when Noor saw them, she jolted and said, "Oh my God," and suddenly she was pulling me toward them.

A home guard soldier stopped us before we could get too close.

"It's them," Noor said, her voice shaking a little, and she raised her arm and pointed at two of the wights: a man and a woman who looked oddly familiar. "Those were the people watching me at school."

I stopped breathing for a moment as it clicked into place. They were the vice principals. The ones who'd stalked Noor and who we had seen again just before the attack on her hiding place in the unfinished building.

The ones H had thought were normal, some secret society bent on controlling us.

"Holy shit," I murmured, and took her hand.

Both of them turned their heads to look at us, and their eyes flashed with hatred. Then they were led through a doorway and were gone.

Later, Miss Peregrine confirmed it: They had never been in ymbryne custody before. They'd been in America for years, unaccounted for, on the ymbrynes' most-wanted list.

They had fooled H. They'd tricked Abe, too—for years—into thinking some other group was responsible for many of the wights' crimes.

I swore to myself I'd never let a wight trick me again.

The ymbrynes, once they had spent a little time settling us back into the Acre, returned to Marrowbone to oversee the end of the negotiations. LaMothe and Parkins had actually come to Hopewell in person with their fighters and, after what they'd witnessed, appeared to be very much on Team Ymbryne. Leo had already been persuaded to make bygones bygones, Miss Peregrine had said, and now there were only a few contractual formalities to work out before a solid peace agreement could be reached and signed.

⁕ ⁕ ⁕

We continued to work on finding V, though our quest didn't carry the same urgency it once had. Our life and safety no longer seemed to depend on it, and I had begun to wonder about H's motivations; whether sending us to find her was more about his mistrust of ymbrynes than V being the key to something crucial. I couldn't know. What I *did* know was that finding V was important to Noor. She was the closest thing Noor had to a mother; a last link to a lost childhood.

Millard, Noor, and I gave the search most of our time, and the others helped whenever they could. Millard seemed to think we were getting close. Another small memory of childhood came back to Noor one night over dinner, something about a strip-mined mountaintop, and it led Millard to rule out Ohio as a possible location of V's loop. That left only Pennsylvania to search. It felt like it was only a matter of time.

Noor and I spent pretty much every waking moment together. Emma, for her part, was mostly ignoring us. She wasn't mean about it. But she was going through something, and it wasn't anything I could help her with. So I gave her space and hoped that we really could be friends again soon.

All seemed well.

Great, even.

⁕ ⁕ ⁕

Noor and I were hunched over rib-eye sandwiches at the Shrunken Head, having just come off a marathon session with Millard in the maps room. We'd been scouring a pile of new atlases the Americans lent us, looking for anything that resembled the topography of H's map fragment. But after five hours of work, the pile was only a little shorter than when we'd started; even Millard's usually inexhaustible enthusiasm for cartography was beginning to flag.

I took a bite of my sandwich, winced, then spat a small metal pellet into my hand.

"Sorry 'bout that," a passing waiter said. "Sometimes they don't get all the buckshot out of the carcass."

I pushed the plate away. "How about a coffee instead?"

He went off to bring me one, and I noticed Noor staring out the clouded window at the bridge head outside. It was barking rude things at passersby.

"Hey," I said quietly. "What's on your mind?"

"We're getting so close to finding her now. Like we're just a step away."

"It's exciting," I said. Then: "Isn't it?"

"Yes," she said slowly, "but meeting her again means talking to her, means facing all this stuff and digging up all these feelings I buried a long time ago."

"You don't feel ready."

"Maybe?" She sighed. "I don't know."

"You know what I think?"

She looked up.

"I think maybe you could use a little break." My coffee arrived with a sudden smack on the wooden table, startling me for a second. "Maybe we could both use some time off. We went through so much, then dove right back into the work again, and you haven't had time to process any of it. None of us have."

But Noor seemed almost afraid to be hopeful. "Maybe just a tiny break? I'd actually been thinking it would be nice to go back to New York to pick up some of my stuff. Clothes, shoes. My back-pack . . ." She shrugged.

"That's a *great* idea," I said.

"I mean, if I'm really going to, like, live here—"

"Let's go," I said.

"Really?" She hesitated. "We could be back in a couple of hours or something, right? Use the Panloopticon?"

"Yep." I scooted back in my chair. "Easy."

◆　　◆　　◆

We got there in less than an hour. We took the Panloopticon door to New York City—at this point Noor and I had pretty much free rein to roam the Panloopticon at will—and then caught the subway to Brooklyn.

The train rattled along underground. Noor sat beside me, our hands mingled in a stack on her lap as we talked about plans for the future. She wanted to finish school. She talked about commuting from Devil's Acre to Bard College in New York, where she'd been accepted into an accelerated student arts program for high school kids. She loved art history and music, but had a knack for engineering and science, too. She was torn. I told her she might have a future in both.

It seemed like we had beaten the prophecy, circumvented the worst outcome, and something like a future was now possible. For her. And for us.

"Maybe I could go to that program with you," I said. "If everything settles down, I'd like to get my degree, too."

"Have a foot in the peculiar world and the normal one," she said.

"Exactly."

All my other peculiar friends had given up on having anything to do with the normal world a long time ago. I had nearly given up on it, too. Until now, I hadn't realized how much I had been mourning the loss of it.

Maybe together, Noor and I could figure out what it meant to be both normal and peculiar, and to be just seventeen among century-old friends, and to be someone whose birth was prophesied and someone who was the grandson of a legend and—as awkward as it made me feel sometimes—someone who was becoming a bit of a legend himself. It was unmapped territory for us both.

We got off at Noor's station, climbed the stairs into daylight, and walked ten blocks along leafy streets holding hands. For a few minutes it felt like nothing in the world was wrong and never had been. Eventually we stopped and Noor said, "This is it."

There was no nostalgia or homesickness in her voice.

She let herself in with a code. We went up three flights of stairs to her foster parents' place. They weren't home, but her foster sister Amber was—watching TV in a darkened room.

Amber barely looked up when Noor came in.

"Thought you ran away," she said. "Who's that?"

"I'm Jacob," I said.

Amber looked me over with one eyebrow raised.

Noor had gone down the hall. "Where's my stuff?" she called from one of the rooms.

"The closet," Amber shouted. "I took over your part of the room after you didn't come back. Dad says I can keep it."

We found Noor's clothes, shoes, some books, and her backpack piled in a wrinkly mess in the closet. She began to pull them out. Then she stood up quickly, looking at something in her hand.

A postcard.

"Where'd this come from?" she shouted down the hall. "The postcard."

"Uh, the mail?"

Noor turned the card over, then over again. Her hand was shaking.

"What is it?" I said.

She handed it to me. On the front was a picture of a tornado. Below it was a town name: WAYNOKA, PENNSYLVANIA.

On the back were Noor's name and address, and below that, in neat cursive: *"Miss you, honey. Sorry it's been so long. I heard the news—and I'm so proud of you. This was the last address I had for you . . . I hope this note reaches you, and that you'll come visit."*

It was signed, *"Love, Mama V."*

And there was an address.

"My God," Noor whispered.

I looked at her, awestruck. "She heard about what you did. She knows you know about her!"

"So you think it's real? You think it's really her?"

I blinked at Noor. That the postcard might not be real hadn't even occurred to me. But then, we'd been through a lot these last few weeks. I understood how Noor was feeling; it'd become hard to trust anything.

But I hated that instinct. I was tired of it. I wanted to remember how to be excited about things again. I wanted to remember what it was like to feel hopeful.

So I sighed. "Yeah, I think it's real. I mean, I think she's telling you, in so many words, that it's safe for her to see you now. That things weren't safe before, but now, because of what we've done, it's possible to reconnect."

"Yeah," Noor said softly.

"You okay?" I asked.

I heard her sniff. She wouldn't look at me.

She tried to smile. "I think maybe I've just gotten really good at doubting the good things in my life."

"I understand," I said quietly. And then I pulled her close. She rested her head against my chest.

Finally, she pulled back. Her eyes were red, but dry. "So— Waynoka, Pennsylvania, huh?"

We typed the address into my phone. It was only a few hours away.

Noor gazed at me with wonder and barely restrained joy. "Want to go visit my mom?"

◆   ◆   ◆

Waynoka, Pennsylvania was two and a half hours away, to be exact, and to get there Noor took (without exactly asking) her foster sister's car. She had taken Noor's space without asking, so the scales seemed balanced; and anyway, we'd bring it back. Probably.

We might've gone back to Devil's Acre first and told our friends. In another situation, I would have brought a few of them along. We probably should have, but it would have cost us an hour of travel there and another back, and my friends had other concerns now—Fiona, primarily, who had only just come back to us—and, in a way, this journey felt like ours. Mine and Noor's. The quest to find V had started with just her and me, and it felt right that it should end that way.

There wasn't much to Waynoka. We drove down a flat, straight country road past fields and farms and lonely houses at the ends of long lanes. We passed some hunters in camouflage pulled over to the side of the road, strapping a dead deer to the hood of a truck. The stump of a giant tree split long ago by lightning. The place seemed a little bit lost. A little bit damned.

Noor had been staring into the rear-view mirror for nearly a minute. "I'm getting the weirdest feeling of déjà vu," she said.

"Like you've been here before?"

She looked uneasy. "Yeah, but—I don't think I have."

We came into a low-density commercial zone. A dollar store, a payday loan place. It was a regular, if rusted-out version, of small-town America. We left the main road and made a few turns, and then finally we came to the address: an old brick warehouse. A sign

out front read BIG MO'S U-STORE-IT. It stood against the banks of a muddy river, which made me think it had once been a mill. Now it was just a parking place for people's extra crap.

I scanned the building's exterior as we pulled into its almost-empty parking lot, making a quick mental map: one main entrance, a big roll door for loading and unloading trucks, old leaded factory windows in rows rising up five floors, and a roof I couldn't see onto, with no fire escape or obvious quick way down.

"If you were a loop entrance in an old storage warehouse," I said, "where would you be?"

"The roof?" Noor said, her eyes locked on it.

I parked and killed the engine. I started to get out, then noticed Noor wasn't moving. She was playing with the light between her knees.

I turned in my seat to face her.

"You okay?"

"For eleven years this woman's lived with me as a memory. A painful, good memory. But the minute we walk in there, she becomes real." She let the light slip through her hands and looked at me. "What if she turns out to be horrible? Or crazy? Or nothing like I remember?"

"Then we'll leave. And forget about her. But if you'd rather not go, there's no reason we have to. Maybe just knowing she's there is enough."

Noor stared up at the building for a few seconds. "No," she said, and grabbed the door and pushed it open. "I have to see her. I want her to tell me what happened that night."

The night she pretended to die.

I got out, too. "You know what happened," I said gently, across the car's roof.

"I want to hear it from her."

◆   ◆   ◆

In a small, fluorescent-lit room, a bearded hipster in a lumberjack shirt sat at a computer.

"Help you?" He looked high.

I said, "What's the quickest way to the roof?"

"The roof's off-limits."

"Okay," Noor said. "But how do we get up there?"

"Uhh, you *don't*. It's off-limits." He leaned back in his chair, squared his shoulders. "Have you got a unit here?"

"Four-oh-four," I said, making up a random number, and I nudged Noor toward the inner door.

The hipster called after us, but we didn't stop and he didn't bother chasing.

We entered the Stor-It part of Big Mo's U-Stor-It, a once-vast mill converted into a claustrophobic warren of wire cages. Long rows of them receded away into gloom, broken at intervals by squares of pale window light. There was chill in the air and a thin, sour smell.

"It's like a tomb in here," Noor whispered, and I thought I heard her teeth chatter.

Her voice, even at a low register, echoed like a penny dropped into a well.

Coming here, I'd imagined something more welcoming waiting for us—perhaps a nice shade-dappled glen in a forest. Just once, something like the portals in kids' books. But this place felt oppressive and unfriendly. As I still had to remind myself now and then, this was usually the point of loop entrances: to keep people away.

Our eyes having adjusted slightly, we began looking for some stairs or an elevator. The instant we took a step, a bank of fluorescent lights above us flickered to life.

"What the—" Noor said, and we both jumped.

I looked up at the buzzing lights, then down the alley of storage units. There were hundreds more lights, all dark.

"Motion-control sensor," I said.

I took another few steps forward. Another bank of lights popped on above me.

It felt weirdly like someone was watching us.

We hurried along the rows of storage units, the lights popping on above us as we ran, until we came to a stairwell and started climbing. The stairs topped out at the fourth floor. The roof was on five. There had to be another staircase somewhere on the fourth floor, so we went to find it.

This floor looked just like the first, long alleys of cages bursting with junk: cardboard file boxes stacked in towers, furniture covered in sheets, heaps of stuff in garbage bags, old sports equipment. Noor held up her arm to slow me, then put a finger to her lips and cocked her head. We stopped and listened.

For a moment, there was only silence, but then a loud bang came from somewhere up ahead and got my heart going, followed by the sound of metal scraping against concrete. Then we heard someone grunting and swearing. We walked on until we came to the right aisle, and paused to look. In a pool of blue light surrounded by dark, an old man was trying to push a hulking beast of an oven into one of the cages, and he was struggling, wheezing for breath.

One of his arms was wrapped in a cast.

Noor shook her head. "I know we shouldn't stop, but . . ."

The old man bent to give it another try. He planted his good shoulder and two hands against the oven and pushed, but his feet slid out from under him and he fell, catching himself with both his good arm and his hurt one.

He rolled onto one side and started to moan.

His back was to us. He hadn't looked at us once.

Noor sighed. "We have a minute. I can't just watch."

We started down the aisle toward him. The lights clicked on overhead as we went, drawing an arrow toward the old man.

He sat up, and hearing us, swiveled quickly around. "Oh!" he said, startled.

"You look like you could use a hand," Noor said.

"I could, God bless you."

He spoke in a Southern twang, and wore a few weeks' worth of gray beard. His eyes were filmy and bloodshot. The cast on his arm was dirty, and his brown Carhartt work jacket and pants were stained with oil or grease.

I gave him my hand and helped him up, and while he muttered a litany of thank-yous, we started shoving his old oven the rest of the way into the storage cage, which was jam-packed with a random assortment of heavy appliances, camping gear, and open cartons of dried food. In one of the only open spaces left, I saw a rolled-up sleeping bag, and I realized he was probably living here.

"I'm in salvage, see," he said, rambling as the oven scraped along, "and when deadbeats . . . we got a lot of deadbeats in this town what don't pay their debts . . . when they don't pay and they lose their units, the manager . . . he and me got an understanding . . . manager lets me cherry-pick some of the good stuff, 'cause I know where I can sell it to get the highest price, and it ain't Craigslist." With his good arm, he directed us toward an open space at the back of the surprisingly large unit, which we were now completely inside. "Right there in the corner, that's it . . ."

We'd just about gotten the oven wedged into the tight corner when I saw a different kind of space farther back—an unnatural blackness in the shape of a door.

I stopped shoving and gaped at him.

He was staring back now with a new acuity, and something in his face had sharpened. "You can go in if you want," he said. "But it ain't a very good idea."

"What are you talking about?" Noor said sharply.

The man nodded toward the darkness. His voice lowered. "That loop door there."

Our jaws dropped.

"What do you know about it?" Noor said.

"I keep watch out here for Miss V."

"You know V?" I said, astounded.

"Sure. Haven't seen her in years, though. She don't come out no more. Tell you the truth, I think she could use a little company."

"We're going in," said Noor.

"It's a free country. But I should warn you—it's a tad dangerous."

"Why?" I said.

"Weather can be rough," he said blandly. "You seem like smart kids, though. I'm sure you'll be just fine."

We certainly weren't turning back now. So we started toward it.

"Are you coming?" Noor said to him over her shoulder.

He grinned at us crookedly. "Hell no."

CHAPTER FOURTEEN

was falling, falling, weightless, enveloped in a velvet void. I tried to count the seconds but kept losing them

One, two

three

four

five

four

I dreamed I was standing in a thicket of Florida woods at night in a summer downpour.

I dreamed I saw my grandfather in his bathrobe holding a flashlight, and I tried to shout at him to stop, go back home, you're in danger. But my words came out in hollowspeak, and when he heard me he looked frightened, then angry, and he lunged at me with a letter opener held like a knife.

I ran, shouting "Stop, it's Jacob, it's your grandson"—

I dreamed he said, *"STOP, YOU MUST STOP."*

And plunged the letter opener into my shoulder.

Pain exploded through me, and then I was being shot into the air in a wide, lazy arc. Bright sky and brown earth traded places as I spun, then landed in a splattering, cushioning puddle of mud. I tried to sit up, but was too dizzy to get it right on the first attempt and fell back into the puddle.

Something heavy landed beside me with a great wet splat, and a wave of mud splashed over me.

It was Noor. We were disoriented and covered in filth, but seemed to be miraculously unhurt.

How far had we fallen? And where from?

I'd never seen a loop entrance like this.

I scanned our surroundings: shed, barn, grain silo, fields. The sky was an ominous sallow gray. Somewhere in the distance, I heard the long whistle of a train.

"How do we get out again?" Noor said, looking around.

"Hopefully V can tell us."

If we find her, I thought. If the rest of this loop was as strange as its front door, it might not be so easy.

We helped each other up and began to scrape the mud off. Neither of us wanted to meet Noor's sort-of mom like this. Then Noor stopped, suddenly, and tilted her head to one side. "What's that?"

It was the same train I'd heard before, but it had grown louder now, with an added layer of sound that reminded me of a ship's sails ripping in a gale.

My gaze wandered upward.

High above us and directly overhead was a small, dark object. It was growing steadily larger.

"What is that?" Noor said.

"It kind of looks like a house," I replied.

The sight was so surreal that it took a moment to process that it was, in fact, a house.

And then I was shouting it—"HOUSE, HOUSE, HOUUUUUUUSE"—while we both tried to escape the deep, sticky mud. I grabbed Noor and yanked her forward. We stumbled, and Noor pulled me up—a two-link human chain grasping for traction.

And then she shoved me and my feet touched dry ground and we were both running, the sound of the train and the ripping sails deafening.

The earth itself seemed to crack, and a sea of mud crashed over us from behind. At that same instant, something punched me hard in the back and I was thrown forward.

On the ground behind me lay a dented doorknob.

I scrambled to my feet again, then over to where Noor was standing. "Are you all right?!"

She was, and I was. And then she was staring at the house, unblinking, with a haunted look on her face.

"I think I used to live there," she said. "In that house. When I was really little."

It was a half-collapsed ruin, of course, despite somehow having landed right-side up.

I didn't know what to say. She closed her eyes and started humming the song she used to calm her nerves, and I hugged her.

I think we were both in shock.

After a moment, another sound broke us out of it. It was like God clearing his throat—a long, deep rumble coming from the heavy cloudbank above.

Behind us, reaching slowly down from the heavens like the trunk of some giant elephant, was the funnel of a tornado.

"Big wind," I said numbly.

"Two of them," said Noor, pointing in the opposite direction.

Two. There were two tornadoes.

They were quiet except for a faraway thrum, a low, almost subconscious droning that made everything around us, even the ground under our feet, vibrate in harmony. A moment later both tornadoes touched the ground, one and then the other, like thunderclaps in stereo. But, unlike thunder, the sound they made never faded. It rolled on and on. They weren't on top of us, but we were pinned between them, and they seemed to be converging.

There was nowhere to run. Certainly not into Noor's old, destroyed house. We could only go forward—but which way?

Frantic, I began pulling her away. "We have to find—"

I was interrupted by a fire hydrant dropping from the sky through the roof of the house, which sent up a fountain of shingles and wood splinters.

The impact seemed to snap her out of whatever trancelike state she'd been in. "We have to find shelter," Noor said. "A deep cellar, or a bank vault maybe."

But there was no real shelter here where we'd landed, only flat fields and grain silos through which tornadoes had already passed, and might pass again, their tracks marked by uprooted trees, wind-dug ditches cutting through rows of corn, and the occasional old truck flipped onto its roof.

We dashed out into the road. Not far away we could see a little downtown.

We ran toward it.

Rain began to fall, hard and pelting.

"Can you remember anything else about this place?" I said. "Something that might help?"

"I've been racking my brain," she said, "but it's all hazy . . ."

I turned to look over my shoulder. One of the tornadoes was directly behind us, maybe a half mile back, zigzagging back and forth across the road. I had never seen one so closely or clearly before, not even on video, and the sight stole my breath. A tight, twisting spiral of cloud connecting ground to sky like a mile-high umbilical cord, and where it touched earth was a terrifying vortex of dirt and debris wider than a football field.

It was heading straight for us. Chasing us.

I screamed it—*It's coming*—but Noor had seen already, or felt it, the waves of negative-pressure crackling the air. We broke into sprints, pumping our limbs until my lungs burned and my legs ached—and we reached the little town.

What was left of it, anyway.

We stopped, gasping for breath, at a square ringed by flattened buildings. Only a few remained. A flock of featherless chickens ran past us, strangely naked and clucking in baffled terror.

On the other side of town, the second tornado was roaring. Trying to decide whether to smash us, to merge with its sister, or to rage alone.

We searched for shelter. I led us inside one of the houses on the square, then Noor chose another, but we abandoned each when we realized neither had a cellar. We had only gotten a hundred feet from the second house when it began to rattle violently and then its roof lifted off, tumbled into the side yard, and exploded into a million pieces.

We're going to die.

The words flashed through my head before I could quash them.

We raced for cover, sprinting back through the square and diving behind a dirt embankment, where we covered our heads as a flurry of windborne shrapnel tore through the air above us. I lay there shuddering beside Noor, waiting for the furious gust to slacken.

"I'm sorry," she said. "I'm so sorry, Jacob. I never should have brought you here."

"You couldn't have known." My hand found hers on the wet ground. "We're in this together, remember?"

There was another massive boom somewhere close, and a plume of fire licked the sky. *Gas station,* I thought.

She began to hum again. And then the humming turned to singing, and for the first time I heard the words to Noor's song.

"One, two, three, there goes Miss McGee . . ."

Just then an old lady—the first person we'd seen—dashed down the road in front of us carrying a cat.

A little shiver went through me. What were the chances . . .

"Keep singing!" I said.

"Two, three, four, run into the store."

The old lady ran up the steps of a grocery, threw open the door, and disappeared inside.

I looked at Noor. She looked back at me, her eyes wide.

"What the next line?"

"Three, four, five, get there alive."

I grabbed her hand. "We have to—"

"Go in the store!" she said.

We jumped up and ran across the street like soldiers darting across enemy lines, and bashed through the swinging door. Miss McGee, or whoever she was, had ducked behind the cash register. Two men wearing grocer's aprons peeked out from a door in the floor, maybe a basement stockroom.

Noor was singing again. "Four, five, six, cinnamon sticks."

I shouted to the grocers: "Where do you keep your cinnamon?"

"Aisle nine!" one of them shouted back—he was in shock, his answer automatic.

"Get over here!" the other grocer cried, waving us toward the cellar door. "You're not—"

The rest of his words were lost beneath an apocalyptic roar. Noor and I dove to the floor. A metallic scream filled the air, and I squeezed my eyes shut and prayed for a quick death, and then it got lighter and louder simultaneously, which could only mean the roof had peeled away. After that I thought I heard the walls go, and then it went quiet, which probably meant I was dead.

Except I wasn't. I uncovered my head and opened my eyes again.

Neither of us was.

We were fine. The entire spice aisle was fine. Untouched, in fact. The delicate little spice jars all in place.

The rest of the store, however, including Miss McGee, had been vacuumed into the sky.

"Your song," I said wonderingly, my voice tiny beneath the ringing in my ears.

"Mama taught it to me. And now I know why." She got shakily to her feet. "It's how I'm supposed to find her."

The first tornado had moved down the street. But another was coming, the sound it made was like a monster chewing glass.

"What's the next line?" I said.

Noor started humming to herself. Trying to remember. She frowned. "I always forget this part."

I waited in silent torment as Noor stared at the floor and sang quietly, the raging tornado drawing closer and closer.

It wasn't Noor's fault. V hadn't mentioned that lives might depend on perfectly memorizing this nursery rhyme.

This doesn't make sense, I kept thinking. Why was this loop so deadly? And why would V invite Noor here without properly warning her about it?

It's a tad bit dangerous, the man watching the entrance had said. Idiot.

Noor had started the song over again. "Four, five, six, cinnamon sticks . . ."

She bopped her head, mumbling to herself. Then clapped her hands and shouted, "Five, six, seven, money come from heaven!"

She turned to me suddenly, grabbed my arms. "Money! The bank vault!"

We ran out into the street. There was a man dressed like a farmer running in the other direction.

"Where's the bank?" I shouted at him.

He pointed to the street behind us. "'Round that corner!"

He looked at us like we'd lost our sanity, then was about to say something else when an object struck him. He stumbled back and looked down, stunned, to see a stalk of corn sticking out of his chest.

As he crumpled and fell, we ran for the bank. Turning the corner, we could see it had already been destroyed. Fire spouted from its windows, and the walls and roof had been breached.

So much for Noor's song. But we had nowhere else to run,

and no choice but to keep going, so we kept on down the street, feet pounding pavement in the vain hope that some refuge would appear.

We'd only just passed the destroyed bank when we saw a bizarre vision ahead—a flurry of what looked, at first glance, like snow.

No. It was paper.

No. It was money. Money from the breached bank vault, whirling down from the sky in a blizzard.

"Five, six, seven," Noor chanted between frantic breaths, "money come from heaven . . . six, seven, eight . . . stand still and wait."

She put on an extra burst of speed and shot ahead of me. "This way!" she shouted. "Come with me!"

We veered into the shower of bills, and when we came to the middle of it, we stopped and stood there.

And waited.

A tornado was coming right toward us, but we waited. Every structure near us had either been destroyed or was in the process of being torn apart. But we had now learned to trust the song. So we stood in the heart of this snowstorm of money, the bills whipping around us, sticking to our muddy bodies while the awful, awesome spectacle of the roaring tornado bore down on us. And then, just before it reached the road where we were standing, it stopped, seemed almost to stare us down for a moment, then turned and tore through a shed.

The roar faded. We had been spared once more.

"Next verse!" I said, shouting through the sound of a million flurrying bills.

"Seven, eight, nine, by the whistling pine!" Noor recalled.

Not far away, towering over the roofs of the houses on the next street, we could see a tall tree waving in the gale. We ran toward it, cutting through a backyard littered with flopping fish, no doubt sucked up from some distant lake, and past a horse whinnying at us from atop the roof of a barn.

The pine stood in a wooded lot at the intersection of two streets, among smaller trees that had snapped and blown away, stumps of jagged wood where their trunks had once been. The one tree that remained was old and enormous and had a trunk twenty feet thick, and the wind whipping through its branches was making a high, keening sound—a whistle, almost a song—its pitch shifting with every change in the wind.

We stared into the upper canopy of the massive pine, looking for a tree house, maybe, or a hidden door—the entrance to V's bunker we were both praying to find.

But there was nothing.

"Now what?" I shouted. "Do we climb it?"

Noor shook her head, brow furrowed, thinking. Then she sang, "Eight, nine, ten, three wise men!"

Neither of us knew what to make of that, and there wasn't much time to figure it out. Could it be a code? A metaphor for something? Every other line in the song had been a reference to some actual person or place, but wise men? There was no one around; every looped normal seemed to be either dead or hiding.

Another tree crashed down in the middle of the street not thirty feet from us, spraying us with sharp pine needles and tiny crystalline hailstones. We covered our faces.

When I dared to look again, I saw a street sign I hadn't noticed before, quivering in the gale.

WISEMAN STREET

Noor cackled with hysterical laughter and clapped her hands, and we ran toward it together.

The house numbers were painted on the sidewalk and started at twenty, but there was only one house left standing on Wiseman Street.

Number three.

It was a cute but humble bungalow—one story, robin's-egg-blue paint, nothing special—except that it had completely escaped harm. There was a clothesline straining against its poles and laundry flapping in the wind. The mailbox shuddered but stood straight. The weathervane on the roof spun but was still attached.

And, there on the porch, sitting in a rocking chair, was a woman who could only have been V. She had short gray hair now, but I saw the same sharp-featured face I remembered from her photo. She wore an old red cardigan sweater over a dress and sat with a shotgun laid across her lap, rocking gently, watching the tornado like other people watch sunsets.

When she saw us, she stiffened and jumped to her feet.

And then she raised the shotgun.

◆　　◆　　◆

"Don't shoot!" I screamed, frozen in place as we waved our hands in the air. "We come in peace!"

V stalked toward us, eyes ablaze. "Who are you and what do you want?" she bellowed.

"It's me!" Noor said.

The gun whipped toward her. V looked surprised, then baffled and sad for a moment as she searched Noor's face—and then her caterpillar eyebrows mashed together into a furious scowl.

"What the hell are you doing here?" she shouted.

Not the welcome we'd been expecting.

"I came to see you!" Noor said, and I could tell she was working hard to keep her voice calm and level.

"Yes," V replied impatiently, "but how did you find me?"

Noor gave me a wide-eyed look. *Can you believe this?*

"We followed the address!" she said.

"From your postcard!" I added.

V seemed confused. Then the blood drained from her face.

"I never sent any postcard."

Noor looked at V like she couldn't possibly have heard that right.

"What?" I said.

V's eyes bounced between us. "Were you followed?"

Just then the clothesline snapped off its poles and went flying over our heads, and we all ducked to avoid being decapitated.

"Come inside before we all get killed," V said, and she tucked the shotgun under her arm and took each of us by the arm.

We ran inside. V slammed the front door and pulled a series of heavy deadbolts, then began darting between windows, pulling down heavy metal shutters. "We almost got killed five times already," I said. "Why do you live in such a deadly place?"

It looked like a cross between an old lady's house and a weaponry museum. Leaning in a rack beside a table set with teacups were three scoped rifles. Hung over the arm of a green-velvet sofa was an ammunition belt. It reminded me of my grandfather's house.

"Because I looped it that way," she said, and pulled on a dangling cord to make a periscope rattle down from the ceiling. "I designed it to be impenetrable. It repeats the deadliest event in the history of this region on the half hour." She peered into the periscope. "Can either of you shoot a gun?"

I nearly fell over. "Wait—you *looped* it?"

She pulled her face away from the periscope and looked at me. "I'm an ymbryne. And of course you can shoot, you're Abe Portman's grandson." She turned to glance at Noor, who seemed almost too stunned to speak, and her expression softened. "We were never supposed to see each other again, dear. Not that I didn't wish it a thousand times . . ."

"But it's not impenetrable," Noor said. "The song."

I was standing next to her, but she seemed, in that moment, very alone.

V let her hands fall away from the periscope. "After all these years, I never thought you'd remember it."

"Of course I did," said Noor. Her voice was barely audible above the wind outside. "You did want me to come."

V smiled and crossed the room to Noor and me, and I thought she might reach out and put her arms around Noor, but she stopped short. "A sentimental mistake." Her smile began to waver. "I knew I shouldn't have let myself grow attached to you, but you were such a dear, sweet child. I knew that eventually, for your own sake, I would have to let you go, but I suppose I wanted to believe that maybe, one day, you and I could . . ." V looked down. Took a long breath. "I never should have taught it to you. And it was meant to be used only in the gravest emergencies." She looked up again. And now she looked afraid. "But only if I reached out to you first."

"But you didn't."

"No."

"I don't understand," I said. "If you didn't send that postcard, who did?"

"That would be me," said a peppy voice from behind us, and we spun to see a man standing by the door to the kitchen. It was the old man from the storage unit. His cast was gone, and he had a gun pointed at us. "I sent several, actually, to a few different addresses. I know the post is a little old-fashioned these days . . . but so is Velya here."

"Murnau," V snarled.

He let out a dry laugh, then untwisted his posture, broadened his shoulders, and flashed a familiar, arrogant grin. And suddenly I saw him, clear as day, through the beard and makeup: Murnau. He had a leather bag slung across his back.

"Did I interrupt a family reunion? My timing is, as always, impeccable." He took a step toward us. His gun, and most of his focus, was trained on V. "All right, sweets. Where do you want to do this? Kitchen floor? Bathtub, save the rug? Not that any of that's going to be here in a few hours."

"Leave her alone!" Noor said. "If you've got some issue with her, you can settle it with me."

"No thanks. You've served your purpose already. But if you try

anything tricky, I'll make your mom suffer more than she needs to."
His eyes cut to me. "And your boyfriend."

"I know what you're after," I said, "and there's nothing for
you here."

He ignored me. "Do you know we've been trying to get into
this loop for years? Wasted a lot of good men, but were never able to
crack it . . . until today." He flashed a grin at Noor. "You forgot to
lock your back door, Velya."

And then he shot her.

◆   ◆   ◆

Before the shot had stopped ringing, before V had even hit the floor,
before I could react at all, Noor ran at Murnau. She had no weapon,
no light stored up inside her, just her two hands and the power of her
hatred. But he was ready: He stepped deftly to the side, drew back
his muscled arm, and slammed her to the floor. And then I was diving toward him—ready to tear him apart—but in the time it took to
close the distance between us, he had snatched another gun from his
belt, raised it, and fired.

It made a soft pop. I felt a sharp pain in my side, and as I
tumbled to the floor I heard a second one—

He had shot Noor.

I couldn't get up.

I grabbed my side. Something was sticking out.

A dart.

I felt searing pain as darkness clouded my sight.

Then, in a moment, or a minute—I don't know how long it
was—I felt rain on my face.

We had been dragged outside.

I forced my eyes open. Willed my vision to focus. I was hand-
cuffed to the porch railing, and next to me, Murnau was cuffing
Noor. She was limp, her eyes half closed.

V lay facedown in the yard, out in the grass. The sky churned.

I managed to slur out a few words. "You're not . . . going to kill us?"

"Unfortunately, I won't have the pleasure. Orders from the boss." He finished cuffing Noor, then glanced over his shoulder at V. "He wants you to watch. And then feel what it's like to have a loop collapse on you."

"It's not . . . going to work," I said slowly. "You don't even . . . have the right in . . . gre . . . dients."

He looked like he'd just remembered something. "Oh, that's right. You children still think—"

He laughed—then I heard a *thwip!* and he winced and bent over. The shaft of an arrow was sticking out of his thigh.

He growled and whipped around to face V.

She was propped up on one elbow, covered in blood, holding a compact crossbow that she had somehow concealed.

She fired again. This arrow went into Murnau's shoulder.

He grunted. Raised his gun and shot her again.

She dropped the crossbow and collapsed.

Noor moaned.

Murnau turned back to look at us. "As I was saying"—he grimaced but seemed barely distracted by the pain—"Bentham thought he could fool us with a bad translation. But we saw right through his ruse. The *Apocryphon*'s original text doesn't mention a mother of birds. There isn't any such thing. What it calls for is the still-beating heart of the mother of *storms*." He tossed away his revolver. Unslung the leather bag from his shoulder and drew out a long knife.

"Speaking of which, I'd better get to work."

He hobbled off toward where V lay in the grass.

The sky was a chaos of funneling clouds.

I tried to shout, to call Noor's name—to turn my head and look at her—but I could not.

My vision tunneled. The world spun.

When the blackness briefly peeled away, I saw Murnau hunched over V's prone form. His arm was pistoning up and down.

Then darkness again, until I felt something slapping my face. Leaves, grit. And I heard what sounded like a freight train. With great effort, I lifted my eyelids.

The tornado was devouring a giant tree across the street, and its branches whipped as if possessed by some devil. Its roots were coming up out of the ground like arms—and Murnau was walking straight toward it. He had the bag slung over his shoulder and something small and dark gripped in his hand, which was raised in triumph.

Just before he was swept away, he stopped and turned back to look at us, and I swear I saw him grinning.

And then he was lifted up by the wind, and he was gone.

I may have blacked out again. What I remember next was a bank of vibrant yellow clouds coalescing toward the funnel of the tornado, gathering into a conical spike that pointed up into the sky. The tree had been ripped whole from the ground, and it hovered there, spinning gently, a hundred feet from the ground, in the center of the funnel.

There was a low moaning that grew louder and louder until it threatened to break my head. It sounded almost like human speech slowed down, a voice inside the wind speaking unintelligible vowels that rose and fell in long waves. The yellow spike of cloud thickened and merged with the levitating tree, and then the clouds around it took a shape, holographically vivid.

It was a face.

A face I knew.

And then its mouth opened, and in a slow, rolling thunderclap, the sky uttered my name.

EPILOGUE

The little girl had been deeply asleep when Pensevus began whispering to her. She did not know how long it had been, but by the time her eyes blinked open, her head was full of nightmares.

She knew just what she had to do.

The little girl rose to her feet and crossed the room.

Pensevus kept whispering. (He almost never stopped whispering.) She carried him dangling from one hand. (She carried him everywhere.)

She had only used the telephone once before, but Pensevus told her just what to do.

He always told her what to do.

She pulled a chair out from the corner and placed it below the telephone, then climbed it so she could reach the receiver.

She made six calls, one after the other. Her task was not even complete when the first ymbryne alighted on the sill of her open window.

When each call was answered, she said only one thing.

"He's back."

ABOUT THE PHOTOGRAPHY

The images that appear in this book are authentic, vintage, found photographs, and with the exception of a handful that have undergone a bit of digital processing, they are unaltered. They were painstakingly collected over the course of several years: discovered at flea markets, vintage paper shows, and in the archives of photo collectors more accomplished than I, who were kind enough to part with some of their most peculiar treasures to help create this book.

The following photos were graciously lent for use by their owners: